Hell

Also by Robert Olen Butler

The Alleys of Eden

Sun Dogs

Countrymen of Bones

On Distant Ground

Wabash

The Deuce

A Good Scent from a Strange Mountain

They Whisper

Tabloid Dreams

The Deep Green Sea

Mr. Spaceman

Fair Warning

Had a Good Time

From Where You Dream: The Process of Writing Fiction

(Janet Burroway, Editor)

Severance

Intercourse

Hell

by
Robert Olen Butler

Grove Press
New York

A portion of this work originally appeared in *Narrative* magazine.
Published simultaneously in Canada
Printed in the United States of America

FIRST EDITION

ISBN-13: 978-0-8021-1901-8

Grove Press
an imprint of Grove/Atlantic, Inc.
841 Broadway
New York, NY 10003
Distributed by Publishers Group West
www.groveatlantic.com

09 10 11 12 10 9 8 7 6 5 4 3 2 1

for my son, Joshua
wherever we end up, let's order the tasting menu

Faustus. How comes it then that thou art out of Hell?
Mephistophilis. Why this is Hell, nor am I out of it.

—Christopher Marlowe

"From Broadcast Central in the Great Metropolis where all rivers converge, all storms make a beeline, and all the levees look a little fragile, it's the *Evening News from Hell*. And now here's your anchorman, looking a little fragile himself, Hatcher McCord." The voice of Beelzebub, Satan's own station manager, mellifluously fills Hatcher McCord's head from the feed in his ear. He squeezes the sheaf of papers with both hands, and he knows even without looking that they're blank by now and he'll be on his own—the last thing he wants is to rely on the teleprompter, though he will be compelled to try—and yes, he's feeling a little fragile—and the three dozen monitors arrayed before him burst into klieg-light brightness with his face pasty and splashed with razor burn and dark around the eyes.

"Good evening," Hatcher says, from the teleprompter. "Good evening, good evening, good evening," he continues to read. "Poopy butt, poopy butt, poopy butt." And he wrenches his eyes from the scroll that is about to drop its baby-talk irony and get into some serious obscenity. Hatcher has been allowed to keep his anchorman ability to improvise, though even in his earthly life when he had to do this, which he did most every night—to cut or to expand to fit the time hole—we're eleven seconds heavy, we're twenty seconds light—he churned with anxiety at the grasp of every phrase. He understands, of course, that this anxiety is why he's allowed to keep the skill. And Satan does indeed seem to want the news to be the news every night. Hatcher knows he gets to pull this off, though that doesn't lessen his worry.

"Tonight," Hatcher says, "a follow-up to last night's lead story: is Hell expecting a Heavenly visitor? Will there be a new Harrowing? Also, a tsunami on the Lake of Fire temporarily incinerates fifty thousand. We'll have an exclusive interview with some of those immediately reconstituted on the beach—Federico Fellini and a dozen fat Italian women in diaphanous gowns carrying parasols. Later, in our ongoing series of interviews, 'Why Do You Think You're Here?', we speak to the Reverend Jerry Falwell and to George Clemens, inventor of the electric hand dryer for public restrooms."

With this, Hatcher suddenly has no more words. He is struck utterly dumb and he stares into his own face arrayed before him six screens high and six screens across, frozen in wide-eyed silence. He started this feature himself—the Why-You're-Heres—and he knows Satan was pleased—the Old Man copied his laudatory e-mail to the "allhell" list—though of course Hatcher also knew that his own personal interest in the feature was transparent. But it serves Satan's purpose to keep everyone worrying and regretting and puzzling, keep them torturing themselves. Hatcher as much as anyone. So he watches his own faces now, and all that cycles in his head is the same question—why the fuck are you here?—and he has no further words to say, even though there's only dead-air going out to all the TVs in Hell. His brow and cheeks and nose before him are suddenly glistening bright with sweat. He opens his mouth and shuts it. He waits and waits, and then he knows he can continue.

"And tomorrow," Hatcher says, "our newly arrived homemaking specialist will show you how to prepare organ meat. Your own. Eat your heart out with Martha Stewart. She'll eat hers."

"Commercial!" Beelzebub booms in Hatcher's earpiece. "Now!"

Hatcher does not flinch. In his gravest evening tone he says, "But first these messages," and he waits and he watches his own face waiting and waiting on the screens, going out like this into every corner of Hell, and just as he has become accustomed to the pain of Beelzebub's shouting in his ear, he has come to wait out this inevitable delay of the cutaway with his lips set in a thin, knowing smile, his eyes steady. I'm learning, Hatcher thinks. I can control this. Because it's trivial. Because it just gives me false hopes.

Finally the red light goes dark on his camera and his face disappears from all but the central four screens, replaced by the "Your Stuff" logo. Hatcher sees it written on lined tablet paper in Prussian Blue Crayola in his own hand as a child. The commercials are tailored for each viewer, reselling everyone all the stuff they ever owned in their mortal life, one piece at a time, but the toll-free order number turns out to be a litany of their childhood sorrows and they can't hang up and they can't take the phone from their ear. Hatcher forces his eyes away from the screens as his complete collection of Marx Toys Presidents of the United States comes up on the screen, all five series of two-and-a-half inch white plastic figures. He delighted in Series Five especially, Ike and his immediate predecessors. Hatcher had them all meet every day to discuss the previous day's news, Ike and Truman and Hoover and Coolidge and FDR, who stood erect and unaided, his legs miraculously restored. And Mamie was there too, to serve coffee. But Hatcher keeps his eyes averted now because he knows about the toll-free order number firsthand. The last time, he tried to buy a book from his childhood, a Wonder Book about a magic bus that could fly, and he heard an hour riff on his father.

Hatcher swivels in his chair and pops his earpiece. His cell phone is vibrating in his coat pocket, the phone bouncing around fiercely, banging the bruise on his thigh from where he walks into the corner of his kitchen table each morning. He grits his teeth at the inordinate pain and he stands up, trying to dig for the phone, which bounces on, briefly touching Hatcher's crotch and initiating what will be an irreconcilable priapismic erection lasting way more than four hours. At last he drags the phone out of his pocket, and the vibrating instantly ends, and he sees from the missed call list that it's Anne. His Anne. She's hysterical still, he knows. He also knows he will never get a signal to call her back. Yet his hands move on their own, trying and trying to return the call, though he has never been able to get through to anyone. And still his hands try. Stop now, he tells his thumbs, which are pushing "end" and "call" over and over.

The phone also shows an unanswered voice mail. This is Satan. No one can get through to voice mail but him. Hatcher tells his thumbs to retrieve the voice mail, and this they finally obey.

The voice is smarmy smooth. "All right, McCord. Your latest e-mail persuaded me. This should be amusing, though I can't promise what I'll let you do with the thing. But tomorrow morning at dawn someone will pick you up at your place."

The Prince of Darkness has never appeared on TV and may still resist—he's notorious for staying out of direct sight—but at last he will do a one-on-one interview. The only unknown is when tomorrow morning will actually get around to occurring.

∝

Hatcher's mind slides away, full of worry about Anne, when the Fellini spot begins. Perhaps she caught sight of Henry in the street again. It's always from a distance and he's never the king she married, he's always the young prince she first saw when she was in the care of Margaret of

Austria at her palace in the Low Countries, when he was tall and still lithe and smooth of skin, and Hatcher holds very still not to cry out from the thrashing inside him, made more acute by his cell phone erection, as he thinks of Henry's hands upon her and how she pants and lifts her eyes when she speaks of him even now, even though he had her head at last, and surrounding the four central monitors showing Hatcher close his eyes against his retrospective jealousy, thirty-two Fellinis are saying:

"The beach was full of the women I adore, the women of the variety shows on the street where I lived when I first came to Rome, San Giovanni, and they'd show films but afterwards there were the live variety acts and it was the women I waited for, the beautiful fat women with their naked thighs and their breasts flushed and moist and swelling out of their clothes, promising unseen nipples—I could only imagine how sweet—and I found them today beside the lake, these very women, the corpulent chorines of San Giovanni, and I arranged them on the shore, and the sea was saturated red, and then the wave came and my flesh and my bones dissolved even as the flesh and the bones of these women dissolved and we howled together in pain, the women of my past and I, and that felt very familiar: the way it feels to make a movie."

Then the fat women begin to speak, one after the other, and Hatcher undoes his lapel mike and wanders off the set into the fetid dark behind the cameras. A tight gaggle of dozens of raggedy bodies, barely visible in the darkness, shuttle out of his way, murmuring softly "Good evening" and "Now the weather" and "A new Wal-Mart opened today." These are the TV news anchors who never got out of local stations, a new group of them each night, Hatcher suspects. They are always huddling nearby, sweating heavily, hair mussed, clothes tattered, unprepared. Hatcher has learned to ignore them.

He thinks how there is always time here for all the news in depth— at last there's time—and how that's hell, as one of the fat women drones on about the mistreatment of the working classes, and another recounts her dream of Fellini riding her on her hands and knees and lashing her bare butt with a horse whip, and another simply screams for her sixty seconds, and the others come on one by one, and as Hatcher stands here in the dark, he finds he can quiet his mind a bit, let Anne go. He will see her when the broadcast is done and his torment can continue then, but for now he has the news.

Though tonight there's less of it than he expected. When the time comes for the big follow-up story about a possible new Harrowing, Hatcher has to move on to other news while the remote crew tries to find his investigative reporter, Carl Crispin, who's dealing, of course, with torments of his own. Crispin was sent to the center of the city, to the intersection where tradition has it the first Harrowing began, the place where Jesus arrived to begin harvesting the elders of the Old Testament to take them to Heaven. Back then, it was a dusty rural crossroads. Now, it is the corner of Peachtree Way and Lucky Street.

Finally, there are no more stories and Beelzebub is chortling softly in Hatcher's earpiece, and they begin the nightly "Lessen the Pain" feature. Tonight's advice, in a grainy black-and-white film clip: when the noontime sulfur and fire storm rains down, just duck and cover, slide under a piece of furniture, or throw yourself into a ditch and curl up and cover your head with your hands.

The piece ends and Beelzebub is breathing heavily in Hatcher's ear. "Guess what I'm wearing," he whispers.

But Hatcher knows his tricks. He keeps his face Cronkitedly calm and fatherly. The end of the show always is a test of wills. He stares into the camera, placid, waiting.

"Oh, you're so good," Beelzebub says. "So here's your boy."

Crispin's face suddenly surrounds Hatcher's on the monitors. It is a gaunt and pasty face. Crispin's eyes are swollen nearly shut from crying and tears are streaming down his cheeks.

"And now," Hatcher says, "reporting live from the corner of Peachtree Way and Lucky Street, Carl Crispin. Carl?"

Carl jerks at the sound of Hatcher's voice and snaps his hand-held microphone upwards, slamming it into his mouth. He tips his head forward for a moment, taking the microphone away, and then he lifts his face and spits out half a dozen broken teeth.

"Carl," Hatcher says. "Are you all right?"

"What the fuck are you talking about, Hatcher," Carl says. "We're in fucking Hell."

"That's right, Carl. And we're doing the news. You're standing in the spot where . . ."

"This fucking spot," Carl says. "Do you know how many Peachtrees there are in Hell, Hatcher? I was most recently at the corner of Peachtree Trace and Lucky Court. Before that Peachtree Trail and Lucky Boulevard, or maybe that was Lucky Street also. And even those seemed relatively distinguishable. There are seven Peachtree intersections along Lucky Street itself, including Peachtree Street Avenue Lane and Peachtree Avenue Lane Street and Peachtree Street Street Avenue. I tried to hurry but I couldn't move my legs to run." Carl starts to sob.

"Carl. It's okay. You're there now. Carl."

Carl shakes his head hard and wipes his face with his wrist, dragging the buttons of his suit coat sleeve through his eyes. "Well, shit. I've done that again," he says. "I may not be able to see the camera for a while, Hatcher." And indeed, Carl is looking off camera to the right now, turning almost entirely into profile.

"That's all right, Carl." Hatcher picks up the sheaf of blank paper from the desk and holds on tight, trying to fight a twitching that wants to start in his hands.

Off mike, the voice of the cameraman calls to Carl, who turns toward the sound, blinking. He is more or less in place now and Hatcher takes a deep breath. He mellows his voice into his best top-of-the-news tone.

"All right, Carl. On our last broadcast you reported on the rumors of a new Harrowing. Certain veterans of the last one were seeing the same signs . . ."

"I lied about all that, Hatcher," Carl says.

Hatcher's throat knots up tight.

"You know I'm a compulsive liar," Carl says.

Beelzebub is chortling again, still softly.

Hatcher sees his own face in the center four screens. It is the face of a man he does not know but has seen around a few times. It's a sad face, he thinks. Sad in the furrowed brow and the tremblingly inverted smile.

∝

Hatcher wedges into the street in front of Broadcast Central. Grand Peachtree Parkway. Teeming with denizens at this hour, whatever that hour is, the air filled with a loud roar of voices and cries. He looks off to the sun hanging behind the sawtooth mountains on the horizon beyond the city. The illusion of the sun, of course. Or a time-fractured view of it. The eye of Satan. Whatever it is. It's been hanging there a long while. He's done several cycles of *Evening News*—he can't think how many, exactly—without its moving. However long that would suggest. Days, by the reckoning of his earthly life. However long ago that life was. His brain is trying to cope, now that he doesn't have the broadcast for a focus. Three bearded men stinking of motor oil and sardines, arms linked, shouting wordlessly at each other, barrel into him and he nearly falls— Hatcher doesn't want to fall—the crowd always surges onto you if you fall—so he tries at least to throw himself a little backward and thumps hard into the stone archway of Broadcast Central, but he keeps his feet, and he tries to fight off a fuckthisfuckthisfuckthis run in his head. Satan relishes that. Worse things always follow. Not yet, Old Man, Hatcher says in his head. Not yet. I'm not going there. Hatcher straightens and focuses on the upcoming interview. He can ask about the sun. He steps into the swift roiling current of the crowd and floats on toward his apartment. He can ask why he's here.

∝

His alley is tight this time, barely wider than his shoulders, and the unidentifiable crunching and sliming beneath his feet would be worse than usual if he was aware of it, but he isn't. He is still turning questions over in his mind for Satan, and he goes up the iron circular staircase and down the outside corridor full of wailing and panting and the squealing of bedsprings and the shattering of glass.

The door to the apartment just before his is standing open. The place is utterly empty but for two overstuffed chairs sitting side by side in the center of the floor, slightly angled toward each other. Mr. and Mrs. Hopper. Howard and Peggy. From Yonkers. Hatcher finds his legs growing heavy, dragging to a halt, as they always do when he passes this door. He stops. He nods. Howard and Peggy look at him. Today they are paunchy and creviced and stooped, as they were in their retirement years in Boca Raton.

"Good evening," Hatcher says.

"I'm with my wife," Howard says.

"He is," she says.

"Forever," he says.

"And I'm with you," she says.

Howard makes a little choking sound deep in his throat. Tears begin to stream down Peggy's face, though she makes no effort to wipe them away.

"Excuse him," she says to Hatcher. "He is always very rude. Good evening."

"You didn't say it either," Howard says.

"You didn't say it first."

"How was I first? Why wasn't it you who didn't say it first?"

Hatcher is happy to find his feet unsticking from where they are, his legs lightening. "Good-bye," he says, but the Hoppers are unaware of him, debating on about each other's culpability.

He moves to the next door, his own, and he goes in.

Anne sits on a cane back chair beside the heavy oak kitchen table. She has reverted to wearing Tudor dress, a gown of forest green velvet with hugely puffed oversleeves of gold brocade and a wide, deep neckline showing her dusky skin, but her naked upper chest rises to her throat and then ceases: her head sits on the kitchen table looking at her own body.

"Anne," Hatcher whispers. "Not again."

She raises her hands and frames her head but does not lift it. She simply swivels her head on the tabletop to look at him. Her enormous black eyes flutter and focus on him and his knees go weak enough to make him nearly collapse there from his desire, and behind his own eyes, he ponders their first moments: *She came to me wearing this voluminous green velvet dress, barely fitting into the tiny studio at Broadcast Central to tape the Why-You're-Here, and she turned those black eyes on me and her eyes were some unidentified deep-space phenomenon, they had a gravitational pull certainly, but I didn't fall into them, they simply stood me up and roused every rousable part, and they gave off light somehow—a dark light that would not lose itself in the crimson light of Hell—and they gave off heat—but a heat quite palpably different from the ghastly ongoing ambient heat of this place—all of which instantly created in me a thing, a feeling, whose name I cannot remember—and I know this forgetfulness is because I'm in Hell—and she sits and we are ready and she begins to speak about her husband and the church and slander, and the voice of the Queen of England is firm and hard-edged but her eyes are deep and soft and she keeps them on mine and will not take them from me, so I slide closer to the camera but I do not stop her, I do not ask her to look into the lens—I want her to keep looking only at me—and now she speaks of the children she carried in her body and how all but one died there and the one was unacceptably a girl and when she speaks of the children, the voice softens, softens and breaks, and I am in Hell—this is a thing I've learned is foremost in all our minds to the exclusion of everything else—the I, the I, the I am, the I am in Hell—but at that moment in our first meeting it strikes me hard: she also is in Hell, this Anne Boleyn of the darkly celestial eyes that will not move from mine, she is in Hell and I ache for that, I want to take her up and carry her somewhere else*

And as these words run deeply in Hatcher, Anne's head sits on the tabletop and looks across the room at the anchorman of the *Evening News from Hell* and she considers another man: *I was but twelve years old when I saw Henry youthful and lank, as I saw him today, and he was the author of all the lies that destroyed me, I know that now, and I am sorry to have been found thus, separated from my body again, by this other man who has entered my life and who powerfully enters into every life in every dwelling place in this nether realm—though it is my understanding that all the others do not experience him directly, as I do—I have learned many new things and ways over the seeming eternity I have already been here—I have learned that a man like this has more power than an earthly king—how Henry would have ruled all the world if he could have but strode into every dwelling each day—and I went to this new man at his bidding, and though I have also learned to wear my cheap, loin-crushing jeans and my shapeless T-shirts with the itchy labels at the back of the neck, on that day it was given me to wear the sort of dress to which I was accustomed in my earthly life and this was a comfort as I came before Lord Hatcher McCord's de-vices, and even as I told my story, as I have done so many times in my own mind this past eternity, I watched him, Lord McCord, his eyes were the gray-blue of an autumn London sky and they clouded and ached for me—I could see that clearly— they ached for me, for me, for me here in this place, for me, for this solitary, be-headed me*

And with this, Anne finds she can pick up her head, which she does, and she sets it upon her neck. Hatcher is happy for this. He knows how things work. Looking into Anne's eyes he had a feeling that one might consider tender or pleasurable, but there is always a dreadful mitigation.

He was filled with desire for her, but that desire, after all—he is acutely aware—was while her severed head was sitting on a tabletop. Now she is restored. She closes her eyes and lifts her chin and swivels her head, first to the right and then slowly swinging back to the left. This is a graceful movement, and he is glad to be in this kitchen, and he is glad she sits before him, but now that she is whole, the rush of his desire for her subsides. He feels it sliding away, and he stifles a curse at Satan so that he might avoid worse, though surely Satan also recognizes the thing being stifled, and surely Satan doesn't have a policy of withholding suffering just because you can suppress your inner criticism of him. He can't give a rat's ass about that, surely.

Hatcher crosses to the table, and he draws the other chair near to Anne, and he sits beside her. She is still swiveling her head back and forth. There is a scurrying behind him, the roaches gathering to listen to the conversation. This is a curious thing. The place is full of roaches, but Anne is oblivious to them, given the century of her upbringing. And as a boy, and even later as a man, he himself never had a serious aversion to the other creatures living around him, no matter how traditionally despised. He once appalled Naomi in their apartment at the Dakota by gently gathering up a large, sluggish, confused, dumb-shit roach from the bathtub with a paper towel and carrying it to the window and setting it free.

He looks over his shoulder now. The countertop beside the sink is full of roaches, a thousand roaches, all of them sitting up on their back legs like begging pups, their heads cocked. Hatcher puts on his best *Evening News from Hell* voice. "Good evening," he says to the roaches. "Tonight, a kitchen table conversation and then one more futile attempt at satisfying sex."

And in a chorus of tiny, brittle voices, the roaches cry, "Poopy butt." Then they laugh.

Hatcher turns to Anne. She is still swiveling her restored head, humming a bit of a pavane from her youth, hearing lutes and tambourines.

He touches her hand just as, in Anne's mind, the courtyard of the Low Countries palace of Princess Margaret, filled with dancing figures and music, dissolves in screaming as a baited bear breaks its chains and charges in, ripping flesh and spattering blood with the wide swiping of its claws. Anne screams.

Hatcher clutches at Anne's thrashing hand. "I'm sorry," he says. "It's only me. I didn't mean to startle you."

"The bear," Anne says.

"It's all right," Hatcher says.

"No it's not," the roaches cry.

Anne looks in their direction. "They're right," she says, though calmly now.

"We're right," they cry.

"It's all the same here," she says, "whether the horror is in my mind or on the countertop."

"We're not horrible," the roaches cry.

Hatcher turns on them. "No you're not. You're pathetic. So shut the fuck up."

Each cockroach eye has two thousand lenses, and now, as one, four million lenses widen in shocked hurt feelings on the countertop, and all the roaches begin to weep, boohooing loudly. And yes, at this, Hatcher is filled with an acute regret. The roaches slump down from their puppy-begging pose and, weeping ostentatiously still, they all pour off the countertop and into the dark joins of the sink and cabinets and the cracks in the wall, and in a few moments they are gone.

The kitchen rings with the sudden silence. Hatcher is slump-shouldered with guilt, and the gravity pull grows even heavier as disgust with himself sets in for feeling guilty about hurting the feelings of a chitinous chitter of roaches. Satan's own roaches, yet. And then he realizes the silence is much larger than the kitchen. Outside, there is silence now as well. It's happening.

Hatcher jumps up and crosses to the door and through to the outside corridor. All down the way, denizens are emerging from their apartments in the dimness of the long twilight. Like them, Hatcher leans out over the iron railing and turns to the street end of the alley, where the passing crowd has also stopped and is turning to look. The sun is not visible to Hatcher from where he stands. But he does see the sky beyond the distant mountains, unchanged still in its twilight pallor. And now the railing, the corridor, the building, the alley, the whole city begins to tremble, and all the denizens cover their ears with their hands, though it never does any good: a sharp blade-stroke of sound punches into their heads—the monumental solar boom of sundown—and everything goes black.

The absolute darkness pushes heavily on Hatcher's eyes for a long while. Everyone waits. Scattered in the distance are the cries of newcomers, unaware of what's next. Then the night sigh of Satan blows through the city—a deep exhaling, as if it were his very breath—and all around, lights come on. In the side streets and alleys, the light is dim, scattered, open flames stinking of kerosene or burning rotted wood, bare bulbs putting out piss-puddles of illumination—when the elder George Bush arrived in the midst of a long night and Hatcher found him in an alley and interviewed him, he would only mutter on and on about the thousand points of light. And in the thoroughfares, stretches of mugger darkness are broken by rotten-orange oases of sodium vapor lamps that fill all the twenty-first-century dead with the sadness of interstate rest stops.

Hatcher steps back into his apartment. Anne sits where he left her, by the table, dressed in green velvet, her head attached. She turns her eyes to him, darker than the moment after sundown in Hell.

"Let's begin this again," she says.

"All right," Hatcher says.

He backs out the door, closes it. He opens the door and steps in. "Darling, I'm home," he says.

Anne Boleyn rises from the kitchen chair. "Darling," she says, and her voice is sad as sad can be.

∞

Later, much later, they still are sitting at the kitchen table and cannot summon an impulse to move. Night is here. "I can't find Catherine Parr," Anne says. "Is she in Heaven, do you conjecture?"

"It's crowded here," Hatcher says.

"The sanctimonious bitch," Anne says.

"Just because you can't find her . . ."

"She was a papal puppy."

"That doesn't mean she's not here."

Anne looks Hatcher in the eyes. "So were they right? Is that it?"

"Who?"

"The Papists. I overthrew the power of the Pope. They called it the Reformation after I was killed by the king. I started that. Henry and I."

"There were others."

"Not that he did it for God."

"Martin Luther."

"I did it for God," she says.

"And others."

"Is Luther here?"

"So I understand."

"You see?"

Hatcher leans to her, pats her hand on the tabletop. "But Hell is also full of popes."

"Borgia and his like," Anne says.

"You'd be surprised."

Anne sighs loudly. "I should've just prayed the rosary and kept my mouth shut."

"It's not that simple," Hatcher says.

She turns her face to him.

He says, "If you really believe God gives a damnation over the dogma, then, for instance, how could John XXIII and John Paul II both be in Heaven?"

"I don't know those," Anne says.

"They can't, is the answer. I've seen one of them around town."

"It's crowded here," she says.

"Yes it is. Maybe they're both in Hell."

Anne sighs again.

"I need to interview a pope," Hatcher says.

"Interview me." Anne flutters her dark dark eyes at him.

"I've interviewed you already," he says.

"'Interview' in the Tudor sense," she says, reaching out and plucking at his left earlobe.

"Ah," he says. "A Tudor sense to 'interview.' This is linguistic news to me."

"I'd like to die," she says.

"You're dead," he says, running his fingertip down the bridge of her nose.

"In the Elizabethan sense," Anne says.

"You died before there *was* an Elizabethan sense."

Anne laughs. "Many times."

The two of them have begun this, and they have begun it often before, and so they are both waiting to see how it will go wrong. For Hatcher, it begins to go wrong now. He has now inadvertently prompted her to think of her previous orgasms, which prompts her to think of Henry, and Hatcher watches her eyes go a little blank before him, and he knows the king just strode into her mind—which is to say, strode into this room—and it will be difficult to get him to stride out again.

But Hatcher tries to banter on. "I would, dear queen, that you could die now in Hell."

"It once was easy for me, the dying," she says.

"But not now."

"Not now."

"Because you're thinking of the past," he says.

This is where it goes wrong for Anne. When a man takes your virginity, you might throw off his memory for your present paramour. But if a man takes your head, you need to be left the fuck alone if you want to obsess about him.

"Because thy member," she says, her voice gone queenly hard, "sleeps when I am awake and wakes when I am asleep."

"Because Satan does not sleep, and he has power over all the members of this club."

"Ah. Satan is the reason. Are you sure it's not my severed head that repulses you?"

"I'm sure."

"It's Satan, you say."

"Satan."

"Not my head."

"Not if you keep it on."

"I never take my head off when we try to play at the beast with two backs."

Another Elizabethanism. Hatcher's jealousy ratchets up some more. "Have you been hanging around with Shakespeare again?"

"He's insufferable," Anne says.

"You sound more and more like him."

"He complains all the time."

"About his member?"

"He weeps for quill and ink."

"Please."

"His hard drive keeps crashing and he loses his plays."

"We all have to keep up," Hatcher says.

"If only you could," she says.

They fall silent. They are each deciding whether to try now. It's less bad when they don't talk first, though that brings its own problems, of course. The night will go on. Sleep in Hell is rare and brief and fitful. And they both know that once Anne finds herself in full Tudor garb, she tends to unlayer herself only very slowly. Not now.

Anne puts her hand on Hatcher's. "It's Satan," she says.

"I adore your head," he says.

"In its place," she says.

∝

Hatcher sits in the kitchen after Anne has gone into the other room. The TV is on now. It's the stretch between news broadcasts, and the same made-back-on-earth episode of a commentary show called *The O'Reilly Factor* has been running over and over for a long while now, full of intense shared sneerings between the emotionally gaunt Bill O'Reilly and a gaunter guest named Ann Coulter. These were opinionators in Hatcher's time, but he never watched them. He ignored most of the rightist ranters. These two are in Hell now but are banned from all but earthly reruns. He understands they arrived together, locked, according to Carl Crispin's report, in a coital embrace in the first class suite of a crashed superjumbo Airbus. This show will continue to run to the exclusion of all else but the news for a long while, Hatcher knows. It replaced the long run of an episode of *Gilligan's Island*, wherein Gilligan bumps his head and subsequently sees everything upside down.

But now this iteration of the O'Reilly episode ends, and Hatcher turns his face toward the sound of the TV. The news will return for a one-minute spot. Beelzebub puts on his most dulcet tone and says, "And now the *News Digest from Hell*, with Jessica Savitch." Hatcher hurts for Jessica already.

"Good evening," she says. "Good evening."

In his mind, he can see her face constrict, as it does every time. She lets the other two good-evenings pass, and then—he understands just how her brain is compelled to work—the good-evenings end, and she expects news text to scroll up, and she reads by reflex.

"Poopy butt," Jessica Savitch says. "Poopy butt." Hatcher shakes his head sadly. He can hear Jessica make a strangling sound in the next room. Then she improvises. "Motherfuckers," she cries. "Motherfuckers. Can't you motherfuckers act like professionals?"

Hatcher knows the answer to her question. He thinks of poor Carl. And he wonders how Carl went wrong on the Harrowing story. Carl's ongoing torment—designed by Satan, of course, not only to torment Carl but Hatcher as well—could have deep ironies built in. Perhaps Carl was made to lie about lying. Hatcher rises. All right. He'll find Peachtree Way and Lucky Street for himself. He bangs his perpetually bruised thigh on the corner of the kitchen table and moves toward the door. "I'm going out for a while," he calls to Anne.

"Motherfucker," Anne calls in return, but rather sweetly, in a Tudor sense perhaps.

∝

Hatcher hopes that the Hoppers' door is closed so he can just move past without pausing. But his legs drag him to a stop, and he looks in.

They are sitting in their chairs.

They are still arguing. They both glance his way, but Peggy finishes her point to Howard, "If you looked forward to being alone for eternity, how did we end up in Boca together?"

"Boca wasn't forever," Howard says.

"It felt like it."

"Now you complain."

"I thought all I ever did was complain, to hear you tell it."

"And where would you have gone if not to Boca?"

"To my sister's."

"Without me."

"Of course without you."

"To Scranton, Pennsylvania, you'd go?"

"Yes, to Scranton."

"Instead of Florida."

Hatcher struggles to lift his feet, to put one foot in front of the other and just keep going.

"You're doing it again," Peggy says.

"What?"

"You're being rude to the famous TV personality."

"Me rude? You talk about him in the third person right in front of him. You think he's deaf?"

Peggy turns her face to Hatcher and she says, her voice abruptly faint, "He had feelings for me once."

There is a long moment of silence. Both Hoppers are looking at Hatcher, though they are seeing through him to a slow page-turning of images from their life together. Howard's voice also has waned. "Who said so?"

"You did."

They fall silent once more. Hatcher struggles to move.

"Yeah, but what feelings?" Howard says, low.

Peggy looks at him. She struggles with something in her mind. "I can't think of the word," she says.

And Hatcher can move. He does. He walks off without a word. He puts the Hoppers behind him. Even in the dark he can see that his alley is wide now, and at the far end is the orange glow of light from the Parkway.

Hatcher McCord, anchorman for the Evening News from Hell, *descends the staircase of his back alley apartment, picks his way through moaning shapes in the dark, and approaches the tumult of Grand Peachtree Parkway. He intends voluntarily to take a long walk through Hell. He will do this for the sake of a story.* Sometimes in his head, when things get particularly intimidating, Hatcher runs bits of voice-over narration to his afterlife. This impulse he's now following, for instance, the passage from his own neighborhood to Peachtree Way and Lucky Street, is intimidating. Of course, Satan knows what he's doing. Satan probably is the one who's doing the prompting. And behind that prompting may be torture of some carefully tailored sort. But Hatcher also knows a few things about how it works down here. And he's aware he has certain privileges. He had privileges in his life on earth for much the same reason. *Hatcher McCord is famous*, his narrator says. This inner voice helps. At that very moment, Hatcher has approached a barrier to the street—a kneeling, twitching body calling out "Mama"—and he leaps over it with something he feels is no less than lithe grace.

On the other side of the body, however, he goes abruptly empty. He pauses. He turns. He looks back. The body is crawling off quickly and it vanishes in the darkness. Hatcher wonders why he has turned. He wonders why he is standing here. *If his newsman's instincts are aroused, Hatcher McCord will never let a good story die.* Hatcher turns back to the bright orange glow, the tumbling, veering, bumping, compressing, stalling, lurching, rushing, outcrying crowd on Grand Peachtree Parkway. *Hatcher McCord does have privileges, thanks to his fame and his importance to society.*

Some other voice in Hatcher's head sighs. Not some other. Also his. Also Hatcher McCord. *Idiot. Hell is full of famous people without privileges. I'm useful. Useful to Satan. If you're listening, Chief, and I'm sure you are, I have to stress that I'm not being ungrateful. You see the anguish I'm in, so surely that makes it all right. I'm useful to you—the Lord of the Flies, the Former Most Beautiful Angel in Heaven, the Infamous Big Cheese—and that's like winning the sweeps with a fifty share. That creature I so gracefully leaped over—I'm right, aren't I, O Supreme One? I was quite wonderfully graceful?—that creature might have been Mick Jagger or Dwight Eisenhower or Dan Rather—not Henry VIII, I suppose—why do you let him flounce around as a young man?—but of course it's to torture me—and Anne too, I suppose—I hope it's torture for her—I leaped over that body quite elegantly, whoever it was, didn't I?*

Hatcher blinks and shakes his head furiously as if a hornet has flown into his ear. He is still subject to great pain, of course, personal and public. Like this. How simple this little inner dialogue is, but it is torture to him. He does know that he can move from one place to another without being waylaid and savaged mercilessly like most denizens. *He is damned, but he is still a journalist. Or, as Hatcher McCord himself might rephrase that as he tries to answer the enduring question of this place—why are you here?—he is damned, so he is still a journalist. Or even, he is a journalist, so he is damned. He will move now as a journalist through the main thoroughfare of the Great Metropolis, and he has the journalist's classic place in the world: he is part of the suffering humanity all around him but really he is not, he is an observer, his pulse quickening at the pain he observes, his deep brain sparking in delight at the possibility of a story and at the gravitas of that, the importance of that.*

"Shut the fuck up," Hatcher says aloud, addressing himself.

He waits. He has indeed seemed in his head to have shut the fuck up.

And so he stands in the mouth of his alley and waits as a megabyte of Internet gossip bloggers lurches by, the men in starlet-at-the-beach bikinis with celluloid-ravaged thighs and acid-seeping hard-ons, the women paunchy droopy naked but for Speedo trunks, weighed heavily about their necks with molten-hot gold pop-star bling, and all of them—a thousand or more—pass by in a long, dense gaggle, pinching and punching at each other. Hatcher's neighborhood has many journalists, and this gossip-blogger group lives at the very edge, at a distant turning of the Parkway where other denizens never actually go in person, where only this subset of bloggers huddle together over laptop screens, zinging each other. At last they pass, and Hatcher pushes onto Grand Peachtree Parkway, turns toward the place of the Ancient Harrowing, and presses into an unsorted crowd of denizens.

He is soon carried into the adjacent neighborhood, where many of the poets and playwrights and fiction writers dwell. He is moving more or less steadily now in a narrow corridor of space at the edge of the great flowing street crowd, squeezing along storefronts and piss-stained apartment stoops, the way often pinching shut from the veering of the crowd but then opening again. He passes by bookstore after bookstore, their windows dark, their shelves full of long-unsold remainders of all the local writers. The stores will open with hopeful new owners at the next sunrise and will be out of business by the next sundown.

Then in front of Hatcher a man lurches from the darkness of a doorway into a sudden flare of orange sodium vapor light. He is draped in a toga that perhaps long ago was white but now is dark with stains and spattered with what appear to be bird droppings, though Hatcher has never seen a bird in Hell. The man's hair is cropped close and his face is pasty and he has no nose, only a jagged outline of one in the center of his face as if he were an ancient marble statue.

"Please, denizen," he cries. "I am here to guide you." His hands flutter up in front of him as if he will grab at Hatcher.

Hatcher pulls back and wonders if he needs to defend himself. But it is more thought than instinct, and so he hesitates.

The man's hands fall, and he says, "Please. I know the way."

"Who are you?" Hatcher says.

"Publius Vergilius Maro."

The name sounds vaguely familiar to Hatcher, but he can't place it.

"I was a poet for the great Augustus," the man says.

"You're Virgil," Hatcher says.

"The Emperor is not so great now."

"Why do I connect you to Hell already?"

"But neither am I. I am but a broken image of myself."

Hatcher remembers. *"The Inferno."*

Virgil wags his head sharply, fighting off thoughts of his own past greatness, and he refocuses on Hatcher. "I'll guide you," he says.

"Like Dante," Hatcher says, meaning it as a little literary joke.

Virgil rolls his eyes. "Oh please. He was a pain in the neck."

Hatcher doesn't understand. "He was really here?"

"You'd never guess it from his poem."

"What Hell was it that you showed him?"

Virgil shrugs. "This one. But low-tech."

"He really came here?"

"And then he lied."

"He's back, isn't he."

"He doesn't go out much. He's still obsessed with the girl, always dreaming of joining her in Paradise."

"His Beatrice."

Virgil steps very close to Hatcher now. He is a surprisingly tall man, for his era, his face fully in Hatcher's. He reeks of rotten sardelles and Cyprian garlic. "You need to come with me," Virgil says.

Hatcher realizes this is one of those oh-right-I'm-in-Hell-and-this-isn't-really-a-matter-of-choice moments. He and Virgil look at each other. The crowd is jostling noisily by, but Hatcher can clearly hear the Roman's whistley breathing through his fragment of a nose. "Okay," Hatcher says.

Virgil turns abruptly and moves off. Hatcher follows. The poet turns in at the next alleyway.

In the narrow passage, the sounds from the Parkway abruptly cease. Hatcher hears only the scrape of his shoes on the pavement. This alley feels almost pristine beneath his feet—none of the offal squinch under-foot of his own alley—this sound echoes back from the tenements in the dark on either side. And somewhere far off he can hear the sound of a police siren. He has never heard that sound in Hell before. Virgil suddenly veers left and vanishes in the shadows. Hatcher stops, and instantly Virgil's voice urges him on. "In here," he says.

Hatcher steps into the blackness. Dimly he can see the poet's toga ahead, and he hears a knock. A door opens, and standing framed there in the jaundiced glow of bare bulb light is a man in a snap-brim and wide-lapeled suit. His face is in deep shadow.

Virgil says to the man, "He's here."

"Thanks," the man says. And from the timbre of the voice and the shibilant "s", Hatcher instantly knows who it is. Humphrey Bogart turns to the side to clear the door. The light falls on his creviced face, and even though his eyes are still in the shadow of his hat brim, Hatcher can see their sad, dark depth.

Virgil vanishes in the shadows. Hatcher steps forward.

"You're late," Bogey says.

Hatcher moves past him and into the back staircase landing of a tenement. The lightbulb juts nakedly from a fixture in a side wall, and mounting the opposite wall is a vast dark shadow of the staircase banister. Hatcher looks around him with the panic of an actor's dream. He's on and he doesn't know his lines.

Bogey steps up beside him. "Her note said 4D."

"4D," Hatcher says.

"One more thing."

"Yes?"

"Put your hat on."

Hatcher realizes there's something in his hand. He looks down. He holds a gun-metal gray snap-brim fedora. He puts it on.

The rasp and hiss of a match turns his face to Bogey, who is lighting a cigarette. Bogey drags once and exhales. He reaches into his inner coat pocket and pulls out a pack of cigarettes. He flicks one partway out. It's a Camel. He offers it to Hatcher.

Hatcher actually hesitates because he smoked as a teenager and then stopped in J-School and he is reluctant to start again. For his health.

Hatcher laughs a sharp, ironic laugh at this and takes the cigarette.

Bogey strikes another match. "I don't expect much from her either," he says, understanding the laugh in a way that Hatcher now also understands. What can this dame have to say?

Bogey holds the flame to the tip of Hatcher's cigarette. Hatcher inhales. As with all the everyday earthly physical pleasures, in Hell there is only a niggling disappointment, though occasionally there is, of course, searing pain of one sort or another. With this drag on a cigarette, for Hatcher there is niggling disappointment. Followed by the brief searing pain of feeling like a teenager.

"Let me do the talking," Bogey says.

Hatcher is suddenly all right. He nips with his thumb and forefinger at the tip of his snap brim. "Right," he says.

The two men climb the stairs. The light at the landing draws the shadow of the banister posts across their bodies first one way and then, when they turn, the other way, as if they are pacing in their jail cell.

At the fourth floor, their two fedoras come up from the light below and into the dark at the top of the stairs. Hatcher and Bogart stop on the threadbare runner that trails down the center of the corridor. At the far end is a thin slice of light at the bottom of a doorway. Bogey nods toward it. They move to the door and Bogey knocks.

From inside, a woman's voice says, "Come in." It's a high, thin, nasally voice.

Bogey draws a sharp breath. Hatcher looks at him, but his face is a mask of black in the dark corridor. Bogey pushes the door open.

The tenement apartment is one room, simple and seedy, as simple and seedy as a cheap hotel room in some dirty little working-class burg. A sagging couch, a desk, a few chairs, a blank wall where the Murphy bed hides, all of it in colors that don't even deserve the name "color."

Dingy grays and tans. And rising from a chair in the center of all this is the dame. A tiny body, fragile, chiseled features and dark, feverish eyes. Her lips are scarlet, painted large, like Satan's own butterfly.

Hatcher and Bogey are standing before the dame and she's looking at the two of them, one at a time, back and forth, like she's trying to figure out which one of them is going to throw her over his shoulder and carry her out of a burning building.

Hatcher waits for Bogey to do the talking, but his partner isn't saying a word. He looks at Bogey, whose face is lambent with repressed anguish, though nobody in the room would know what "lambent" means, even Hatcher at that moment, who is now very much Bogey's fellow private eye. Hatcher lifts an eyebrow and rolls his shoulders in his wide-lapeled suit, wondering what's going through his partner's mind. Bogey doesn't act like this around dames.

Finally Bogey speaks. "You're not who you said you were."

"Who'd I say I was?"

Bogey hesitates. "Nobody."

"That's me," she says.

"You're not who I thought."

"I got no control over what you think."

Abruptly Bogey turns to Hatcher. "You talk to her." And Bogey heads for the window, which looks out into utter darkness. "I thought she'd be someone else," he says, low.

Hatcher looks at the dame. She looks at him. She's wearing a flimsy little flower-print button-front dress, and the buttons are big and dazzling white, just asking to be undone.

Hatcher still doesn't know his lines, but he's catching on.

He takes a drag on his cigarette, and being a gentleman, he turns his head slightly, blowing the smoke just past the dame's right ear. He flips his head at the chair behind her, and she does what she's told. She sits. Hatcher stands over her, but he parks his Camel in the corner of his mouth, casually brushes his suit coat open, and eases his hands into his trouser pockets. Just to put her a little at ease.

"So?" he says. The cigarette loosens and starts to fall from his mouth. Hatcher grabs for it.

Meanwhile, Bogey stares into the nothing out the window as if it was something, and the voice in his head speaks: *I thought it was going to be her. I don't have any reason in this forsaken town to expect anything to turn out right, but somehow I thought it was going to be Baby at last. What a sap I am. Of course this is the way it ends up. You drink a lot. You crack some heads. Even to get her, there was the price of running out on your wife, and then maybe you even run around a little on her, out in the middle of the ocean heading for Catalina. You wouldn't have done that except for Baby getting seasick and never being able to go with you on the ocean in the boat you enjoy so much. Even if it's a little screwy, you try to keep a kind of a code about things. And you try to do your job straight. And you're true to your friends. You give away your last two fingers of bourbon. But you find yourself running into a brick wall. The thing they call your flawed humanity. So you end up in a cheap room in a hot climate and your cigarettes all taste like dust and it looks like you've got an extended booking. Still, I wanted it to be Baby real bad. I wanted her to have her back to me when I came through the door and there's just that thin long body and the rip curls of her dirty blond hair and she waits a beat or two before turning. Baby is Bacall, after all. She has a swell sense of timing. So she turns, and the hair falls a little over her face but you can see both her beautiful eyes, those wide-set eyes, and she gives me that little half smile and we're together again. That's what I wanted real bad. I may be a sap but I'm not stupid. I know what I'm wishing for. That Baby is spending eternity in Hell. I should be wanting real bad never to see her again. I should want her to be in Heaven playing a harp and looking swell in a white gown and wings. But I don't want that. I want her with me. Which probably is why I'm here.*

And Hatcher has caught his falling cigarette. But it has tumbled around and the tip of it touches his palm and the fire sears through his eternal skin and into his eternal capitate bone. Hatcher drops the cigarette and grits his teeth against the pain and tries not to cry out. He knows it would ruin the scene. He stays quiet. He's a trooper. Then abruptly the pain stops, and he's panting. But the dame doesn't seem to notice. He takes a deep breath and stubs the cigarette out with the toe of his wing tip brogue.

He starts over. "So?"

The dame shrugs. "You already said that."

Hatcher shoots his cuffs. "Listen, babe, you got something to say, say it."

"I need your help," she says.

"Everybody needs help in this town."

"I want to get out."

Hatcher answers her with a short guttural laugh, like hawking up phlegm from the back of the throat.

"Go ahead and laugh, wise guy," she says. "But there's a way out."

"Yeah? Who told you that?"

"My ex-boyfriend."

"And how does he know?"

"He did it once."

"So he's gone?"

"No. He's back."

"Why doesn't he go out again?"

"I don't know. Maybe he forgot how. Memories are short around here."

"And there are plenty of liars."

She shrugs. "That's why you private dicks stay in business. To sort out the lies."

"So where is he now?"

"I don't know. I try to avoid him."

"I'd think you'd want to stay close. In case he breaks out again."

"I avoid him."

"Why?"

"Because whenever I get near him, I have to reach into his chest and pull out his heart, and it bursts into flames, and when it's done burning, I eat it."

For a moment, not surprisingly, what film theorists call the "aesthetic distance" has been broken for Hatcher. This is, after all, still Hell.

But before Hatcher can think further about this, Bogey is beside him again. "So you're that kind of dame, are you?" he says.

The dame rolls her thin shoulders, which makes Hatcher reach inside his coat pocket and pull out a pack of cigarettes. "I guess I am," she says.

Somewhere far off a police siren wails.

Hatcher pops a cigarette, puts it in his mouth, stuffs the pack—his brand is Lucky Strikes—back into his coat, and he finds matches in a side pocket. He strikes one. He lifts the flame to the tip of his cigarette, and he realizes the conversation has stopped. Both Bogey and the dame are watching him. Hatcher takes the cigarette out of his mouth and turns it around, elegantly, and offers it to the dame. She opens her mouth slightly. Gently he puts the sucking end between her lips. She closes them on the cigarette, and they brush the tip of his finger. He draws his hand away slowly.

"Thanks," she says, real low.

Hatcher feels a hot tidal wave of unfocused regret wash over him. He aches.

Bogey says, "So you want us to locate this boyfriend and find out what he knows."

"I just want out," the dame says, lifting her face and blowing a thin plume of smoke into the shadows above her. "You figure out how."

"It won't be easy," Bogey says.

"If it was easy I'd do it myself," she says.

"This town," Bogey says.

"Yeah," she says.

"The walls have ears," he says.

"Don't I know it," she says.

"So you have to figure somebody already knows you're trying to blow the joint."

"Maybe."

"And he knows we're supposed to help."

"I don't care. I'll take that chance."

"But will I?"

Hatcher looks at them. He understands that they're talking about Satan. A chill passes through him, a physical reaction that's rare in Hell. It occurs to him that perhaps this whole scene isn't just another fleeting fabricated form of torture. Perhaps this is Bogey's ongoing life here, and the dame's. So why the chill? It's the newsman's chill, he realizes. As if there is a story. A big one. A way out. The young woman's face is angled toward Bogey, partly eclipsed in dark shadow. "What's your name?" Hatcher asks.

She turns to him, her full face flaring bright. She takes a long drag on the cigarette and blows the smoke out through her nose, never moving her dark eyes—as dark as Anne's—off his. "Beatrice Portinari," she says.

"You're Dante's girl," Bogey says.

"In a manner of speaking," she says.

Hatcher says, "He's the guy who's supposed to know a way out?"

"That's right."

"He lied," Hatcher says. Maybe there's not a story here after all.

Beatrice shrugs. "He's a poet."

"He made the whole inferno thing up."

"But the lies were true," she says.

Hatcher wags his head at this paradox he has never understood. "That's why I hate interviewing writers."

"Down here he's trying to write a novel," she says.

Inside Hatcher's head, he is answering himself: *You understand the journalist's paradox well enough. That truths can be put together to make a lie.*

"Look," Beatrice says. "He came and he went. You think his fourteenth century audience would have understood the real Hell? You should have seen this place when I arrived. Not that electric lights and the Internet haven't made things just as bad in their own way. But back then it was a nightmare version of the same life we all already knew. You think Dante could have written about what really goes on? All of us huddled together in the long night in a walled city burning our filthiest rags soaked in animal fat from who knows where and everybody compulsively reciting bad poetry in broken meters. With the smell and the sound of that stuff filling you up, you'd just throw yourself in the Lake of Fire to clear your head. But back in Florence they would've laughed that off. That can't be Hell. That's just daily life in Siena. Dante gave them the tortures they could believe in. But it was still torture."

Hatcher feels his newsman's twitch again. Maybe Dante really knew something. And maybe even the neo-Harrowing thing is related. This little noir scene has quickened him to the possibility of the biggest story in Hell. And he knows to try to turn off his brain, though it may already be too late. Satan is listening.

The police siren is wailing louder now.

Beatrice closes her eyes and pinches her mouth and shakes her head. At first Hatcher thinks she's just remembering Hell from the old days. But she stands up abruptly, turns, and moves to a door at the end of the room. She throws it open. Inside is a naked old man, his hands racing up and down his body scratching some terrible itch. He is howling like the police siren on about a 1941 Ford.

"Will you shut the fuck up?" Beatrice cries.

The man immediately shuts the fuck up, though his fingers continue to dig furiously at his body.

Beatrice slams the door and returns to her chair and sits.

She shakes her head in disgust. "He won't say which one, but he claims he's a pope. Boniface VIII is my guess."

The room is absolutely silent. There isn't even the buzz of a silent room in anyone's ears. Hatcher can't remember actual silence since he came to Hell. All three of them stir uncomfortably. They all three think they can hear Satan listening.

Then Bogey says, "Fuck you, Old Man."

Beatrice and Hatcher brace themselves. That will do it. A whirlwind of flaming sulfur will rush through the window now and they'll have to decompose and recompose in agony for a while and then get back to the old chaos. But the silence goes on. And on.

Beatrice whispers, "See?"

"What?" Hatcher says, low.

"They'd never have understood this."

"I'm not sure I do either," Bogey whispers.

Beatrice says, "We're still alive."

They all rustle around a little in their skin to verify that.

"So it seems," Hatcher says.

"That's the real torture," Beatrice says. "Just that."

Bogey says, "You've been eating too many flaming hearts, sister."

"Get me out of here," she says.

"We'll do what we can," Bogey says. He looks at Hatcher and nods toward the door.

"How can we find you?" Hatcher says.

Beatrice smiles faintly and blows smoke into the air between them. She looks past Hatcher. "You know what I'm about to say, don't you?"

Bogey puts a heavy, searingly hot hand on Hatcher's shoulder. "Don't let her say it."

Beatrice smiles.

"I could smack a woman around a little in life," Bogey says to Beatrice. "Think what I can do in Hell."

"You won't touch me," Beatrice says. "You're soft inside. Face the facts. The problem of one little man finding his dame doesn't amount to a hill of beans in Hell."

Bogey pulls at Hatcher's shoulder. "Let's get out of here." But Hatcher can't seem to move and neither can Bogey.

Beatrice looks at Hatcher. "If you want me," she says, "just whistle," Bogart moans.

"You know how to whistle, don't you?" she says. Bogey's hand, which has been burning hotly into Hatcher's shoulder all this while, goes suddenly cold. "You just put your lips together and blow."

The two men find they can move. They cross the room and go out the door. They head down the dark hall, not saying a word. But all around them now, sounds are coming from behind the passing apartment doors. Moaning sounds. Keening sounds. Classic gnashing-of-teeth sounds. And then, from behind the last door this side of the stairwell, comes the pittering of a computer keyboard. Hatcher slows and stops. Bogey goes on around the corner. The neighborhood is full of writers. Hatcher has the impulse to open this door. He does.

The room is black except for the radiance from a computer monitor. In profile, a man's head hangs in the light, the darkness shrouding the rest of him. It's not even clear there is a rest of him—as if he were like Anne, arrived in Hell from a beheading—though the sound of furious typing clatters from the dark where his hands and keyboard would be. He is a bald man with the fringe of his hair cut very short and with a faintly aquiline nose. He does not take his eyes from the computer screen.

Hatcher understands that the man is a writer, and he seems vaguely familiar for some reason or other, though maybe not for his writing exactly—from tabloids and gossip columns, perhaps—maybe there was a woman involved somehow—but Hatcher can't place him.

"I don't know who you are," Hatcher says.

"Neither do I," the man says. The head floats closer to the screen, the eyes narrowing. "Though I yearn to."

The typing, fast already, begins to accelerate, faster and faster until the individual keystrokes blur together into a low moan. "I'm in here somewhere," the man says.

Hatcher watches for a moment, thinking to go but once again is unable to move. Then, even as the typing moans louder, the writer turns his face to Hatcher and says, "Back out of the room now and gently close the door."

Hatcher backs out of the room and gently closes the door. He steps into the stairway landing, and Bogey is gone. He listens for the man's footsteps below, but hears nothing. "Bogey?" he calls. There's no answer. Even the corridor behind him is quiet. They're all suffering in silence now, and it's time to move on.

∝

He calls again, in the dark outside the alley door of Beatrice's tenement, but this time for Virgil. Anything Dante knew about Hell, Virgil knows it too. Hatcher tries to stop overtly thinking about the matter any further: he focuses on the distant din of Grand Peachtree Parkway. This back-alley episode seems to be finished, and maybe Virgil is gone. But he found Hatcher out there in the street. He's of that realm too. "Virgil," he calls again. "Publius Vergilius Maro!" Hatcher cries. But still there is no answer. Except from the invisible rats of Hell. All around him he hears the stirring of their feet, the clatter of their scrabbling claws like the sound of computer keyboards, a million keyboards, all the writers in Hell typing frantically away.

Hatcher hurries off in the direction of the Parkway.

When he emerges from the alley, he makes note of the place. The whistle crap was simply to torture Bogey. Hatcher might want to try to find Beatrice again. Of course it's possible for anything suddenly to change in Hell. But for the most part, change is gradual, and the quotidian details—from backed-up toilets to confusing street names—stay torturously the same. So. Directly opposite, in the Parkway median, full of construction rubble and gouged earth, some concrete blocks mount narrowly upward to a twisted tangle of rebar—all of it vaguely in the taunting shape of a tree. There are no trees in Hell. To his left is a run of bookstores, the nearest with its name on a tattered standing sandwich board: **Hell's Belles Lettres**. To his right is a shop with a red neon sign jutting over the sidewalk, bloodily illuminating the area, spewing sparks: **BURGERS**. He shudders to think of the meat in those. He is grateful that, of all the things he is compelled to do in this place—knowing even as he does them how badly they will turn out—he is not compelled to eat the hamburgers of Hell. And this thought scares him. He braces himself for that very impulse now, to go in there and order the double cheeseburger as a punishment for thinking he has something to be grateful for.

But the impulse does not come. Hatcher can imagine Satan having his little laugh. He won't let his subjects anticipate him. And the fear of punishment is torture aplenty. Satan knows what he's doing and why he's doing it. And with that thought, Hatcher recognizes the contradictions of trying to remember how to find this alley again. If the Old Man wants him to find Beatrice, he will. If he doesn't, Hatcher's remembering these landmarks will do no good.

Meanwhile, struggling along at the near edge of the passing crowd, approaching Hatcher, is a deeply disgruntled Jezebel, former wife of King Ahab of Israel. Though personal age can shift abruptly in any direction in Hell, she is perpetually dressed in rags and she is old, as she was when

36

she was pushed from her balcony by eunuchs and then eaten by dogs, and inside her, a voice is always speaking. *It's not the Tishbite Elijah or his false god who has put me here, never, his people are here too, in abundance. As are mine, but I was as true to my gods as he was to his, and his god was an angry old man who adored the waste of the desert, and he was a savage god. My husband spoke of these traditions of his: the rape and murder of every man, woman, and child of any nation in the path of their wandering—Midian and Bashan and Heshbon and Makkedah and Libnah and Lachish and Gezer and many more. And I built sweet gardens where my gods dwelled among the almond trees and the pomegranate trees and we worshipped naked in beds of narcissus and cro-cus and henna and we consecrated the poplar and the palm and the tamarisk, as Baal would have us do to join like a newlywed with the sweetly, blessedly bur-geoning world around us. And for this, the foul old man stinking in haircloth spoke as if he were a god himself and cursed us with a long drought, raping and murdering even the flowers and the trees. And how powerful was the god he spoke for? Even after the Tishbite took my husband and all my priests up to Mount Carmel and worked some magic trick with the weather upon them and then slaughtered all eight hundred and fifty of my devout holy men, my simple woman's wrath scared him away for years. Elijah fled at the mere threatening of his life. What was the point of a stroke of lightning from his god and some cooked bullock and the murder of eight hundred and fifty sincerely devout men, if the triumphant effects lasted half a day? And even years later, after his people finally succeeded in murdering my husband, their king, I ruled his Israel for fourteen years, and when I knew they were finally coming for me, I died with dignity, painting my eyes with black kohl and anointing my skin with opal balsam. Okay. We did our share of slaughtering. Okay. But so did they all, in all the following millennia as well, apparently, because they're all here in Hell, the big shots of all the religions. So then who is the true god who judges us all so harshly? He gave me my time and my place to be born and a daddy who was a king and a priest and who stroked my hair and kissed my brow and who I had no alternative but to believe, when he said what life was about. Whoever that god is, he set me up to be who I was. So why for eternity do I have to wear rags and stink like a Tishbite? And why oh why am I compelled to figure out how to do e-mail?*

Keeping up with advances in technology is one of the great tortures of Hell for the old-timers, and as Jezebel's mind works itself around to this, her increased agitation makes her veer from the edge of the crowd and she steps heavily on the foot of a man standing at the mouth of an alley. This is Hatcher McCord, whose foot suddenly flares wildly in pain, the source of which, an old woman in a bundle of rags, lurches against him and seems about to tumble to the ground, where she will be routinely crushed by the crowd. Though the pain she has caused is shooting up his leg and making his knee cap feel as if it is about to explode, Hatcher's hands rush out and gently hold the old woman at the shoulders, which squish and shift as if he has grabbed handfuls of maggots. But he perseveres in his hold in order to keep her from falling, and she steadies herself and passes on without a word or a glance at him.

He watches her go.

Something just happened, he realizes vaguely, this gesture with someone who has just hurt him, something that he should stop and consider. But things are getting muddled in his head. Satan's work. The Old Man doesn't like too much thinking. Everyone understands that. Though Hatcher stands there thinking about how he can't think. He wants to stop. Not for Satan's agenda but his own. He wants to stop thinking in order to fully experience something important to think about. The immediate physical and emotional encounter with life in Hell sometimes begins to add up in certain ways, and maybe this should yield the most important ideas. *It all has to come back to these ways we exist in our moment to moment encounters with consciousness—even into eternity—even if the moments leap and circle and combine, we are still along for the ride, and we have company—like the woman who stepped on my foot—and we have to figure out how to deal with all that. But Satan won't let me think about not thinking,* Hatcher thinks, and so he stops.

And what's next? The night is young. He has a story to pursue off in the direction of Peachtree Way and Lucky Street, one that got as far as the official *Evening News from Hell* lineup. Satan seems to be going along with this for now. He turns to the right and rides along with the crowd.

∝

The night streets teem with bodies and screams, though the screamers are different from the screamers before the setting of the sun. These are the denizens with night terrors, taking over from those with the anguish of twilight. There are cars now as well, the automotive technology often retro, the center of the street jammed and blaring with Cords and Fords and Moons, with Vauxhalls and Maxwells and Fiats and BMWs, with Hondas and Renaults and Zims, their drivers and passengers sealed inside, banging on the windows and crying out in rage at the drivers and passengers in the cars around them, and none of them moving, except intermittently to lurch forward several feet to crush a few pedestrians in the eddies flowing around them, only to stall again, while beneath their tires and body frames, the crushed denizens wail away until the next lurch of traffic allows them to rise and reconstitute.

For a time, Hatcher loses his knack for mobility and gets sucked from the margin of the flowing crowd and toward its center. He wonders if this means his Big Boss has now decided this story should be dropped. There are never editorial meetings as such. Things come up. Things get pursued until something—often painful—occurs to stop them. Being crushed in the center of a nighttime crowd would be one of the simpler terminations to a story. Hatcher figures the initial tolerance of the neo-Harrowing item was simply to build false hopes anyway. Even if, as Hatcher's news nose faintly whiffs, there is some sort of something true behind this, it would involve such a small number of denizens that covering it would have a torturous effect on the vast numbers once again left behind. But it wouldn't have to be true to be torture. Maybe this was all simply to arrange that public, humiliating disavowal of the story by Carl. And the news nose whiff will be a purely private disappointment.

Hatcher keeps his mind thus desperately occupied amid the multitude of gropers and pinchers and farters and bleeders, the maggoty and the pustulant and the leprous and the Botoxically botulinal. He is worried because he knows they are entering Hell's tenderloin, and soon all these bodies about him will begin to cast off their clothes and grow desperate with unscratchable itches. As unpleasant as the crush of bodies now is, it will get far worse when they are naked. Is Satan pissed with him? But now Hatcher feels himself twisted by an eddy of the crowd and borne to the margin, and he is dumped flat on his back in the mouth of a side street.

A long-bearded old man's face appears, hovering over him. The man is clothed in a gunnysack, and he lifts a hand-scrawled sign on a stick and floats it before Hatcher. It once read "Repent. The end is nigh." But one letter has been scratched out and replaced and a new word has been careted in, and the man now slides away to gyre endlessly on the corner urging the denizens to REPEAT. THE END IS NEVER NIGH.

Hatcher struggles to his feet and faces the Parkway. It is utterly clogged, the crowd ground now to a halt, the air above it filling with the rise and fluttering fall of shed clothing. Hatcher turns around and looks down the side street. It is a dead end leading to splashes of neon on a large building, obscured, from this distance, by the dark. He takes a step toward it, and from the darkness at the top of the building comes an abrupt bright red sparking flare and a clap of sharp sound. Hatcher hesitates, but the flame evaporates and the afterclap subsides, and he moves on.

Soon the building shows itself in the red glow of its neon signs: a wide ground-floor facade of colonnaded arches and two dark-windowed upper floors and minarets at the front corners rising into the night. The neon proclaims: LIVE! NUDE! THE HOUSE OF VIRGINS! YOU'VE MADE IT! 72 FOR U!

And now beside Hatcher is an unmistakable, forced, drawly chuckle: "Heh heh heh. If it isn't Hatch the Snatch."

Hatcher turns and finds the ship-anchor nose and narrow eyes and heavy brows of a familiar face. "Mr. President," Hatcher says, reflexively using the honorific, though he likes the irony now. This was the last president he covered, and for a moment, at the very end of Hatcher's life on earth, as his heart attack began, he felt his own imminent premature death would be mitigated by not having to live out this one's full second term.

"Hatch the Snatch," George W. Bush says.

"Mr. President."

"Snatch the Hatch."

"Welcome, Mr. President. I didn't know you'd arrived."

George turns his eyes to the House of Virgins. "He's inside. I got him now."

"Who's that?"

"Osama. I got him now."

From the House of Virgins, a wail begins—a man's voice—and at first, briefly, it sounds like sexual fervor, but quickly the sound morphs, the voice clearly is crying in intense pain, and around his voice begins the sound of female voices, ululating together, a chorus of trilling excitement—a chorus of seventy-two, no doubt—and then suddenly a third-floor window flares bright with flame and an explosion punches through the air and the flames leap out of the window and carry with them disassembled male body parts—legs, arms, a torso, a wide-eyed head—that fall to the ground before the building. The flames flicker out in the window, the women's voices fall silent, and the body parts lie motionless for a moment. Then abruptly the parts all rise into the air and reassemble into a naked, darkly bearded young man. As soon as his body is recomposed, he begins screaming again in pain but without a moment's hesitation he dashes for the front door of the House of Virgins and disappears inside.

"That wasn't him," George says. "See, this happens every couple of minutes. Osama's waiting his turn, like we used to in the back of Spunky's in Crawford. How's about that for pointyhead ironicky? My intelligence report says they have to wait in line for the seventy-two virgins."

"Your intelligence report?"

"Somebody gave it to me when I got off the boat."

"Who was that?"

"Some guy who met me right there at the dock. He says, 'Mr. President, here is your intelligence briefing.' See, I'm back in the saddle here, Hatch. A little heavenly reward."

"Pardon me?"

"I'm just wondering how, if they keep doing the same seventy-two virgins over and over again, then you know, how they're actually virgins when, like, the second guy does them and so on."

"You mentioned a heavenly reward . . ."

"Well now, Hatch, a reward can't be the explanation. See, that's Hell you're looking at there. Inside that Arab looking building. Osama and those virgins and those other boys are all in Hell."

Hatcher turns to George. "Mr. President . . ."

"Though maybe you're right. Satan could turn those girls back into virgins each time. That would certainly be Hell. Right, Hatch? Heh heh heh." George's chuckling ceases with another male voice baying in pain from the house and then the women ululating and then the exploding and the afterclapping and the thudding to the ground of the body parts. George watches in wonder.

"That's not him either," George says.

"Mr. President . . ."

"I'm sure glad I'm not in Hell," George says.

"Sir, you are."

"Looks pretty rough in there."

"Mr. President, it's Hell out here too. You're in Hell."

George turns to Hatcher. "Heh heh heh. You've got your disinformation all wrong there, Snatch."

"That was the River Styx you came over on the boat."

George puts on a you-poor-dumb-shit smirk. "The reports are clear. You see, we're standing here in Heaven, and those boys inside that building over there are in Hell."

"Look around," Hatcher says. "Does this look like Heaven?"

George doesn't move his eyes from Hatcher's. "We're searching now for the WMDs—Wings Made Divine—and we expect to find them soon."

A man's cries, the women's cries, the explosion—louder this time—and George keeps his eyes on Hatcher, keeps the smirk fixed, and Hatcher feels a sharp hot burn on his forehead, his cheek—a splash of boiling liquid—and another—glowing red—and it's falling on George too—a splashing of blood on his hair, his face, searing Hatcher and George—and the former president's eyes widen, though he does not move a muscle. And then a small, flaming object plops onto George's shoulder. It is a raggedly severed penis, smoking and glowing red, the flames dying at once. George moves his eyes very slightly to look at the object, and then he returns his eyes to Hatcher and waits. Soon the blood strips itself from the two men and coalesces in the air and the penis rises from George's shoulder, and then the blood and the penis fly off to join the reassembling of the exploded man.

George's smirk fades, and Hatcher knows the former president is realizing at last where he is. Then, after a long moment, George clears his throat. His voice is barely a whisper. "So this is where I am?"

"That's right."

George nods. "Have you seen my dad?"

"Yes."

"And my mom?"

"I haven't seen her."

George nods again. "She's probably in the other place."

Hatcher holds his tongue.

"If she is here," George says, "she's going to find me and whip my ass. Heh heh heh." This time the chuckle is small and sad.

Hatcher wants badly to move away from George now. But before he does, his journalist's self makes him say, "I do the evening news here, Mr. President. When you get settled, stop by Broadcast Central and we can do an interview."

George says, "I'm pretty much on my own here, right Hatch?"

"That's right."

George nods. "Thanks for asking, but I don't think I'd know what to say."

Hatcher mutters a good-bye and moves quickly up the street, thinking about the hell of not knowing who you are and the hell of suddenly knowing.

∝

The Parkway is stalled, dense with naked bodies, their private parts jammed into the private parts of whatever body is pressed against them, wedged there and flaming. Nighttime is the wrong time for this journey, Hatcher realizes. And the sadness of George Bush and the anguish of the jihadists and the priapic pain of the crowd before him turn Hatcher back toward his own neighborhood: *Hatcher McCord understands that sometimes the time is right for a particular news story, and sometimes it isn't. Sometimes larger issues present themselves. He is, after all, spending eternity in the same place as George W. Bush. Who can tell him why?* George certainly has refreshed this question, and in spite of the din of voices all around Hatcher and the sucking sounds and the fleshy squeegee rubbing sounds, when his voice-over pauses for dramatic effect, Hatcher's head goes utterly silent for a long moment. Then: *Naomi can. Wife number*

*three. And Deborah. Wife number two. And Mary Ellen. Wife number one. They all
would have thoughts on the subject of why he's here. He might deny the reliability of
these sources, but obviously he didn't get it right, either. Here he is forever with Osama
and George and all the rest. And with Naomi, surely. And Deborah. And Mary Ellen.
Surely these women are somewhere in town as well, or soon will be. If Hatcher McCord
approaches the Big Why? as if it were a news story—and it is, in a certain way—the
instinct he has to track down his former wives is a natural one, journalistically. But by
now he knows this instinct in himself as something else: seek the fresh torture. Yes, he
will try to find his ex-wives. He is the very model of an intrepid newsman. But also he
is driven to suffer.* There is a swelling of cheesy music in Hatcher's head, and
he is glad the voice-over is finished. That voice was right, however. He squares
his shoulders. *Okay, Old Scratch. You've got some new thing in mind for me. Scratch
the Hatch. Hatch the Scratch. But fuckitfuckitfuckitfuckit, I'm going home to Anne
first.* He squeezes into the near margin of the crowd, his back to all the naked
suffering, and he creeps off, thinking that Satan even wants this, of course,
for him to go to Anne, old torture before fresh.

∝

Anne is naked and whole in their bed in the dark, the TV and the hanging, bare, low-watt lightbulb both turned off, and she looks up at Hatcher
as he crosses to her, her eyes so dark they register as light in the lesser
dark of the room. As soon as he sees her, he is wanting her, wanting to
touch her and finally finally die with her, but with the step before the
step before the last step, he thinks how he is wanting her, wanting to
touch her, and wanting finally finally to die with her but how this always
goes wrong, and with the step before the last step he thinks how thinking about how the wanting her, wanting to touch her and wanting finally
finally to die with her is often the very thing that makes it go wrong, and
with the last step all he is doing is thinking about thinking about wanting
her. And his body is no longer wanting her.

He stands there. She lies there. They look at each other.

"It went away," she says.

"Yes," he says.

Her eyes are so beautiful, he thinks.

"For me too," she says.

"Yet again," he says.

"I was in my mortal life a woman of strong will," she says.

"Yes."

"And you were a powerful man."

"So I thought."

"You still are."

"No. Even on earth, I observed power. I spoke of it. Merely that. My own power was celebrity."

"That is great power."

"Only an illusion of power."

"We are ourselves illusions now, forever."

"And even those who had true power in life," Hatcher says, "it was in a narrow alley and for a passing moment. They're all here now, I think. All of them."

"But I remember what it feels like, to have a strong will."

Hatcher says, "What did it get you, though, my darling Anne. Look at how it ended. Henry's will was even stronger, and yet even he could never get what he wanted, and now he's in Hell like everyone else."

She closes her eyes.

Hatcher squeezes at his forehead. He himself has brought up Henry. "Why did I say that?"

"Because you are powerless not to," she says.

But her voice is soft, and Hatcher says, "You're not angry."

She thinks on this. She opens her eyes. "That's true."

"And I'm not jealous, even having brought up the king."

Anne rises onto an elbow. "Render thyself naked now, Lord Hatcher, and come lie beside me. Quickly."

He throws off his shirt and his pants, working his way down toward merely skin.

"No thinking," Anne says. "Look me in the eyes."

He does. He does. And he is naked and he is beside her.

Tonight the mattress is gravelly hard. He ignores this.

They have gotten this far before.

They both start to lift their arms to embrace and there is a clash of wrists and elbows. They stop and wait.

"You start," she says, falling onto her back and putting her arms alongside her, as if she were in a coffin.

Hatcher twists around and slides an arm behind her at the shoulders, his hand vanishing there and instantly snagging on a coil of her unfurled hair. Anne gasps.

"Sorry," he says, withdrawing the arm quickly.

"You're pulling my hair," she says.

"Sorry."

"The headsman lifted me like that, just after."

"I'm sorry."

"Those very roots you just pulled. They held my head aloft."

"No remembering," Hatcher says. "Look me in the eyes."

She turns her eyes to him.

Hatcher slides his arm under her, farther down, at the shoulder blades. She shifts a little toward him and a shot of nerve pain runs from his elbow down his arm and into his hand. He gasps.

"Did that hurt?" she says, lifting up. "I didn't know."

He pulls his arm out.

They both sit. They put their hands on each other, gingerly, at the shoulders. They are sweating. There is a sound from the alley. A voice.

"Someone's singing," Anne says.

"They're weeping," Hatcher says.

"No," she says. "Listen. There. 'Pastime with good company, I . . .' something ' . . . and shall until I die.'"

"It's a woman crying," he says. "There. Hear that?"

"Henry wrote that song, just after he became king."

"That little trilling sob."

"What was the word in the lyric? I *what* until I die?"

"It sounds like Mary Ellen crying."

"I couldn't hear."

"Listen."

And they both listen. But the alley is silent.

They look at each other. Their hands are still on each other's shoulders. For a moment, they're not sure why.

"We were trying," Anne says.

"Yes."

"I'm actually sleepy," she says.

"You're never sleepy," he says.

"I am now."

They let go of each other, and they lie down, side by side.

And soon Anne is asleep. To thrash and dream badly, of course.

Then, rare as well, Hatcher falls asleep.

And after a time, he rises to wakefulness from another rare thing. Indeed, a first for him in Hell. He is having an unmitigatedly good sexual feeling. He opens his eyes, and he is on his back and staring at the glowing filament of the bare lightbulb hanging above him. Instantly, he knows three things: he is awake, Anne is not beside him, and he is presently the recipient of an ardent and expert blow job. He closes his eyes again. He thinks briefly of his boyhood in Pittsfield: a shower nozzle, stove-warmed Vaseline on an oven mitt, an actual girl from a double-wide out along the Illinois River. But he is with a queen now. So he opens his eyes and lifts his head slightly and looks down his naked torso to Anne, her mouth working expertly, her beautiful eyes looking back up along his torso into his own. Then her eyes close and release his gaze, which drifts up and slightly to the left, and there, across the room, sitting in a chair, filing its fingernails, is Anne's headless naked body.

Hatcher does exactly the wrong thing. He screams and jumps up. Anne's head—having limited motor skills and, in its detached state, being more prone than usual to being startled—clamps its mouth tightly shut. Hatcher leaps about the room now, knocking into the bed stand, the window, the wall, Anne's head whipping up and down and back and forth with each movement. This being Hell, there is nothing to prevent Anne's teeth from actually biting clean through Hatcher's distressed member, for him subsequently to be reassembled. It occurs to him that this would actually be preferable, in that it would put a clear end to the present ordeal. In this instance, however, Anne's head bites only hard enough to hold on, and so Hatcher—though movement is not in his ongoing best interest—compulsively continues to leap and spin and pirouette and, within the confines of this very small room, even execute two unmistakable grand jetés, one from the window to the opposite wall and then another back again.

At last he lands in front of Anne's body, and with great force of will he holds himself steady and grasps her head between his two hands and pleads for her to release him and reattach. Anne's hands do rise now, and they grasp her head, and she releases Hatcher, who crumples to the floor. Anne puts her head onto her body, stretches her neck, looks down at Hatcher, and says, her tone criticizing *him* and not her, "Nothing I ever do in bed is right."

∝

Meanwhile, in the alleyway, the voice that Hatcher and Anne heard is still silent. It both cried and sang, though not like Hatcher's ex-wife and not King Henry's "Pastime with Good Company." Ernest Hemingway stands even now out there in the dark. He is looking for a good bar—he has been looking for a good bar for pretty much as long as he's been in Hell—and he can't find one and, as it often does, his failure has made him weep for a time. A little girlishly, it's true. This is Hell. And while he wept, he sang in a mumbly, untuned voice, easy to misunderstand from a distance, it's true. But the song, in fact, was from the Spanish Civil War, "A las Barricadas," the hymn of the Anarcho-Syndicalists. And now Ernest Hemingway stands in an alleyway in Hell and his head is full of words.

It was late and everyone had come into the café. The place was dim and full of bullfighters and Gulf fishermen and boxers and Upper Peninsula Indians and some boys from the Lincoln Battalion who died at Jarama. No one could see anyone's face, the bar was so dark. The old man sat at a table by the window. The only light in the place came from a lamp on the street and it shone on the old man. He was dressed in a white poplin empire dress.

The two waiters inside the café watched him. "He committed suicide," the older one said.

"Why?"

"Look at him."

"That's why?"

"His mother put him in that."

"How do you know his mother did it?"

"Who else? If he wished it for himself, he wouldn't be wearing it here."

The younger waiter nodded.

The old man wanted another drink. He wanted a first drink. But there was nothing to drink here. There were only all the men he ever knew or ever thought about. Then his wives came into the café. He knew they would come. And the women he slept with and didn't marry but wanted to. And the women he didn't sleep with but wanted to. And the women he slept with but didn't want to. Everyone was here. Everything he'd ever done was here, inside his skull. What did he fear? It was not fear or dread. It was an everything that he knew too well. It was all in darkness but it was all here, and it needed that, the dark, and the heat.

The light in the street went out and he was in darkness now too. He had always been in darkness. He knew it was all todo y pues todo y todo y pues todo. Our todo who art in todo, todo be thy name, thy kingdom todo thy will be todo in todo as it is in todo.

And in the dark of an alley in Hell, Ernest Hemingway whispers aloud, "Forgive us our todo as we forgive the todo who todos against us." With this, Ernest looks into the darkness above him, thinking about who might be hearing his words—he has always wanted at least to be heard—and his hand goes reflexively up and palms the back of his head, which he once blew off with his favorite Boss 12-gauge shotgun. Then the hand falls and he lowers his face. He begins to cry once more and he begins to sing once more, but he does both things very softly, so softly that no one around can hear.

∝

What appears to be the sun in what appears to be the sky in Hell usually teases its way up in the morning, repeatedly tantalizing and disappointing the denizens, showing just the merest upper edge of its corona, drawing a trickling blood-flow of light from the dark above the mountains, brightening the streets and the windows ever so slightly, just enough to be noticed, but then falling back, snuffing it all out, only to almost appear again and then vanish again. It behaves this way over and over before it finally provides an actual dawn—having suckered the denizens each time—and it does all this after what is always a long, long night. So when Anne reattaches her head and folds her arms across her naked chest and closes her eyes and when Hatcher is able to quit writhing in pain and rise and stagger into the other room to sit, naked still, at the kitchen table, their reasonable expectation is that they will sleep almost not at all but sink into bored stupefaction and that they will have plenty of warning that the night is beginning to struggle to an end.

But not this time. They doze inopportunely. And the sun comes up abruptly. And their apartment booms with heavy hands on their door. Hatcher has time only to convulse awake and jump up to full dangly nakedness as the door slams open and in rush Robin and Maurice Gibb in powder-blue jumpsuits. They leap apart to frame the open door, striking mirror disco poses, their outer arms lifted up, their outer legs cocked, and they sing, in intensely vibrating falsettos, "Staying ali-i-i-ive, staying alive." The powder-blue jumpsuits are a common uniform for the official minions in Hell. That the Gibb brothers have already attained this status tells Hatcher something he suspected on earth about the ascendance of disco in an era of rock and roll. The brothers Gibb fall silent and shakily hold their poses. It now registers on Hatcher that it is dawn and it is time to go to the interview with Satan. As the dead disco dandies totter in embarrassment—even Hell's minions, of course, are still subject to torture—Hatcher will shortly regret not taking this opportunity to slip into the bedroom and grab some clothes. But before this thought has a chance to form, into the open doorway, also wearing a powder-blue jumpsuit, steps the former director of the FBI, J. Edgar Hoover.

He takes two steps into the room, placing the Gibb brothers in the position of backup singers, strikes the same disco pose as theirs, and sings, "What you doin' on your back, aah?" The room fills with drum machine thumping and brass-section riffing and the Gibbs' background quavering, all in service to J. Edgar Hoover's lead vocal, which is complete with echo chamber effects. Hoover ratchets up his falsetto with "You should be dancin', yeah," and the three do a perfectly synchronized arm and leg switch and sing on.

At some point in his tenure in Hell, Hatcher noticed how, though many millions—indeed, no doubt, billions—of the dead are teeming around the place from all the eras and places in the history of the planet, the ones who primarily come his way tend to be the people he is in some way familiar with. Though freshly rendered interpersonal torture does occur—Anne Boleyn's with him, for instance—that tends to be rarer. The torture of the familiar is the norm. And so, given the musical sensibilities Hatcher treasured in his earthly life, it is hard to exaggerate the severity of his torture at standing naked in his tiny kitchen in Hell as former FBI director J. Edgar Hoover sings a Bee Gees disco song backed by a full studio orchestra and Robin and Maurice. Hatcher wants to run and hide. He wants at least to go put some clothes on. But he is unable to move, even through the dance interlude, where the three do a line hustle together, pumping their arms furiously, and through the endless repeats of the you-should-be-dancing chorus, and even as Hoover and the Gibbs simulate a studio fade, singing in smaller and smaller voices until they are silent.

Now Hatcher tries again to move but can only teeter.

"Oh no you don't," J. Edgar says. "You're coming with me."

Hoover steps to him, crushes Hatcher's elbow in a fist, and guides him, naked, out the door, down the spiral staircase, and into the backseat of a waiting 1948 Cadillac Fleetwood limousine as black as the night that has just passed.

∝

Once inside the Cadillac, Hatcher understands the unique infernal possibilities of being shut up naked in a tight private space with J. Edgar Hoover, given the long-understood but dangerous-to-pursue story of the man, which even included rumors that the Mafia had photos of him flouncing in a feather boa and a little black dress at a private party. Indeed, Hoover instantly begins to sing in a tiny falsetto, "Nobody gets too much heaven no more," and Hatcher tucks his private parts out of sight, tightly crosses his legs, and slides over against the door.

Beyond the black privacy window separating the driving compartment there is a scuffling sound and chirpings of pain as the Gibb brothers crowd in. The unseen driver grinds the car into gear and Hatcher is thrown back from the acceleration down the alleyway and then thrown toward Hoover with a sharp turn into Grand Peachtree Parkway. He quickly recovers his ball-crushingly modest pose. Alarmingly, though, Hoover has stopped singing and is now panting heavily. Hatcher presses his face hard against the window and squeezes his legs painfully together. He has no chance to stop the thought to Satan: *Come on, Old Man, I'm just trying to let you say what's on your mind and you have to turn it into this.* "Oh shit," Hatcher says aloud, certain that his rashly critical thought will now prompt Satan to fully unleash the libido of the former director of the FBI.

But instead, Hoover's panting stops with a groan. He cries, "And if thy right eye offend thee, pluck it out, and cast it from thee" and Hatcher does not listen to the sounds that follow this but concentrates on the extraordinary rate of speed the driver is maintaining through the dense crowd in Grand Peachtree Parkway, the thumping of bodies against the car coming so fast as to blend into a low roar.

Behind the wheel, Richard M. Nixon could be expected to draw some pleasure from the carnage he is wreaking—perceiving, as he does, all the denizens of Hell as his personal enemies—but in fact he is distracted by the acute discomfort of physical contact with the Gibb brothers, who are pressed against him, obsessively jutting their hips and hustle-stepping and shooting their arms up in disco poses that are gradually crushing all the bones in their hands against the roof of the car, their falsetto screams ringing in the driver's compartment. And inside Dick Nixon: *My old man's cheeks and forehead would flush bright red and my saint of a mother knew what was coming and his fists rose and I backed out of the kitchen door and I put my hands over my ears because of the sound that would follow, and even the touch of my own hands startled me, nauseated me, made me drop them, and then there was only the running away from the sound. What a coward I was.*

I ran as fast as I could, but I knew I would be tough someday, I knew I would never back down. And this is perfectly clear. I am not an abuser. With Pat it wasn't about being tough, it was about touching. When I hit her, it was about touching, and it was about touching whenever I sought out the backseat of White House limo SS100X, my favorite, the one I always insisted on. I was the President. It was the restored midnight-blue Lincoln Continental where Kennedy was shot. I would ride around right in that same backseat. The very spot. They touched him there. And they could touch me if they wanted to. I wasn't going to run away.

And up ahead, among the denizens in the crowd only a few moments away from suffering the blunt trauma of Dick Nixon, is Patricia Dankowski, once known professionally as Trixie Smith, a Chicago prostitute from Avondale, reared only a few blocks from Saint Hyacinth's Basilica in a brick semidetached where she was touched for a few years by her father—he's now, unbeknownst to her, in the basement of a brick semidetached in a very rough neighborhood of Hell where the rapists perpetually rape each other—and she is oblivious to the indiscriminate touching all around of the jostling throng of denizens. She squeezes an arm out of the press of bodies and runs a hand through her over-bleached hair, great clumps of it tearing loose in her fingers, but she does not notice, as she is thinking of the night of September 26, 1960, when she was touched for a brief time by the future President of the United States: *Call me Jack, he says, and he smiles a lot of teeth at me and he's a good looking man, even better looking than his photos, and we're at the Ambassador East, which isn't a first for me, though it's not a place I've been in lately since they've come to know me by sight and I advise against it for any clients, so as to avoid a scene. Not that I've ever been in the Presidential Suite, where they've put him, and he's got Peggy Lee playing on a phonograph when I come in, though he switches it off as soon as he motions to the bedroom door, which is too bad because I'd like to hear her go on singing "I Got It Bad, and That Ain't Good" while I'm working Jack Kennedy, and he asks me "Do you have a TV, Trixie" and I say "Yes, I do, Jack" and he says "I'm going to debate that fellow Dick Nixon on TV in about an hour and a half" and I say "I didn't just fall off the hay wagon, Jack" and he laughs and he says "Well then, what do you think I should do about Quemoy and Matsu" and I say "Nuke 'em, Jack" and he laughs again and he's naked real quick and so am I and I'd just as soon take a little bit longer because when John Fitzgerald Kennedy is inside me I get it in my head that I'm somebody after all but I'm only somebody for what's got to be less than sixty seconds and then I'm nobody again, just like my old man always said afterwards, but when I'm dressed and passing through the sitting room I get up the nerve to ask Jack to play my favorite song and he waves off all his men already coming in from the other bedroom and he smiles and he goes to the phonograph and he puts the needle on the vinyl and he and I stand there together and Peggy sings to me about how a man is always going to end up making you sing the blues in the night.* And now there is, very nearby, a roaring engine and then a wild flinging of bodies and Patricia Dankowski is hit and shattered by Satan's chauffeur. She tumbles over the right front fender and along the side of the car, and for a very brief moment, as she hurtles past, she and Hatcher look each other in the eyes.

∝

Having seen the eyes of this woman flying past, Hatcher turns his face from the street. Hoover is moaning—not yet reconstituted from his eye-plucking—and so Hatcher closes his own eyes and waits, and waits. Eventually, the sucking and tucking and zipping sounds of a reconstitution begin and Hoover falls silent. Outside, the roar of body-thumps eventually ceases and there is only the sound of the engine for a while. And when Hatcher finally opens his eyes to look once again upon Hell, he is no longer in the Great Metropolis.

The car is climbing a narrow, curving, empty road into the mountains that Hatcher heretofore has seen only on the horizon. He puts his face to the glass and tries to look back to the city. He sees the slick gray lumpings and soarings and plungings of the mountains as the car twists with the road. And then Hatcher gasps as the city jumps into his eyes: a vast sudden everything: the far horizon and the extreme periphery of his vision, as if he has been plucked into the middle of the air and he dangles before the immense compressed jumble of a billion rooftops and tenement facades and webs of streets and all of it shimmering—not shimmering, quaking—not quaking, writhing—writhing with vast throngs of bodies, tiny from this distance, but Hatcher knows what these great stretches of huddling masses are: millennia of individual bodies and minds and hearts born into life and cast now into this place, shimmering, yes, shimmering from his view in the mountains of Hell like a scrub fire on a vast plain. He hangs and sees and hangs and he tries to figure out where his body is so he can pull back, and then the city vanishes and it's just cliff faces and the huddling of boulders until at last the car rushes into a great level plain hidden among the mountain peaks. And there are stands of trees and a vast grassy meadow, or what appear to Hatcher as these things, which he did not know existed in Hell.

He feels a slight nudge on his arm and Hatcher looks to Hoover, who has averted his face. But the G-man is holding an upturned hand to him with a stack of three golden-brown squares. "You'll need these," Hoover says. "Honey cakes for the dog."

Hatcher takes them and they are densely heavy and sticky and their smell is so sweet that it makes Hatcher's teeth ache. He holds them in his palm and puts his other hand over them just as the Cadillac brakes sharply and fishtails to a stop. Before him is a rustic-style hunting lodge— classically shaped in one story of stacked rough logs with a low-pitched gable roof—but even from where Hatcher sits, a hundred yards away, the lodge is so massive as to utterly fill his sight, the rough wood trunks of its walls as large as sequoias. Hatcher has an instant stab of sadness, realizing that the seeming utter absence of nonverminous animal life and growing things in Hell has always given him a sweet little dangerous pulse of pleasure, that whatever the reasons are for a very high percentage of humanity seeming to be here, there is some code of justice—however severe—at work, since the nonhuman living things of that previous life are spared from this place. What were the sins of these trees? he wonders now, with the bloom of a sharp pain behind his eyes.

And having wondered about the unworthy sequoias, he suddenly finds himself face to muzzle with three dogs. Or, more precisely, the three heads of one dog, Cerberus. The faces of the Hound of Hell are not, as they are variously portrayed in the earthly life, like combinations of lion or bear or wolf or, in latter days, pit bulls. Cerberus is a rabid, grossly outsized Jack Russell terrier, slobbering and barking and leaping incessantly, his three heads each as big as a midsummer watermelon. For the moment, however, he has ceased his jumping and is concentrating on slobbering and barking at Hatcher's window.

"Roll the window down just a bit and feed him," Hoover says.

Hatcher grasps the window handle and starts slowly to turn it, bits of slobber instantly flying in and burning acutely on his forehead, the tip of his nose, his chest.

"Watch your fingers," Hoover says.

Hatcher does, opening the window just enough to thrust the end of a cake out, averting his face from the slobber, and he starts feeding the heads. Each one falls silent in turn, and then Cerberus abruptly backs away and trots off, chewing laboriously at the sticky cakes.

"Now," Hoover says and he pushes Hatcher's shoulder.

Hatcher opens the door and steps into the driveway before Satan's mountain lodge. He is acutely aware once more of his nakedness as two powder-blue jumpsuited minions rapidly descend the long front stairs and head toward him. He crosses his hands over his crotch and looks away. In the field to the side of the lodge he sees rows of pickup trucks, a hundred or more. And then gunfire flurries from behind the lodge. This brings Hatcher's face back to the approaching minions, and the two mustaches are unmistakable. One a modified Walrus and one a classic Toothbrush. If asked which two people in history he would least wish to be naked before, Hatcher would probably have answered something like "my mother and Hillary Clinton." But now that Adolf Hitler and Joseph Stalin are at each side of him and grabbing him firmly by the elbows and, at once, lifting him off the ground and reexposing him, he has a new respect for Satan's insight.

Joe and Adolf tote Hatcher across the drive and up the steps and through the front door, and striding toward them, framed in the light from enormous veranda doors behind him, is Satan, wearing a red-and-blue-plaid flannel shirt, Armani jeans, and a **RUTTIN BUCK** camouflage hunting cap with tied-up fleece earflaps. Against his chest he carries a Ruger Deerfield 44 Magnum autoloading carbine with a smoking muzzle. Hatcher expected that through the anticipated long night he would have a chance to prepare himself for this moment. But the abruptness and the intensity of his gathering up and passage here, culminating in his hanging in dishabille six inches off the floor in the grip of two of the most prolific murderers in history, has prevented any preparation for what is, in fact, his first actual physical encounter with Satan. Till this moment he has had only the traditional earthly iconography and Satan's e-mails and cell phone messages to conjure up the Prince of Darkness. And now: Hatcher thinks of some typical politician with whom he's only vaguely familiar and who's declared his candidacy for president and is scoring about four percent in the polls and Hatcher finally meets him in an American Legion hall in Dubuque or Cedar Rapids on a brutally cold December afternoon as the guy benightedly campaigns to win the Iowa caucus vote. That is say, a classic, middle-height, middle-age man with a squarish, slightly pasty, faintly jowly, smarm-ready, white-guy-in-power face. Except in the moment after this face registers on Hatcher, the face flares bright red—nothing else changing, not shape or jowls or even the smarm factor—but it all becomes instantly, luminously, arterial-blood red.

"This one's late!" Satan roars. "Set him loose out back!"

And before Hatcher can quite get his mind around this, he's being whisked past Satan and across the floor toward the veranda windows. This much is clear at once: Satan either is mistaking him for someone else or he's pretending to.

As Hatcher passes through the doors and sees the field before him, he starts to understand. A hundred—or a bit fewer now—naked men, mostly white, mostly paunchy, are running madly in circles in a dozen acres of low, stubbly canebrake. Originally there was one man per pickup truck parked in the front of the lodge, but now there are a dozen or more bodies twitching here and there on the ground, each with a major magnum-hole in head or chest. No doubt, all were hunters in life. Hatcher is being taken for one of these.

"Wait!" he cries, twisting his head over his shoulder to try to address Satan. "I'm Hatcher McCord! Your anchorman! Your interview!"

Joe and Adolf are quickly descending the back steps, Hatcher flopping between them. At the bottom they rush on, across the yard toward the canebrake, and Hatcher is thinking this is what it's always been about, doing this to him. He was getting to be too important in Hell. But why the hunting motif? He hunted with a couple of presidents over the years but only for show. He never even shot anything. Now he can see before him the whites of the eyes of the naked hunters running around making sounds of terror like the cries of wounded moose. Hatcher tries to reassure himself: it's only more pain and humiliation. If it wasn't this way, it would be some other.

But now Satan bellows from behind, "Wait!"

Joe and Adolf stop and turn around, Hatcher still hanging between them.

"Put him down," Satan says.

They do.

In his desperate relief, something registers on Hatcher about what is beneath his feet, but not quite consciously.

Satan is standing at the top of the stairs to the veranda. His face is pasty white again. "Hatcher McCord!" he cries.

"Yes. That's me," Hatcher says aloud, while his inner voice declares *The grass isn't real.*

"The anchorman." Satan has stopped shouting. There is even a tone of dawning recognition in his voice.

"The *Evening News from Hell.* Hatcher McCord. I'm here for the interview."

Perhaps the logs in the lodge aren't real either.

Satan says, "I didn't recognize you. In person, you're naked."

Hatcher is attuned to tones of voice. As an interviewer in his earthly life, he prided himself on being able to discern all the little audible clues that a subject is lying. Hatcher has the odd impression that Satan truly made a mistake about who Hatcher was. Certainly Satan would be adept at feigning his confusion. But why would he bother?

Satan begins to drum the fingers of his right hand in the air. "Come here," he says. Hatcher is free of the grip of the two tyrants now, and he moves to the veranda and up the steps, Satan continuing to elaborate on his invitation: "Come. Come. Hustle along, Hatcher Thatcher Snatcher. Come to Papa do. Come along comealongcomealong. Here, boy."

I'm spared for now, and at least trees are innocent.

As Hatcher reaches the top of the steps, Satan backs up a few paces and motions him to stop. "Now," Satan says, "Hatcher, old bean. Tell me why you come to visit your Papa Satan in the nude."

"Hoover . . ." Hatcher begins, and Satan waves his hand to silence him.

"Oh dear oh dear, have you been doing naughty things with Eddie?"

"No. No. Not at all. He burst in unexpectedly . . . Morning came . . ."

"Morning came," Satan says. "Ah, morning came indeed. I made the morning to come, my boy."

"I didn't have a chance . . ."

"Please. Papa understands. Morning. The clarion call of the feathered creatures." Satan pauses, lifts his face, and makes a bird call of some sort that Hatcher cannot recognize.

"Treedle eedle eedle oodle oodle!" Satan calls, and from behind Hatcher all the naked hunters in the canebrake are compelled to answer with the same call.

"I am riven with guilt at mistaking you," Satan says. There is a sly overripeness to his tone that clearly signals his insincerity. Hatcher understands he knows nothing, really, but hearing the meaning of this tone makes him have about a twenty percent confidence in his previous impression of Satan's confusion. There are things to think about in all this, but he does not have time.

"I'll make it up to you," Satan says, striding up to him and shoving the rifle into Hatcher's hands. "Step aside."

Hatcher does. He turns and watches as Satan lifts a hand and drums his fingers again, and Joe and Adolf approach at a trot. Satan stops them with a wave and then begins to point from one to the other and back again, moving his lips silently, doing an eeny-meeny-miny-moe. Stalin and Hitler begin to quake. Hatcher realizes that both of them have large, liquidy, creepily fetching, feminine eyes. Satan ends with his forefinger pointing at Hitler.

"Strip," he orders.

Hitler tremblingly complies, peeling off his jumpsuit and then standing straight-spined and naked before Satan, his face rigid in terror. Hatcher, newsman though he be, consciously does not confirm the earthly reports that Hitler had only one testicle.

"Shoot him," Satan says to Hatcher.

"Shoot him?"

"With the rifle in your hands," Satan said. "Shoot Adolf Hitler. Shoot him in the face."

Hatcher is trying to catch up with all this. He looks dumbly at the rifle.

"Are you more anti-Communist than anti-Fascist?" Satan asks. "You can do Joe instead."

It's not a preference for someone else that makes Hatcher hesitate. Hitler would do just fine, if he has to shoot someone in the face for Satan. But Hatcher feels some vast thing opening up in him.

Satan thumps his own forehead with the heel of his hand. "Of course. Ofcourseofcourseofcourse. Pillars of fire and smoke. Big TV news. Round the clock." He throws his head back and does an inept fire engine siren impression—"Weeeooo weeeooo"—and then resumes, "You're on. Smoking skyscrapers behind you. Undo your tie. The nation turns to Hatcher McCord." And now in a high girlish voice, "Oh please do your face just that way again. So grave, so compassionate. We all ache together." Abruptly he leans near to Hatcher—smelling, yes, generally of something burnt, of brimstone even, but also, from his breath, of Frosted Cherry Pop-Tarts and, from his face, of Old Spice After Shave—and his voice swoops down into a conspiratorial baritone: "You want Osama bin Laden? I'll get him for you. It'll only take a moment."

"It's not that," Hatcher says.

"He's small beans, though. Comparatively speaking, yes? Comparatively. Numbers, boy. Numbers."

Hatcher does not understand his own hesitation. Adolf Hitler, after all. Big numbers.

"You're a sportsman, is that it? Adolf. Run around."

Hatcher looks at his rifle once more, the stock and the forearm a smoothly unbroken run of apparent walnut.

"You can do it," Satan says. "You're a great shot here. Just point and shoot. Squeeze, don't pull. Point and shoot, anchorman."

Hatcher lifts his eyes and Adolf Hitler is running around in circles twenty yards in front of him, with each circuit lifting that famous face to Hatcher with wide, frightened eyes. Adolf fucking Hitler. Hatcher puts the rifle to his shoulder and squeezes the trigger. Hitler's head explodes in bloody fragments and the body falls.

Hatcher pants heavily. He trembles. All the muscles of his hands and arms and chest trill with jumpy happiness. "Go ahead," Satan says.

Stalin turns his face from the fallen Hitler. He looks Hatcher in the eyes with that familiar avuncular smugness. Big numbers. And Hatcher pulls the trigger again. Stalin's head vanishes in a pulpy red plume and the body falls.

Hatcher's chest pumps up instantly full, as if he was drowning and has unexpectedly leapt into the air. The headless bodies of Hitler and Stalin lie shuddering beside each other. And now, before Hatcher can even lower his rifle, one of the hunters—a corpulent jowly man with a Brylcreem-rigid pompadour—dashes this way from the canebrake, as if to run up the veranda steps and past them and escape out the front door.

Satan rattles a rapid ID: "He shot his best friend to death in a planned hunting accident so he could fuck the wife in their double-wide with her twin eight-year-old girls locked outside in the snow."

Hatcher hesitates. The man's dash has suddenly turned into gluti-nous slow motion. Every one of us had the trying-to-run-but-can't night-mare on earth, Hatcher thinks.

"One man or a million," Satan whispers. "It's the same. Fuck big numbers. The nova of a star or the splitting of an atom. In the great scheme of things, the difference is inconsequential."

Hatcher hears this and it seems true and the pompadour's best friend deserved better, but when it comes down to it, Hatcher is simply still holding that big, beautiful chestful of air from Stalin, and it needs a proper release. He pulls the trigger. The man flies backward, his belly blown open. Hatcher's full chest huffs happily empty, and he breathes deep again as a lanky, hatchety-faced man leaps through the steam of the gut shot of the fallen hunter and heads for the veranda.

Satan says, "This one never ate a thing he killed. He just got off on seeing those cute little birdies explode."

Hatcher pulls the trigger and catches the lanky man in a shoulder, spinning him around screaming.

"Again," Satan says. "We shall not forget even one sparrow."

Hatcher shoots once more, cutting the man in half at the middle of his spine.

This time he sighs a calm, sweet, quiet sigh. Poor little birds.

Hatcher feels the rifle being gently tugged from his hands. He resists for a moment. But it's Satan.

"Look how talented you are," Satan says.

Hatcher lets go of the rifle.

"And righteous," Satan says. He looks away from Hatcher, toward the lodge, and flicks his head to someone.

Hatcher is in a state of calm quietude, like after a sauna and a massage and about four glasses of wine with a Xanax dissolved in the first one. Hands are upon him, squaring him around at the shoulders, poking at the back of a knee. "Lift your leg," a woman says. He does. "Now the other." He does. His arms are lifted one at a time and there is a zipping.

His head begins to clear. He looks down. He is wearing a powder-blue jumpsuit.

∝

They sit in the lodge great room with a walk-in fireplace roaring intensely behind Satan. Hatcher sinks deep into an overstuffed chair before the Old Man. He crosses his leg. He realizes he is also wearing powder-blue-coordinated Nike Dunks. Behind him is a top-of-the-line Sony HD Camcorder set up on a tripod. The camera was unattended when they sat down a few minutes ago and Satan has been rattling on and on ever since about how this is the first-ever interview he's granted, that even William Randolph Hearst tried unsuccessfully to get an interview for the

Hell Times Herald Examiner Journal Standard, which Hearst published for a long while until the Internet came along and he was forced to shut down and now Hearst's off in a blogger cubicle writing about his own dick and its previous billionaire adventures, weeping at his loss all the while, and he can't turn off his keyboard Caps Lock and is thus the object of severe and constant ridicule by his fellow bloggers for always shouting.

But Satan stops talking abruptly, looking at something over Hatcher's shoulder. Hatcher turns. Adolf Hitler is standing beside the camera. His head has been reconstituted, but imperfectly, his face a maze of raw scars. An old, bleached-blond woman, her arms and face and neck a dense patchwork of liver spots, is hovering beside Adolf with a bottle of iodine and a dingy wad of cotton. She heavily doses the cotton, the burnt-orange liquid splashing everywhere, and she swipes at the join-lines of Adolf's face. He cries out in pain and she cries out in the same pain, and she does the cotton again and they cry out together again. He seems unable to stop her from these painful ministrations, his hands hanging unmoving beside him, his head held rigid. Both Hitler and the woman are wearing blue jumpsuits—hers short-sleeved to feature her age-and-sun-ravaged arms.

"Stop stop stop!" Satan cries to the woman.

Hatcher expects that the woman will back away and Hitler will operate the camera. But it's Hitler who bows. He takes the bottle and cotton from the woman, and he withdraws. The woman looks to Satan and Hatcher, for a moment blinking hard, trying to focus on them. The face seems familiar, but in a mid-seventies, heavily made-up, heavily nipped-and-tucked New York-to-Miami retiree way—his second wife Deborah's people. The woman looks away to where Hitler is marching out of the room.

"Leni," Satan says sharply. "Focus. Glory times have come for you again. This will be your masterpiece. Marching millions in the dark. Torchlight. And naked racing bodies. Leaping and soaring and running. All captured solely in my words. The grandiloquence of the Prince of

Darkness. Now turn that thing on and back away and hold very still, you bitch. No fucking with the camera."

And Leni Riefenstahl focuses. She bows from the waist and steps behind the camera. Hatcher turns to face Satan, whose eyes are lasered on Hatcher's. He's reading even this thought that I think he's reading this thought, Hatcher thinks.

"Any time," Satan says. "Shoot." He laughs loud. "Shoot. Shoot. Quick." Satan jumps up and pantomimes shooting and he roars on. "Point and squeeze. I'm out running in the canebrake. Shoot quick. Shoot me with your questions, Hatcher McCord. Shoot me with your 44-magnum brilliance."

As Satan is going on, Hatcher tries to focus on the questions, the notes for which he left behind with his clothes. But it's difficult. He has an image caught in his head: Adolf and Leni beside the camera. And what Hatcher is seeing are collegial powder-blue figures, minions of Satan, joined with the Old Man, and here Hatcher himself sits dressed in the jumpsuit of a minion and he's about to willingly—eagerly—give Satan a wide, public voice. But. But. *I'm a journalist. I do not judge. I report. Let the public judge. And it takes an informed public to make good judgments.* This all suddenly sounds to Hatcher like bullshit of a very strange sort, and he shakes his head sharply back and forth.

"Pee-kow. Pee-kow." Satan is still shooting his invisible rifle. His bullets apparently are ricocheting. And then he abruptly stops and falls back into his overstuffed chair, the fire behind him flaring up, the flames rushing out of the fireplace to lollop over Satan's head for a moment and then recede. "I feel so much better after that," Satan says. He leans toward Hatcher, narrowing his eyes at him, smiling faintly, and he wiggles his eyebrows. "We all have so much satisfying fun inside our heads, don't we."

By Hatcher's deepest reflexive assumptions, this should reinforce his conviction that Satan is hearing every thought. But it doesn't. To his surprise. On the contrary.

This new impression is oddly reinforced by Satan now saying, "You don't want me to say 'shoot' again, do you? You know how I can go on." Hatcher does indeed know how the Old Man can go on. But his throwing it in now suddenly seems like a shrewd guess at Hatcher's thoughts, the kind of thing a self-conscious manipulator can use to feign insight, or an immortal ruler to feign omniscience.

But Hatcher doesn't have the luxury of considering this further at the moment. Satan does have his powers. He waves his hand and the jumpsuit begins to burn and itch.

So Hatcher begins. "Why you?" he asks. "Why this job? We all want to know about ourselves, but let's start with you. Why are *you* here?" As soon as he asks the question, the jumpsuit stops burning and itching and, in fact, even stops troubling his mind, which, however, troubles his mind.

"I've got father issues," Satan says. "Oh boo hoo. Oh boo fucking hoo, you say. You've got your own father issues. Everybody down here has father issues. Yes. It's true. And mother issues. Boy, don't even ask me about that. Think of me and women. Talk about an absent mother. Think of poor me. But think of poor you. All of you. Parents. Holy shit. What a mess. It's what makes us all down here one big modern extended family. We have to help each other. Give me a hug. Huggiehuggiehuggie."

And Satan jumps up and throws his arms open wide.

Hatcher knows he has no choice in the matter. He stands and as soon as he's on his feet, Satan is upon him, holding him, pounding in a manly way on his back with both hands, bussing him on both cheeks. To Hatcher's surprise, none of this is physically painful. It's just the lumpy awkward thereness of a drunken-party farewell. Satan continues to pound and buss and Hatcher doesn't know what to do with his hands. Do you hug Satan? What could it hurt now? Your fate is already sealed. Hatcher lifts his arms and puts them around Satan and gives the Old Man a couple of light pats on the back.

Instantly Satan stops. He says, "Good. There. Doesn't that feel better? I'm okay, you're okay. It's all about family values." And Satan throws himself back down into his chair. Hatcher sits.

"Next question," Satan says.

"Can I ask you to talk a little more about your father, how that went wrong?"

Satan rolls his head and digs a knuckle into the corner of an eye. "It always goes wrong, doesn't it? Somehow? It's just some sons deal with it more indirectly, more hypocritically, if you will, though far be it from me to criticize. You mortals have to play your little games. But me and my dad. I was his Lucifer. I was young and beautiful. He made his face to shine upon me. He made my face to shine. Yes. He made me the man I am today. He made it all, don't forget. I just do his dirty work. See, he doesn't have an editor in his brain. Things pop out and he makes things go in a certain way and then the next moment he steps back and goes whatthefuck. When that happens, he can blame it on me. Sometimes he goes whatthefuck and then a moment later he just goes wellfuckit and takes the credit for it. Same kind of shit, either way. He and I talk all the time. 'Here, you want the credit for this one?' he says. 'Nah,' I say. 'Not that.' 'Really,' he says, 'this one's yours.' 'Okay okay,' I say. But I don't have any choice. What kind of relationship is that? When it comes down to it, he can do no wrong and I can never do anything right. Fucking shit happens in the world, but if *he* does it, fine. That's Dad's holy fucking will. If *I* do it, then it's, 'I'm so disappointed in you.' Fuck that. Next question."

Hatcher's philosophy of smart interviewing employs a process he thinks of as reincorporation. Get some things on the record in one realm and then reincorporate them when you get to the questions about a different but inconspicuously related realm, the latter being what you're more interested in. So Hatcher's instinct now is to press Satan on his own reasons for being in Hell. He says, "But things did change between you. Was there some event . . ."

Satan waves his hand to stop Hatcher from completing the question. Hatcher clenches in anticipation of some sort of serious pain. Punishment for presuming to press the Prince of Darkness himself for personal information. *Go ahead, Old Man.* Hatcher waits. Satan hesitates. Then, on a dangerous impulse fed by a number of little clues—Satan's mistaking him for a hunter being the most recent—Hatcher's inner voice goes on. *Don't you hear me, motherfucker? Give me your best shot. Bring it on.*

But Satan begins to answer Hatcher's question. "So we were sitting around the dinner table, and he's going, 'The whole meat thing, the burnt offering thing, the cut-the-throat-this-way and the drain-the-blood-that-way thing, I've had a bellyful of that.'"

Satan himself is working one realm to get at another, and it would be wise for Hatcher to listen carefully if he wants real answers, but instead, he's got a new line of inquiry shaping up and he's testing it some more. He keeps his face earnestly fixed on Satan raving on, but mostly focused on his own inner voice, which keeps trash talking. *You can hear me, Old Scratch. Old Scratch-your-crotch. Old Scratch-up-your-butt. Blow my head off. Toss me in that fire behind you. I dare you.*

But Satan raves some more. "So I go, 'Eat, old man. Eat your meat. Yum.' And he goes, 'Maybe all this sacrifice shit has got to stop.' And I go, 'You're just saying every dumbshit thing that comes into your infinite fucking mind. And since it's infinite, there's going to be some major dumbshit things that come up.'"

Go ahead and fix my ass good for these fuck-you thoughts I'm having. Do something to show me what an immortal omnipotent omniscient bad-ass you are.

"And of course it wasn't too long before the old man came back around. Kill the other guy. Kill yourselves. Kill anything that moves. That's the way to please You-know-who and get to You-know-what."

Whoa. You can't hear me.

"But it was too late for him and me."

We all assume you know what we're thinking.

"He realized I saw through him and he didn't like it."

But you don't.

Satan suddenly leaps up from his chair. His face flushes as red as the throat blood of a bullock before a tabernacle.

Hatcher gasps and recoils. *I'm wrong. Now it comes. The worst thing ever.*

But Satan simply cries, "I did it in defense of the double cheeseburger! Those cows died for you!" And he throws himself back into his chair. His face turns white. "Next question."

Hatcher is panting. This is a dangerous moment, he knows.

Satan sees the state Hatcher is in. He cocks his head at him, and again Hatcher fears he's been wrong.

But Satan says, "Yes. Exciting. It's all very exciting. Ray Kroc's in the kitchen even as we speak. Cooking up a firestorm of Big Macs. Calm down now and ask me the next fucking question."

Hatcher has to put aside what he's learned unexpectedly and go on as he'd intended. He takes a deep breath, quells the panting, and says, "There are so many of us . . ."

"A multitude. A teeming multitude. Your brothers and sisters. Give me your tired, your poor, your huddled masses yearning to breathe free. *Yearning*, I tell you. I lift my lamp beside the flaming door." He's on his feet again, and suddenly a torch appears in his hands. A torch with a flame of what looks like red neon, but throwing out great swirling clusters of sparks. "Sacrifice. Kill. Pray. Come to me, my little ones."

A spray of sharp pointillist pain rains onto Hatcher's forehead. The sparks from the torch. He cries out and he smells his hair burning and he beats at his head with his hands.

"Oh pardon," Satan says, and instantly Hatcher's pain ceases. "Pardon. Breathe free and get burned. Always the way, yes? Always."

The torch has vanished.

Once more, Hatcher starts to doubt what he thinks he's come to understand. Breathe free and get burned. This is a warning. But why such indirection? Hatcher can't worry now. Interview. "So you invite your multitude, yes?" Hatcher hears himself reflexively picking up the Old Man's locutions. "Do you have to take the souls you're given?"

"Have to? I want you. I want you all. I choose you, my darlings."

"Doesn't *he* decide who gets in?"

The fire behind Satan flares up, rushes forward over Satan and all the way to Hatcher, does a bullwhip snap at the top of Hatcher's head and sets his hair on fire again. This time Satan simply watches as the top of Hatcher's head rages in such pain that his sight shuts down and his brain is about to. Then Satan says, "Okay. Okay."

The flames go out and Hatcher can see again: the thin, hard, upturned line of Satan's mouth, his narrowed eyes. Hatcher's head still aches and smolders and his hair is gone for now, but his brain is working again. He is exhilarated. How quick Satan was to punish him for pressing the point about his father's higher authority. Hatcher takes this as proof of the privacy of his own thoughts. *Prove me wrong, asshole.*

And Satan doesn't. He says, "Don't go 'he' with me. He he he— I'm not laughing. He he fucking he. It is I. I who choose. I do so because I want you. I want you in my family. Doesn't that warm the cockles of your heart? Not to mention the top of your head. I want you all." Satan looks straight into the camera. "Isn't this a Hallmark moment? Send me a card now, all of you. Go find a sweet little greeting card with family thoughts and mail it to me." Satan blows a kiss. He turns back to Hatcher. "Next."

"Your power is so great," Hatcher begins.

"Now you've got it," Satan says. "Good interview technique. Win the heart of your subject with noble cosmic truths about his power."

Hatcher says, "How do you choose?"

"You mean how did I choose *you*," Satan says.

This time Hatcher has not even a flicker of worry. He swells with the importance of the place of a journalist—his place—in any life or afterlife, ennobled by the fundamental right and need of all people to be fully informed. He straightens his spine and in spite of his charred and denuded head still wispily smoking, he says, "I'm a newsman." with the intention of going on to explain how he speaks for everyone.

But before he can, Satan cries, "Right! Righteously right! And an exemplary newsman you are, my boy. Look what you've done. You've been able to ask the Great Dark Lord all these questions and you only had one little hairdo malfunction along the way. And I'll make that up to you."

Instantly, the pain on the top of Hatcher's still-smoking head ceases, as does the smoke, and he becomes intensely aware of every hair follicle dilating and excreting. His hair grows and grows and he feels it descending over his ears, the back of his neck, his forehead, and into his eyes, and it falls on his shoulders and finally stops.

"You see? All fixed. Your girlfriend will absolutely adore it. The first man she fucked had hair just like that. You can both reminisce. Such fond memories. We all have such memories. I sat on a cloud once, metaphorically speaking. I hate sitting on clouds. Fucking idiotic. Strum strum on your harp. Flap your wings. What bullshit. But I have memories just like your headstrong, footloose girlfriend. Or should I say footstrong, headloose."

Hatcher brushes the hair out of his eyes. Already he's wondering who Anne's fuck with the long hair was and starting to churn about it. *I won't let you do this, Old Man.* And the power of having the privacy of his thoughts actually helps him move away from his retrospective jealousy. And this was good, this challenge to him. He needed the reminder that Satan can still see and know. Almost everything, no doubt. He's just not listening.

"You've been a great newsman today, Hatcher," Satan says. "What integrity. Doesn't that make you proud? I haven't had such fun since I brought old Billy Graham out here—he's a crack shot—and the son of a bitch tried to get me to do an altar call."

Hatcher McCord pictures the aged preacher trying to convert the Devil himself, and inside, Hatcher laughs wryly, sadly, at the quixotic pathos of the human condition.

"That led to some serious malfunctions of various sorts, I can tell you," Satan says. "Don't ask."

Hatcher McCord's interview with Satan is an unparalleled journalistic landmark, and the irony is that he has to keep his biggest investigative break to himself. Fuck you, Satan, he says casually in his head. Hatcher's head is a precious haven in the midst of the maelstrom of Hell.

"Not that it pleases me," Satan says. "I sometimes get a bellyful of the malfunctions. I feel for you all, my little children. You are all so pathetic. I do care." And Satan digs knuckles into the corners of both eyes. "Boo hoodie hoo," he says.

By the genius of his interviewing, he has learned a secret that is both dangerous and empowering.

Satan abruptly drops his hands and lifts his face. He closes his eyes in faux agony and cries, "Satan wept."

Hatcher McCord, whose likeability rating even at the time of his death was second only to Oprah Winfrey . . .

Satan opens his eyes and lowers his face. Hatcher is not so far gone in the overvoice of his life that he misses this moment. He sorts quickly through what's been going on and recaptures enough at least to say, "Wonderful. Yes."

"Of course," Satan says. "Of course. But as the broadcast interview ends—and that will be the end, that touching moment right there—I want you to do a voice-over thing, and you say it just that way."

Hatcher nods knowingly at Satan, though there's a rustling of panic in his chest because he's not quite sure what "that way" is. Worse, he's not even sure what the "it" is.

"Say it," Satan says.

"Yes," Hatcher says.

"Now."

"Of course," Hatcher says.

Satan is waiting. Hatcher is in high, blinding panic. But he is free to scramble around in his own head, he knows now. He can find a way to finesse this. One of his other great newsman talents has always been the ability to act as if you know a lot when, in fact, you know very little. Satan is such a fucking poseur. And Hatcher says, "You are so brilliantly expressive. I want to study that one more time so I can capture every nuance."

Satan cocks his head. Hatcher braces himself for more fire. At least he might get rid of this long hair.

And then Satan smiles a vast, radiant smile. "Good. Yes. Oh I chose you well, Hatcher McCord. We should work on this. Of course, I'm totally fucking insincere, you know. I don't really give a very hot damn about you all. But I want you all to think I do. If I want to be *seen* as sincere, then that's basically the same thing as *being* sincere. I respect the image and want it for myself and I care that you think I'm sincere and so that shows respect for you and so it all adds up to the same thing, yes? Of course yes. Here we go."

Satan lifts his face, closes his eyes, and he says, "Satan wept."

Hatcher gets it. "I'm very moved," he says.

"I knew you would be," Satan says.

"I'm ready," Hatcher says, preparing his most telling, throbbing, compassionate anchorman's voice—nightly employed back on earth for the final two-minute feature with the dying child or the starving laid-off worker or the courageous amputee athlete—by using the voice in the privacy of his own mind: *Little does Satan know that the experienced and brilliant newsman can, for the sake of a story, feign respect even as he knows his subject to be a fool.*

Satan lifts his face and closes his eyes.

And Hatcher says, with aching mellifluousness, "Satan wept."

Satan squeezes his eyes more tightly shut and scrunches up his shoulders in appreciation. Then his eyes pop open and he says, "I could kiss you." He leaps up and levitates Hatcher from his chair. Hatcher's feet grope for the floor and find it as Satan grabs him and ends the interview with a flurry of cheek bussing and back-thumping, and he personally elbow-hustles Hatcher past Leni Riefenstahl standing at severe attention just out of arm's reach of the camera.

She moves her eyes slightly to the two men as they pass, but she looks inward: *It was February and it was cold in Berlin, it was very cold and the snow was drifted up and when the speech was done I had the urge to strip off my clothes— every shred till there was only my quaking naked body—and leap into a snow-drift to sweetly temper the intense heat I was feeling from him, and this was at the Sportpalast where he spoke and I was near the front of the crowd, a little to his left, looking up at him from an angle that made me tremble, the angle of a daughter with a father, I know, the angle of all of us as a nation in our needy submissive solidarity, and what ghost may have passed through me of my commonplace father my bourgeois Kaiserreich father my keep-your-place-girl, quick-with-his-fists father, this ghost passed on instantly now as this man strode to the podium and saluted us, drawing his flat open hand straight from his heart and out to us all, and I looked up at him and I saw him from this angle below as if through the lens of a camera and he beamed sternly all around and he was the father of us all and then he began to speak, and he had me at "Fellow Germans."*

∝

Hatcher is alone in the back of the car as it comes down the mountain. Beyond the privacy partition, Dick Nixon is driving fast. Alone in the front seat, with no bodies threatening to touch him, he can relax. He looks forward to driving the crowded streets ahead, plowing through them, though he knows to try to squelch the pleasure of that thought, fearing Satan, who Dick assumes knows every thought. But at this point in time, all is good for Dick Nixon, considering where he is. He lifts his face and begins to sing "Big wheel keep on turnin', proud Mary keep on burnin'" and somewhere ahead, in a back alley of the Great Metropolis, Ike Turner sits before his TV set, unable to move. He watches Richard M. Nixon singing this song, though on the screen, Dick is not driving a 1948 Cadillac Fleetwood, he is on a stage vibrating his thighs in a miniskirt. Ike cannot look away from the screen no matter how hard he tries.

Nixon's singing would be torturing Hatcher too, except Hatcher has found the solid mahogany door to his mind at last and shut it and he's taking no calls. He is aware of the rock-naked slopes and crests and cliff faces passing by and then the flat, arid run up to the city, and he is aware the sun is now vast and high overhead and he knows the forecast for noontime from last night's news—scattered sulfurous fiery storms—but all of that is vague in him for now as he sits in the prime corner office of his mind and all is silence there. *What to do with this freedom in my head, what to do. I got away from my old man. On the pre-dawn morning when I was supposed to kill a whitetail with a shotgun out in the river bottoms and start growing up like he wanted, me his only son, his only child, carrying all of his hopes, I burrowed deep into the absolute dark of the back corner of the attic guest-room closet with the smell of old wool and mothballs and shoe leather and I huddled up tight and I wasn't afraid of him and I knew I could think what I liked and I interviewed President Eisenhower in my mind—grilled him about the Suez and the Eisenhower Doctrine and I wouldn't let him off the hook about actually taking military action to stop communists merely on the suspicion of a problem—and I could hear my dad calling downstairs, but I was going to think what I wanted. And it may have led me straight to Hell. He would have predicted that. But now I'm huddled up and free to think again, and I saw my dad here in Hell once, trapped inside his traffic-jammed Studebaker, giving the finger all around, and I didn't care one way or the other, really, that he was here too—of course he was—and I didn't even try to catch his eye. That's one thing I can do with my freedom. I don't have to expect it to be torture if I want to figure out why I'm here. And if I do and if somebody really is coming to take a few souls away to wherever else there is, then maybe I can know how to be one of those to go. And maybe even Beatrice and her boyfriend are right. Maybe there's a back door somewhere. I can think my way through that. And nobody can hear me. Not a word. Faces flashing at my window now and they can't hear me. The sky has gone black but I'm in Satan's own Cadillac. The sulfur rains are starting to pour down out there and the eyes at my windows are widening, the mouths are opening to cry out, and now the flesh dissolves all around and the eyes melt and there is only bone and tooth and then not even that and it's getting a little warm in here but the car rushes on and I am thinking and thinking and it's too bad what's happening out there but it's high noon in Hell and there's nothing to be done about that and one way or another I've just got to figure out how to get the fuck out of here.*

∝

Hatcher waits quietly in the Cadillac in his alleyway until the rain ends and the steaming puddles that are the denizens who were outside begin to coagulate back into bodies. Then he steps from the car and goes up the staircase. Ahead of him, the Hoppers' door is closed, and behind it, Howard and Peggy are sitting in their overstuffed chairs. They are outwardly silent. But inside Howard, there is a voice speaking, unheard even by Satan: *The rugs have gone threadbare in Yonkers, the back door sticks in the heat, she talks nonstop through breakfast and lunch about every little thing that can possibly go wrong in the kitchen cabinets and in the world, and at dinner she will pause only to look out the window at the maple trees, which she's been worrying about for years though we've never seen even a trace of the blight, and she'll say "I'm sad," and I'm supposed to do something about it, and I know what she's thinking right now, that if I was worthless then, think how worse than worthless I am in Hell, but in Yonkers I go down to the basement to spend another long sweet Saturday restoring vintage fountain pens in silence and I am applying the heat gun to open a turquoise Waterman Lady Patrician I bought in an estate sale and she slips into the room, the woman of the Patrician, whoever she was, long ago she carried the pen in her purse with her powder and her lipstick and her handkerchief and her perfume—her perfume—the heat awakens the smell of her perfume—her smell—rose and moss and patchouli—and she is beside me, I have resurrected her, she is alive again and I breathe her into me.*

And inside Peggy, her own voice speaks, unknown to Satan or to Howard either or even to herself, most of the time, and when it is known to herself, it serves only to torture her: *This must be hard on him even with our door shut against the sulfur out there pouring down, the smell gets in anyway and it's bad and he's got a nose on him and I don't know how he got it but he's always had it, like early on, maybe our fourth or fifth date, and I know we're going to kiss and it's night and we're racing along the Hudson in his Ford Roadster and he's sniffing at the air and I say what and he says dogwood and I can't even pick it up, and later we're parked and we're kissing and he puts his nose against my throat and he says rose and he says jasmine and he says there's something smoky, like an animal, and he hopes it's okay, his saying this, he hopes this doesn't make me mad, and it doesn't, it's actually something okay in a way that I can't even begin to put into words, but I slap him a little just the same* and for Peggy this is so long ago and utterly lost and whatever was okay is so very difficult to think about that she says now, aloud, "You've always been so rude," and he says, "Me rude? You never stopped yammering long enough for me even to begin to be rude," and they start up, while outside, Hatcher passes their closed door and approaches his own.

He hopes Anne was safely in the apartment for the rain. If she's waiting inside for him, he has to figure out now what to tell her about her own mind. He stops before the door. He recognizes the assumption he just made. Perhaps this privacy of mind he has isn't universal. Maybe it's a rare gift. Like good hair and straight teeth and a killer broadcast voice. Maybe if he lets anyone know about it who doesn't have the gift, Satan will find him out through that other mind and deal with him.

He opens the door and steps in. Anne is not in sight. "Darling, I'm home," he says.

She appears from the bedroom, head attached, wearing jeans and a TUDOR HOOLIGAN T-shirt. As soon as her eyes fall on Hatcher, she gapes and gasps such that Hatcher wonders if the rain misted into the backseat and he wasn't aware and he is standing before her half dissolved.

"It was your investiture," she says.

"What?"

"When they grabbed you full stark naked, I worried for your fate. But it was to . . . " She pauses, trying to find a word, but both her hands have come up, their fingers fluttering at him.

He looks down. He is clad still in the powder-blue jumpsuit of a minion. Of course he is. He was hustled into the car after the interview and borne along like this. He lifts his arms, rotates his hands, considers himself up and down. Has he become a minion? Is this how it's done?

" . . . enable you," Anne says, finding the word she wanted. "Is this so? Did they give you new powers, my darling?"

He looks at Anne. Her T-shirt now reads GOVERN NAKED.

"No," Hatcher says. "I don't know."

Anne angles her head to the side ever so slightly, narrows her eyes and smiles faintly. "Even Henry goes about in mufti. He is a king no more. And my anchorman, powerful already, entering every dwelling in Hell, is elevated even higher now." She has begun to purr.

Hatcher looks down once more at his uniform. Everyone in Hell knows what this means. Perhaps this will help him too, in what he must do. He feels Anne drawing near, and he is happy suddenly about his apparent new status. Maybe real status. He thinks to pat at his hair. It's been restored to its normal anchorman length without Anne ever being reminded of the first man she had sex with. All is well. He lifts his eyes and Anne's T-shirt reads KISS ME, I'M A BRIT IN HELL and she is upon him, putting her arms around his neck and her mouth on his.

Hatcher wonders if minions get to have satisfying sex. He wonders if the thing that actually makes the sex go bad in Hell is the notion that an immortal is not only watching but listening to every intimate thought. He wonders if that often didn't apply back on earth as well. He recalls that it certainly did apply in the back of the Pittsfield American Legion Hall a week after the first Kennedy funeral when he was driven to bind together the passion for a girl with the passion of world events and the girl was driven to listen for God, who was inside her mind telling her to look at her dirty little self and feel ashamed. He even recalls the impression on that night that JFK was there with him, not just watching but inside Hatcher's head where they could talk, and Hatcher asked *Mr. President, do you mind?* and Kennedy said *You should proceed with vigah* and Hatcher wonders if Anne even considers Satan's putative presence in her head, wonders if maybe for her it's Henry VIII in there listening all the time. And with all this wondering and recalling, of course, Hatcher is missing quite a bit of kissing. His lips are working but he's missing their primary intended effect.

And Anne recalls with the first kiss of her newly invested Hatcher how her first kiss with Henry was at Hampton Court in the King's Long Gallery and how he wore a robe of Venetian damask and silver tissue and gold cloth and no one in the realm could wear such a thing but him— it was all his power draped upon him—and she wonders at how a man's power gives off a palpable emanation, a thing in the air that enters through her very gown—not to mention through her very Bangladeshi jeans— and goes straight to all the excitable spots on her body and excites them. And she wonders at how that excitement is like the excitement of seeing a beautiful snake suddenly among the flowers, crimson and black, and its beauty is made vivid by the poison you think is in its fangs and you want to touch it and it coils for you and its round-tipped little head rises and swoops for you and then it bites and you go quite numb and you lose all the excitement, and then you stop and ask yourself why you shouldn't be the one who bites. And Anne, wishing to make this thing go right for herself at last, is moved to bite her semipowerful man on the lip and he cries out and they both remember the last time her teeth got involved in sex between them and she suddenly can't understand why she wants this anyway and she lets go and backs off. Her T-shirt now reads HELL IS LOSING YOUR HEAD.

From the bedroom Brünnhilde in the Götterdämmerung begins to send Wotan's ravens home in her final aria before riding her horse into her own flaming funeral pyre, sung, however, in this version, by a very large chorus of Satan's cockroaches directed by Richard Wagner himself, which is to say that Hatcher's cell phone rings. He knows who it is. He steps past Anne, who is looking a little distracted, the look she often has before removing her head.

"Please keep it on," he says in passing.

"Okay okay," she says, trailing her hand along the blue sleeve of the passing minion jumpsuit.

He goes into the bedroom and flips open his cell phone. It's Beelzebub. "Showtime," he says and is gone.

∝

Since they sometimes do several cycles of the *Evening News from Hell* before evening actually comes again—the hot afternoons often linger for a long, long while—the cell phone call Hatcher has just received is his routine summoning for work. Always in the past, he has left quickly to get to Broadcast Central after the summoning, but he has often gotten there only after long delays on the Parkway. And yet there never seems to be an issue of time. When he arrives, they prepare. But he has never willfully hesitated in his progress. He has his own investigative agenda now. There are some stops he could make along the way to work. Dare he do it? He knows his inner thoughts are his own. But is he always being watched? And listened to when he speaks? These might be separate matters.

He is pacing and twitching around the bedroom floor, he realizes. What further consequence is there to fear when he has already been dismembered and incinerated and acidly dissolved? Pain is life here. There is always the reconstituting to be available for more pain. His hands fly into the air, clutching at nothing. He says aloud, "Pain pain pain fuck fuck fuck." A figure is in the bedroom doorway. He stops. Anne watches him, her brow furrowed. Her T-shirt is blank. Pure white. Wordless.

"What is it?" she asks, softly.

He could tell her now, what he knows about minds in Hell. But maybe it's only his own. Maybe he's special. Maybe he's unique. To make her think she can think might be dangerous for her.

"It's time to go to work," he says.

"You're special now," she says.

He starts. Did she read his mind? No. He realizes she's referring to his apparent minionhood.

"No reason to be anxious," she says.

"Thanks," he says. "No."

"I'm sorry for biting," she says.

"It's okay."

"My head is on."

"Yes. Thanks."

"I'm sad," she says.

Hatcher's hands fly up again. He twitches. But in excitement now. He might be able to do something about her sadness. If he finds a way out, he will take his Anne with him.

∝

A few moments later Hatcher is standing in front of the open closet, a little surprised at how reluctant he is to even temporarily remove his blue jumpsuit, when Brünnhilde begins to sing again, in his pocket. This time, however, she is rendered by Michael Jackson in a seriously inadequate falsetto interrupted shortly by a banging of metal and guttural German cursing—interpretable, if Hatcher were so inclined, as Wagner flailing away at the King of Pop, who is dressed in full Brünnhildean armor for his ring-tone recording session. Hatcher answers the phone. It's Beelzebub again, who says, "Business suit, comrade. And wear your new tie," and he's gone.

Oops. Hatcher feels as if his mind was just read. He flushes as hot as a sulfurous rain. But. But. All that really suggests is Beelzebub knows about Hatcher's minion suit. It would be a simple thing that he was told. Bee-bub and Old Scratch surely are both adept at guessing what their subjects are thinking, like bebangled fortune tellers in a carnival. Beelzebub knows in conventional ways that Hatcher just got home and how he was clad. He knows Hatcher's facing the choice of doing the news in anchorman suit and tie or the minion uniform. In spite of the little scare, Hatcher still believes he's right about omniscience. And now he even thinks to try a first test of Satan's omnipresence. Hatcher lifts his face and says aloud, "Fuck you, Bee-bub." He waits. Nothing happens. "Fuck you, I said." Nothing. "And your boss too. Fuck you, Satan." He gives the finger to the north, south, east, and west, to the ceiling and to the floor. He braces himself. Nothing.

Hatcher takes a deep breath. The fear is subsiding. He's cool as mortal life inside. And now Beelzebub's throwaway bit of fashion advice finally registers on him. What new tie? Hatcher steps into the closet doorway and peers inside. Hanging directly in front of him on a hook in the shadows of the back wall is a tie. He puts his hand to it and takes it out. It is powder blue. It's official. He takes off his jumpsuit of exactly the same color and rolls it carefully and tucks it deep in an upper shelf corner of the closet.

∝

The writers' neighborhood is on the way to Broadcast Central and Hatcher is making good time along the edge of the throng in the Parkway. The smell of sulfur is still strong in the air, but the puddles in the street have vanished—reconstituted—and the city is teeming in a way that feels almost comfortable to Hatcher in its tortured normalcy. He has a little bit of evidence that not only is Satan not hearing everything, he's not seeing everything either. Hatcher thinks about Virgil. The poet guide is a good place to start in his quest for Hell's back door.

Along the street, a few of the transitory bookstores are open, and as Hatcher is wondering how to go about looking for Virgil, he sees a hand-lettered sign in a bookshop window: SHAKESPEARE AND COMPANY. He stops and goes in.

The bookshelves here are full, unlike those in most of the shops along the street, though Hatcher does not glance at the titles. He is immediately struck by a figure sitting at a desk at the back of the shop, a small woman with thick, wavy hair cut off at the collar of a tattered brown velvet jacket. In a sitting area near the desk are a couch and several chairs, all empty, all canary yellow or avocado green Naugahyde, gashed and covered by what appear to be piss stains. Before Hatcher wanted to be Walter Cronkite, he wanted to be Ernest Hemingway, so he instantly recognizes Sylvia Beach. He approaches her.

Sylvia looks up at him. "Are you a writer?" she asks, rising from her chair a little in hopefulness.

"No," he says. "Sorry."

She sinks back down.

"Well," he says, "I published a memoir once, partial, from childhood to forty or so, but I didn't actually write it and it was full of invented anecdotes."

Sylvia furrows her brow and cocks her head.

"The writer called it 'creative nonfiction,'" Hatcher says.

"I don't understand that term," Sylvia says.

"I hear he lives in this neighborhood."

"I hear there are many writers around here."

"Oh yes."

"They don't come in."

"This is Hell, Ms. Beach."

"I only get book reviewers. They come in and sit around, and they all seem unaware of who or where they are. I don't know them. They clearly read too fast and in the wrong frame of mind. They miss so much. Perhaps that's why they're here."

"You haven't had any writers at all?"

"Herman Melville came in."

"Have you seen Virgil?"

"He's working on a new novel."

"Melville?"

"Yes." Sylvia shrugs. "He can't get past the first sentence. 'Call me E-mail.'"

"The old-timers have trouble adjusting."

Sylvia waves her hand vaguely at the shelves. "No wonder they stay away."

Hatcher looks at the shelves. Each of the books, throughout the shop, has the same spine, a familiar segmented stacking of rectangles, differing only occasionally in color.

"Every volume I have. Reader's Digest Condensed Books. It's all I can get." Sylvia begins to weep softly. "Is it because of Adrienne, do you suppose? That I'm here, with these?"

"Adrienne?"

"Monnier. The woman I was with for many years."

"From all that I can tell . . ."

"My father the pastor . . ."

". . . it would have been no different if she'd been a man."

". . . perhaps he was right."

"Your father's probably here too. There seems to be a multitude of reasons, for all of us."

Sylvia is crying harder and Hatcher steps close, puts his hand on Sylvia's shoulder. She looks up. "You wouldn't recognize Adrienne if you saw her? No, of course not."

"No."

"How about Ernest? Hemingway. Is he here?"

"I don't know."

"And Jim Joyce?"

"I haven't seen either of them."

"Perhaps they'll find me."

"Only if they can inadvertently bring you pain, I'm afraid."

"Oh, I'm used to that," Sylvia says. She pats Hatcher's hand.

He says, "Virgil is here."

"Of *The Aeneid*?"

"And *The Inferno*."

"As a character. Yes."

"He's in a toga. His nose is mostly missing, like a statue. If you see him, please ask how Hatcher McCord can get in touch with him."

"You're on the television, aren't you," Sylvia says.

"Yes."

"You seem a nice man," she says. "Why are you in Hell?"

"I don't know exactly," he says. "But if you're here, Ms. Beach, then I was a sure thing."

She pats his hand once more and he gently pulls away. They say goodbye and he goes out her door and up the street, his mind still on the question she raised. The big Why. His second wife, Deborah, fancied herself a writer. Wrote a bad memoir about the two of them, full of lies. Wrote a bad novel about the two of them without enough lies. Creative nonfiction and uncreative fiction. She could be living nearby. Virgil could be nearby. There are people to find, but he isn't going to do it stumbling into shops and leaving messages.

Hatcher is approaching the alley now where Virgil first took him. Up ahead, the neon **BURGERS** sign is popping and sparking and radiating brightly in spite of the intense sunlight all around. He slows. He stops. He waits, hoping for Virgil to appear again. But he knows this isn't going to work. Then it occurs to him. If the upper management in Hell does not have omniscience and isn't omnipresent, then they might need some sort of physical record-keeping. Somebody knows where the denizens are. Hatcher presses on toward Broadcast Central.

∝

Hatcher enters the vast marble-block building that is Broadcast Central, and about three stories up inside the towering atrial reception hall, Albert Speer is chained to the back wall with large feathery wings strapped to his arms and a Nazi eagle's head fitted on top of his own with the beak curving down in front of his eyes. Broadcast Central is based on a Speer architectural plan, and on most days he is up there explaining his innocence to anyone whose attention he can get. Hatcher glances up at him and Speer shouts down, "You have to understand. I didn't know how bad it was." Hatcher never knows how to respond, so he simply lowers his face and passes under the man and through the high arched doorway and down a long, dim marble hallway to the elevators.

On the top floor he steps from the elevator, neatly but barely missing the abrupt snapping shut of the doors—visitors often lose limbs here and have to wait for the elevator to return to be reconstituted—indeed, the floor underfoot feels blood-sticky even now—but instead of heading for the studio, Hatcher turns toward the corridor of offices. He treads lightly. He feels a blip of pleasure at treading lightly. It will do good to tread lightly so that Beelzebub will not know of his approach. No one will know. It's Hatcher's own little secret, moving from here to there. His mind is careening now. He is tiptoeing like a cartoon cat sneaking up on a mouse. He is enjoying this a little too much for his own good.

But he settles down as he approaches Beelzebub's outer door. And there are voices from within. He slows and stops and then eases forward. He is next to the open doorway.

From deep inside the office, faint but clear, is a man's familiar voice. "Your situation is very similar."

"The superior number two man," Beelzebub replies.

"May I ask a blunt question?" the voice says. Hatcher feels close to identifying the speaker.

"I've brought you here for that very thing," Beelzebub says.

"I've spent an awful long time already down a drill hole full of boiling oil." Dick Cheney. It's Dick Cheney.

"By way of initiation," Beelzebub says. "You'll suffer differently now."

"But to speak like this, when . . . you know."

"You're with Beelzebub now. I'm the Supreme Ruler in this office."

"All right," Cheney says. "Let me ask this. How stupid is he?"

"Ah. Yes. Well." Beelzebub hemming and hawing is a new thing for Hatcher to hear. The "he" must be Bee-bub's boss.

"With mine, you kept waiting for the slightest glimmer," Cheney says. "But." Even outside the door, Hatcher can hear the shrug.

"Oh I know. I know," Beelzebub says. "Mine is stupid. Yes. But crafty, I'd say. Smart in that way."

"Ah," Cheney says. "I didn't have to deal with that."

"Nevertheless."

"We'd float the rumor that in private he was different from what he was in public. One-on-one he was so Texas-backslappy shrewd he was some sort of smart. He liked the reputation."

"Flattery then?"

"Of course," Cheney says. "But the fundamental process for men like you and me is this. The stupider the president—or any leader—the more power you arrange for him. And the more secretive you make him. Don't disclose a thing. The insular, unitary leader. Finally he's got so much in front of him but at the same time he's so cozily private that even the stupid man who's too stupid to realize he's stupid will realize two things. He needs somebody to do the real work for him, and nobody will know the difference."

"Yes, I see that," Beelzebub says. "This is good. Reassuring. I think I'm on the right track."

"If there's anything I can do."

"You were a hunter."

"Yes."

"I'll set up a hunting date in the mountains with the Old Man. We can get that Texas attorney you already diddly-plugged and put him out in the canebrake."

"Pardon?"

"No need. You'll be found innocent down here."

Hatcher backs quietly off, down the hall a ways, and then reapproaches noisily. He turns in at Beelzebub's door.

Hatcher has only rarely visited this office. The last time, the secretary in the outer office was Messalina, empress of Rome and notable nymphomaniac. Now, crossed on the desktop, are the bottoms of a pair of wide, bare feet, each, however, cloven down the center. They are attached to a large bleached-blond woman with a round, heavily-made-up face rendered oddly beautiful by enormous dark eyes. In between, she is naked, with breasts the size of Iowa pumpkins, and when her eyes move to Hatcher, she demurely draws bleached-blond bat wings from behind her and folds them over her chest.

Emerging from an inner office are the former vice president of the United States, dressed in the blue jumpsuit of a minion, and the eternal vice president of Hell, dressed in a charcoal-gray pinstripe suit and white shirt with a neatly-knotted maroon tie sporting a McDonald's Golden Arches motif. Beelzebub's massive and cratered face bulges above his tightly buttoned collar, with deep-set neon-red eyes and lacquered black faux hair. He sees Hatcher and smiles. "Hatcher, my boy. I think you two know each other."

Cheney has a faint red glow, and one side of his mouth pinches up into a smirky smile like his last boss. "My favorite debate moderator," he says.

"My favorite puppeteer," I say.

"Oh you boys," Beelzebub says, and he looks past Hatcher. "Lily," he says to the secretary. "Go to lunch."

There is a stirring behind him and Hatcher turns his head to see. The naked, bat-winged blond rises from the chair, sets up a small desktop pedestal sign that says **gone for sex**, rises from the floor, and thinks of something. In midair she rotates to look at Beelzebub.

"Need anything?" she says in a venereally husky, chain-smoking, truck-stop-waitressy voice.

"No."

"Fries? A Coke?"

"I'm fine," Beelzebub says.

She nods and then gracefully drifts out of the office.

"She looks familiar," Cheney says.

"She's the girl of your dreams," Beelzebub says.

Hatcher looks back in time to see the furrow of puzzlement pass over Cheney's face.

"Literally," Beelzebub says. "She's a succubus."

Cheney still doesn't get it.

"She's off now back to the mortal realm to fuck the new prime minister of France. In the middle of his dreams, you see."

Cheney shrugs.

Hatcher says, "Perhaps the former vice president will do a 'Why Do You Think You're Here?' interview."

Beelzebub says, "Hatcher's got the nose for news, doesn't he? What do you say, Dick?"

Cheney shuffles his feet. "I have no comment on that, really. I had other priorities in life." His face goes more or less blank, and he waits.

Beelzebub glances at Hatcher and winks. Then he says, "Well, Dick, thanks for stopping by. Go on out in the street now."

Cheney nods and without another word or gesture slides past Hatcher and through the office door.

"So, my boy," Beelzebub says. "Congratulations."

It's official. Hatcher takes a deep breath. "Thanks."

"I see your minionhood has emboldened you to come by the office." Beelzebub waits one beat and then another, clearly to make Hatcher worry about his attitude toward this.

Hatcher is exhilarated to realize that he doesn't give a fuck. He keeps his face placid.

"I'm glad," Beelzebub finally says. "What's up?"

"I was interested in my encounter with J. Edgar Hoover."

"Ah yes. He has his ways, doesn't he?"

"Yes he does. I'd like to do a 'Why Do You Think You're Here?' interview with him. In his office."

Beelzebub takes this in, and his face begins to vibrate ever so slightly. His eyebrows are great, flaring arcs of needle-rigid hairs, and the right one lifts high while the left one sinks low. He leans toward Hatcher and cocks his head as if he's reading Hatcher's deepest thoughts.

Hatcher knows better. He cocks his own head now, lifting his own right brow and lowering his own left brow. He leans toward Beelzebub, splitting the slight remaining distance between them. After a long moment of silence between the two faces, Hatcher says, "Hoover and his earthly power are known to a great many of the denizens. Imagine how all-powerful it will make our Big Boss look for everyone in Hell to see Hoover whimpering around trying to understand his eternal damnation. On his own administrative turf."

Beelzebub's eyes widen. Both eyebrows pop up together as high as they will go. He pulls back a bit. "Dude," he says. "You surprise me. Not surprise, of course. Delight. I am just delighted to see how you are coming along. The surprise I refer to is that your pansy-ass world is capable of now and then sending along someone with something on the ball."

Hatcher returns his own eyebrows to their default position and he smiles an aw-shucks smile. "Thanks," he says, thinking, *If any office in Hell keeps track of where everyone is, it's got to be Hoover's.*

$$\infty$$

Shortly thereafter, Hatcher sits down in the recording studio and finds a script waiting for him. Beyond the glass window, Dan Rather is fidgeting in work overalls and a Lone Star Feed & Fertilizer ball cap, trying to figure out the mixing board before him. The former CBS anchor has been around Broadcast Central for a while, but Hatcher hasn't known where he's been working, exactly, and when he's seen him in the halls, Hatcher can never approach him. Rather is clearly banished from the air, and whenever anyone seems to be approaching him, he backs frantically away, crying, "I don't know the frequency!" With the glass partition between him and Hatcher, however, he stays put but fumbles around at the knobs and sliders on the board.

Hatcher looks at the script. It's for the Satan interview. There is a brief introduction—the segment isn't even called an interview here—and there is the final "Satan wept." Hatcher is simply to record his voice and the piece will be assembled, with someone else no doubt stepping in technically after Rather has suffered long enough.

Hatcher puts his headphones on. Rather notices this and reaches to remove his cap. He instantly starts wrenching mightily at it—he's tried unsuccessfully to do this before—but the cap won't budge. Finally, Rather puts his headset on over the cap, leans forward, and presses the talk button. "Courage," Rather says.

Hatcher doesn't quite know what he means by this, never did quite know when Rather occasionally used it to sign off from his evening news.

Rather's hands are fluttering and hesitating and fluttering again over the mixing board. He says, with his best West Texas twang, "Me and this job are like a hen trying to hatch a cactus," though the remark seems not to be directed outward.

"Dan," Hatcher says.

Rather looks up.

"Good to catch up with you," Hatcher says. He's not sure Rather recognizes him, though they spent years vying for the same viewers.

"I'm Hatcher McCord."

"I know who you are."

They look at each other through the glass for a long moment.

"Can I ask you a question, Dan?"

Rather nods, but he instantly asks his own question. "Are we all here?"

"We?"

"The newsmen. In Hell."

"I haven't seen everybody."

"Murrow?"

This is a sad thing for Hatcher. "So they say. When I asked about him, Beelzebub said he was smoking."

"Why don't I think this has to do with Ed's cigarettes?"

Hatcher nods at Rather with his face scrunched to say, I know what you mean.

Rather thinks for a moment and then says, "You know, there wasn't a single person on earth who didn't have millions of other people expecting them to go to Hell."

Hatcher hasn't thought of it this way. "You're right," he says.

"Courage," Rather says.

"Courage," Hatcher says. This was the question he had for Rather, about this word. Oddly now, it feels apt.

"I think I can start this thing up," Rather says.

Hatcher picks up his script. "All right."

Rather nods and Hatcher begins to read, "When I visited your great Father, the Supreme Ruler of Eternity, in his comfy cozy . . . "

Hatcher stops. "Let me start again," Hatcher says into the microphone.

Rather's hands move to the board, and he says, "Whenever you're ready." Hatcher looks at the words before him. Until a short time ago, whenever they gave him something to say, he'd read it out as is. He dared do nothing else. But all of a sudden, with this typically overwrought script before him plumping up Satan—like so many that Hatcher's done before—he can barely make his mouth shape itself around the words. He knows it's because he feels his thoughts are his own. This is a serious danger, he realizes. Breathe free and get burned. He still can't make his publicly verifiable deeds his own. He still dare not change a thing in his work. He topples his head forward in this recognition. Then he lifts his face once more, takes a deep breath, and looks Rather in the eyes.

"Hatcher McCord take two," Rather says.

And Hatcher starts over. "When I visited your great Father, the Supreme Ruler of Eternity, in his comfy cozy living room, he greeted me with a hug, so typical of his magnanimity."

The script asks him to pause. He does. Then he reads, "Not that he didn't charmingly remind me who was the boss."

Another pause. "Then he spoke with passionate eloquence."

Another pause, and now the big climax. Hatcher summons his will, unctions-up his voice, and says, "Satan wept."

He stops. He looks through the glass, and Dan Rather gives him the thumbs-up. Then Dan looks sharply down at his mixing board with acute concern. "Whoa Nellie," he says. "It's doing something."

This could mean anything. This could be a routine step in the editing process. The technology around the station often seems to have a mind of its own, or at least an automated sophistication that its surface—in this case, a rather old-fashioned mixing board—does not fully reveal. Or it could easily mean the onset of a bizarre and intensely painful incident typical of life in Hell. Hatcher is calm inside as he waits to see which it is, and this is new. He realizes the isolated privacy of his mind is what lets him wait for the pain without the thrashing panic, but he's not sure why. Courage.

And it turns out to be the routine step. "It seems to have just edited itself," Rather says.

The two men look at each other and then Rather does the obvious thing. He plays it. Each of them turns his face to his own monitor.

The comfy cozy stuff is spoken over an establishing shot of the lodge's great room, empty.

The magnanimous hug shows Hatcher from behind with only Satan's arms around him, pounding him manfully on the back, and little fragmented glimpses of Satan's head bussing Hatcher's cheeks. These glimpses seem off somehow, but they are gone too quickly for Hatcher to figure out why.

The charming reminder of who's the boss is spoken over a shot of Hatcher with his hair on fire.

Then, as Hatcher says that Satan spoke with passionate eloquence, a face comes up on the screen, framed against the lodge's walk-in fireplace, and it begins to speak. The face is the face of Hatcher's father.

"Come to me, my little ones," the face says. "I want you. I want you all. I choose you, my darlings. I do so because I want you. It's what makes us all down here one big modern extended family. I want you in my family. We have to help each other. Doesn't that warm the cockles of your heart? Isn't this a Hallmark moment? Send me a card now, all of you. Go find a sweet little greeting card with family thoughts and mail it to me."

The face—Hatcher's father—blows a kiss.

Hatcher's father says, "I feel for you all, my little children. I do care." And he digs knuckles into the corners of both eyes. Then he abruptly drops his hands and lifts his face. Hatcher's father closes his eyes.

"Satan wept," Hatcher says in the voice-over.

The face freezes in its pose for a moment before the frame fades to a roiling bright red. Then the monitor goes blank.

"Some part of me always suspected as much, given the banality of evil," Dan Rather says.

Hatcher is still trying to deal with the shift from routine step in the editing process to bizarre and intensely painful incident, so he does not respond.

Rather says, "That Richard M. Nixon was Satan himself."

Which means everyone will see his or her own personally tailored image when Satan speaks. Like the "Your Stuff" commercials. And right now Hatcher is so full of his dad that he simply takes off the headphones, rises, and goes out of the studio without another glance at Dan Rather, who is swelling with pride at having once stood up snarkily to Satan himself in the White House pressroom. Literally swelling. But Hatcher does not hear the dull pop, as he is not only down the hall but also on the front porch of his boyhood home in Pittsfield, Illinois: *Fireflies in the dark yard and the smell of tar and gravel dust from the pavers having gone through the neighborhood that afternoon and my dad's home early for a Friday and I don't get up and get the hell away like I should when he comes and sits beside me on the porch while I'm thinking about something he'd despise—Adlai Stevenson maybe having a real chance to win the second time, now that they've nominated him to try again—and I made the mistake of speaking up about politics at dinnertime earlier in the week, saying what a relief it'd be to have a man with an actual brain in the White House, this after my dad gave me a bad whipping in the backyard for not going out to shoot a whitetail, which he claimed was about my not minding him instead of my not shooting, though he said I should easily guess what he thought of my piss-ant little girl's ass about that, and now he's back from the bar by nine or so and I've seen that before, when he gets an early start with business slow and the deliveries done and with the McCord Hardware Transtar pickup parked at the door of The Pitt, advertising his drunkenness, and tonight he sits down beside me and he's quiet for a while and I'm not letting him drive me off and then he says, almost softly, "Your mother thinks you're goddam perfect, you can do no wrong." I don't answer. What he says is true but I don't let myself think about that and still I just wait like an idiot for what's next. Do I actually think it will be any different? "She's wrong, you know," he says. I don't answer. He says, "She's a goddam woman, so who is she to measure a man? She sees herself in you and so of course you're perfect. I'm a man, and I see that you'll never be enough of a man to spit past the end of your dick. You're doomed, boy. You'll never be anywhere near what you're supposed to be." He says all this low, which is rare, and, except for the one small outburst of metaphor, he says it with a veneer of logic, which is even rarer. Still, I'm taking a little bit of comfort in its being Friday night. And he seems to read my mind. "You think I'm saying this drunk," he says. "Come here." And he leans across to my chair and reaches out and grabs me by the back of the head. He yanks me right up to his face. "Smell my breath, boy." And I do. There is no liquor there whatsoever. None.*

∝

After the news, Hatcher goes to his steel-gray cubicle and phones J. Edgar Hoover's office.

"Minion Hoover's office." The husky female voice on the other end is instantly familiar, though he's heard only a few words from it before. Beelzebub's succubus.

"Lily?" he says.

"Lulu," the voice says. "I'm Lily's sister."

"Lulu, hello," Hatcher says in his best swooping, hello-upscale-groupie tone, trying to figure a plan already. "I'm Hatcher McCord, anchorman for the *Evening News from Hell*."

"I'm Lulu, spawn of Grand Mater Lilith," she says, putting on his tone and then giggling. "I was expecting your call."

"Ah. Bee-bub," he says.

Lulu giggles again. This giggle of hers is more like a little trilling in the deep back of her throat, as if she's gargling something back there. "Bee-bub," she says. And again. "Bee-bub."

"You have an enchanting laugh, Lulu."

She giggles some more. "I watch you on TV every whenever," she says. "Do you sleep well?"

"You thinking of a little visit, you sexy Lulu?" he says.

Her voice goes instantly clear and reedy fine. "You bet your squeezable ass, anchorman," she says.

Hatcher's breath snags. She seems to him the only clear way to get the addresses he wants. But there may be a heavy price to pay, he realizes. "We'll have to talk about all that," he says.

"Ohhhhh yeahhhhh," she says, extending the words like a tongue down his throat.

"I'm a minion now," Hatcher says.

"This I know," she says. Then she adds, with one more giggle, "Bee-bub."

"Well, good. I want to interview . . ."

"There'll be a car ready for you right after your broadcast," she says. "Do linger a moment at my desk, minion McCord."

∝

Hatcher finds a 1932 Duesenberg LaGrande Dual Cowl Phaeton sitting in front of Broadcast Central, and he steps up onto the running board and through the back door. A hand-held camcorder lies on the seat. He takes this as an encouraging nuance of his minionhood. He is on his own with the camera. All the other off-site "Why Do You Think You're Here?" interviews involved somebody being tortured by don't-dare-move-the-fucking-thing camera duty. Martin Scorsese was the last one, for the recent Bill Clinton episode—yet to run—shot in a cheap hotel room where the former president is presently eternally waiting in vain for a young woman to arrive, any young woman. On the way to Clinton and on the way back, Scorsese wouldn't stop talking about how he himself could have avoided all this if he'd gone to the seminary as he'd once planned, and nothing Hatcher said about Hell's vast population of priests and pastors, monks and magi, rabbis and imams and shamans, both minor and major, from all the world's religions would assuage his regret, though night came upon them and Scorsese's agony shifted from his abandoned vocation to not having a camera of his own when the sun went down because this was so clearly his kind of town.

Now, however, Hatcher is on his own. With, of course, his driver, who is dressed in a button-over leather coat and leggings and a visored chauffeur's cap and is staring fixedly down the long hood of the Duesenberg to its chrome-plated bronze leaping Pegasus hood ornament. He is Porphyrius Calliopas, the greatest charioteer of the Eastern Roman Empire, whose vast bronze commemorative statue at the Hippodrome in Constantinople was the only one ever erected while its subject was still racing and who personally incited the biggest riot in chariot-racing history, with ten thousand Green and Blue team hooligans killing each other.

Hatcher is ready, and he waits, and then he says to the driver, "You know where we're going, yes?"

Porphyrius snaps his head around to Hatcher, tries to focus. "Yessir," he says. He looks back out past Pegasus at the crowd blocking the way before him, squeezes his steering wheel tightly, and they move off, creeping through the clogged streets, the charioteer never having been able to figure out how to drive fast enough in Hell even to shift out of first gear.

∝

Eventually they arrive at Administration Central, another neoclassic, deco-pimped, marble-block building near the center of the city, not far, Hatcher realizes, from the Old Harrowing site of Peachtree Way and Lucky Street that he'd set off for earlier. Hatcher takes up his camera and steps out of the car and walks across an empty plaza—even the dense flow of denizens eddies away from this place—and into a reception hall and elevator corridor so similar to Broadcast Central that he expects to see Albert stuck up on the wall.

Hoover's office is on the top floor at the end of a hallway. Hatcher hesitates before the outer door. He knows who waits inside. But he also knows what he needs from her. He opens the door.

Lulu rises from her desk instantly, rises above the desk, actually, levitating so that Hatcher has to crane his neck upward to see her. Lulu's bat wings are folded across her body like a button-over coat. They, unlike Lily's, have raven streaks in their bleached-blond fur. "Ooooh, Hatcher McCord," she gurgles, and she opens her wings to flash her naked body. Hatcher concentrates on her beaming face, consciously not looking directly at her body, though he is very aware of it, nonetheless—a peripheral blur of massive breasts and other swellings and ripplings and gapings.

"Business first," she says and closes her wings. She descends to her desk sits, and her arms emerge from beneath her wings to put on a pair of horn-rimmed glasses and, with a serious pout, pick up some blank papers before her and shuffle them around. "Impressive, oui?" she says. "How I am so very efficient an executive secretary?"

Hatcher is listening to Lulu but thinking about the addresses. Over her shoulder he is aware of her computer. The monitor presently shows the Windows Blue Screen of Death, though this does not alarm him, as the BSoD is the universal screen saver in Hell.

"Oui?" Lulu repeats, with an edge.

"Ah. Mais oui, Mademoiselle Lulu," Hatcher says. "Très efficient."

Lulu giggles. "Creep up on the door and go right on in," she says. "Don't knock."

Hatcher goes to the door—not quite creeping, but he is quiet—and faces a little dilemma. Lulu seems to have an agenda. To embarrass Hoover, no doubt. Hatcher doesn't like to think what Hoover might be doing in there alone. Hatcher is hesitating, and he hears a faint hiss from Lulu. He looks at her. She puts a long, scarlet-tipped forefinger to her lips to insist on silence, and then she shoo-shoos the hand to get him to go in. At this point, he'd rather irritate Hoover than Lulu, so he pushes open the door.

At first glance, Hoover does not seem to be in the office. But four strides away, at the far wall, is Hoover's massive desk, and the high-backed executive chair is turned with its back to the door. From the other side come gurgly squishy sounds that Hatcher does not want to hear. So he clears his throat loudly. The chair jerks and there are scuffling sounds and one sharp bark of pain and then some whimpering and some more scuffling and some ruffling and chair squeaking, but the chair does not turn for a long moment, and then it swivels quickly and Hoover is dressed in a wide-lapeled dark gray suit and white shirt and powder-blue minion tie and he has set his face in its stern Mr. G-man pose, this whole effect undercut only by the neon red lipstick on his mouth, applied, by all appearances, with meticulous precision.

"McCord," Hoover says, ducking his chin a little to find his manliest tone.

"Mr. Director," Hatcher says.

"You look good in a suit," Hoover says.

Hatcher goes a little icky at this, and whoever or whatever is under the desk apparently acts up, with a brief thumping and rustling, and Hoover squirms a bit in his chair as if he's kicking something under there.

Hatcher says, "I'm sure you're busy," and he makes sure to say this respectfully and without lowering his eyes to the desk. No sense getting into a pissing match with J. Edgar Hoover. He gestures slightly with the camera. "We should get started."

Hoover pushes back and rises. "Over there," he says, nodding to a wall covered in wide, floor-to-ceiling drapes. He moves to one end and pulls a cord, and the drapes open to a twentieth-floor panorama of the center of the Great Metropolis.

Hatcher moves to the window and looks out: the sun is still high, denizens throng the web of streets between rubble-strewn rooftops, dense black smoke plumes up from the complex of tanks and pipes and furnaces of the Central Power Station, a vast building-top motley of stone and wood and brick sprawls toward the sawtooth horizon bearing unseen multitudes, and a jumper falls past the window—suicides often come to Administration Central to replay their grief—and then another flashes past, a thin woman feet first with her skirt collapsed over her upper body like a cheap umbrella on a windy day, and Hatcher thumps his forehead hard against the glass trying to follow her, though he can't see anything immediately below from the angle and she quickly plummets out of his view, and he lifts his face to the nearest street, overflowing with souls, and he strains to look more closely, trying to resolve the dense mosaic into hats and hair and even tiny pointillist suggestions of faces. If your mind is bugged and an Immortal with attitudes and preferences is eavesdropping, how do you go about experiencing the very moment you're in the midst of living, the thereness of the landscape all about you and the grinding yearnings of the people nearby? If the He or She or It is listening in, you are bent, bullied, persuaded, muddled, and intimidated into certain feelings, and you don't have a clue whether they're actually yours or not. But now, looking out this window in the privacy of his mind, Hatcher feels a hot swelling inside him, as if every pore on his body is dilating, and at first he thinks it's the start of an Immortal's rage, it will be judgment and pain and more pain. But no. He watches the people in the street and he knows that each head down there is carrying within it its own throng of people and places and feelings from a mortal life once lived through a billion rich and complex moments. And the swelling in Hatcher opens into a bloom of sadness. Because he knows his mind is his own, he knows he is alone, and so he is free to feel this now. He spreads his arms wide and leans heavily against the window, and if one could weep in Hell out of pity, he would be weeping now, but his body won't do that. Nevertheless, there is a strange stopping inside him, a settling, a fleeting moment's feeling that in mortal life he would have called contentment. This is Hell as far as you can see. It is Hell for everyone. *We are all utterly alone, but we are alone together.*

"How about here," Hoover says.

Hatcher looks at him. Hoover has struck a pose with the city as backdrop and his hands clasped behind him.

"That's fine, Mr. Director," Hatcher says, and he wonders if Hoover really intends to do the interview with his lips painted. "Before we begin . . ." Hatcher hesitates. He doesn't know how to ask this, and he regrets even trying—why the fuck should he care if the man chooses to appear like this?—but Hatcher is looking at Hoover's lips and Hoover suddenly realizes what this is about.

"Ah," Hoover says. "Of course." He pulls a handkerchief from an inside coat pocket and half turns and wipes the lipstick off his mouth. He puts the handkerchief away and strikes his pose again.

Hatcher lifts the camera and Hoover is looking fiercely determined to do whatever manly G-man thing he needs to do, but from his lips, which barely move, comes a soft, clear, "Thanks."

Hatcher, perhaps still under the influence of that moment of contentment, says, "You look good."

Hoover pushes his lower lip up ever so slightly—into a little pout of thanks—and then he hardens again and nods, "Ready."

Hatcher turns his camera on and says, "There's just one question and you can talk for as long as you wish. Why do you think you're here?"

And J. Edgar Hoover says, "I was needed. Can you imagine how many Communists there are down here? Do you want Hell being run by Communists? They'd destroy us. Satan was an angel. He had a falling out with his father, but who hasn't? Some fathers just up and go crazy. Others have it out for you. Satan was set up, if you want to know the truth of it. Somebody had to deal with the vast hordes of damned humanity. The proof is out that window. Look at the citizens he has to deal with. Look at the elements within that citizenry. Now look at the organization Satan has built. He knows everything about everybody. All the time. Every second. You think there's a question about why I belong here? What would I do in a place where everyone is so high and mighty and perfect? You think I'm not needed here? You don't think it's lonely for men like Satan and me? We understand each other. I have to suffer like the rest of you. You don't think I deserve it? You don't think a real man can't like something a little frilly? You don't think I look stunning in a feather boa and a tasteful basic-black dress?"

Hoover stops. He hears where he's gone with this. Hatcher lifts his face from the camera and Hoover looks at him and then at the camera and then back to Hatcher. "Nothing we can do," Hoover says.

"I have no control once it goes in," Hatcher says.

Hoover nods. "I guess I'm done." He turns and moves off to his desk.

Hatcher looks out the window once more. The streets are full of thousands of years of souls endlessly pressing on to destinations they do not know, from promptings they do not understand. Hatcher has a brief, sweet, newsman's fantasy: he scores the greatest scoop in history—the discovery of a back door out of Hell—and he breaks the story on the

Evening News from Hell and they all go, every last soul, they all escape from Hell. And he wins an Emmy. And then a Pulitzer Prize.

Hatcher turns from the window and crosses Hoover's office—the man sits behind his desk and waits, and whoever is under there waits—and Hatcher is out the door and instantly vast furry bat wings enfold him and press him into hot naked rippling womanflesh.

But only for one dart of a tongue halfway down his esophagus and then an unfolding of wings and a quick float back to the desk and a putting on of the horn-rims and a fluffing up of papers. Hatcher stifles a faint gagging still going on down his throat, and he steels himself and moves to her desk.

"Well," he says. "You said to stop by the desk."

"Oui oui," she says.

"Are you French, Lulu?"

"No. Lily and I did a three-way nooner with the prime minister of France. So we oui oui ouied all the way home." She giggles her deep throat giggle and winks. "So. I want to take you home to meet Mama."

"Mama."

"I know what you're thinking."

She couldn't possibly, of course. Not just because of what Hatcher now understands. But also because his mind has basically shut down about what he's getting into for the sake of these addresses. And yet he can't think of a better way to proceed. But oh my. Mama.

"She's old as can be," Lulu says. "But sexy as Hell." And clearly Lulu believes Hell to be sexy.

Hatcher has no choice but to push on. "Would you do me one little favor, Lulu?"

Lulu flutters her bleached-blond eyebrows at him. "What would you like?"

"I've got some interviewing to do. Denizens. It'd help if I can get a few addresses." He nods to the computer behind her.

"Wellll," she says, cocking her head to the side, laying the tip of her forefinger into the center of her cheek, lifting her eyes to the ceiling, and then twirling the finger. "Since it's you. But no screaming when I bite a little."

She is already whirling in her chair and her hands flash over the keyboard, calling up the directory. Hatcher is panting in panic, but one pain is like another in Hell, when it comes down to it. And so he gives her all the names he can think of that he might need to find the back door, and to understand why he is here, which may not be unrelated if another Harrowing is truly imminent. Virgil and Dante. And Beatrice, in case her back-alley noir apartment was temporary. Hatcher's three wives. These names come quickly. And then he says his father's name, who turns out to have no address at the moment but is out somewhere stuck perpetually in traffic, roadraging at other drivers. Hatcher has a little surge of relief that he won't have to find the old man. And he says his mother's name. They are all of them in Hell. And now he's glad he thinks of this, for Sylvia: Adrienne Monnier. Then he hesitates. But yes. If it's what Anne needs, to resolve things one way or another. He says Henry VIII, King of England.

∝

Hatcher steps into the elevator at the end of Hoover's corridor. His head is buzzing with Lulu's promise to come for him soon, to meet Mama. As the doors are about to close, there are hurried footsteps and then a trim man with an elongated face and broad-bridged nose slips in. At first his dark eyes sharply focus on Hatcher, but they quickly go blank. He wears a cream linen suit and a wing collar and spectator shoes. There is a smear of blood at the corner of his mouth. He turns and stands shoulder to shoulder with Hatcher as the doors close. A hunch shoves even Lulu to the back of Hatcher's mind for a moment.

"Mr. Tolson?" Hatcher says.

The man turns his face to Hatcher. "Yes."

This is Clyde Tolson, Hoover's longtime assistant at the FBI and his intimate companion for more than four decades.

"I'm Hatcher McCord."

"I know."

Hatcher nods at the blood beside Tolson's mouth.

Tolson takes out a handkerchief and dabs there and looks at the spot of red sadly.

Hatcher says, "It never quite works down here, does it."

Tolson looks sharply at Hatcher. But then he smiles a faint half smile, puffing once through his nose. "Never," he says.

The two men look back to the front of the elevator until the door opens, and they part without a word, Tolson heading deeper into the building on the ground floor and Hatcher going out the front.

The Duesenberg sits at the curb. The sun is still high. Hatcher is in the center of the city. He crosses the plaza to the car and reaches into the backseat and lays the camera there and then moves to the front passenger door and leans in at the window. Porphyrius Calliopas is staring intently down the hood of the car at Pegasus leaping. *My horses. How long has it been? My palms and my waist are wrapped tight with the reins, the crowd bellows, I fly behind my horses and two of them are loaned to me by Neptune himself I am sure, with their wings tucked secretly away they came to me as Parthians, my sweet palomino Pyrros and my cranky chestnut Euthynikos, they are my legs, they are my breath, they are my fame, I call to them and they fly, and though others are running near us and many voices cry out my name, the moments that I am lashed to them move slowly, I can count the beats of my heart, I can smell their dank earth smells, I can feel their heavy sweat against my face, one drop and another and another, and I am certain that when we die, we will die together, the three of us, trying to make the far sharp turn in the Hippodrome, on the inside lane with a clot of chariots around us, but I am wrong: Pyrros dies beneath my grieving body in a stall and Euthynikos bolts and runs alone and is found*

later, and I am cursed to die in a bed as an old man and then I am quickened
again in this place and I cannot find them and that is the worst of the tortures,
that for all this eternity already and forever more, they are nowhere to be found,
there are no horses at all, no horses.

"Driver," Hatcher says.

Porphyrius rears at this and his hands flail and he turns his face to
Hatcher and he calms down. But Hatcher hardly sees these things. He is
focused on what he must do and he sees the driver looking at him and it
occurs to him to ask, "How do you find the streets, when you are driving someone?"

Porphyrius reaches to the glove box and opens it and pulls out a
folded map.

"May I have it?" Hatcher asks.

Porphyrius hesitates.

"You'll wait for me till I return," Hatcher says.

Hatcher can see the man thinking. Porphyrius looks at the map.

"You know who I am?" Hatcher says, touching his powder-blue neck-
tie for emphasis.

Porphyrius nods. He reaches his hand across the seat and extends
the map, his brow knit tight, his hand trembling slightly. Hatcher reaches
into the car, takes hold of the map, pulls it free. And the hand of
Porphyrius bursts into flames, roiling, heavy flames that rush instantly
up his arm.

Hatcher recoils, pulls his own hand and arm and the map safely
out of the car. There is no possibility of giving the map back. The driver
is vanishing utterly in the flames that race wildly up his arm and over
his shoulders and head and down his torso and legs, and then as abruptly
as it flared up, the fire vanishes, leaving only a pile of ashes and a
chauffeur's cap.

Hatcher stares at them, stunned for a moment but happy to have
the map in his hand. The ashes are beginning to stir a bit. Reconstitution

is beginning. But Hatcher uses his newsman's instincts: the source gave what he gave, which he shouldn't have given, and he paid the price. But you've got what you need for the sake of the story. Hatcher walks off.

∝

Before he leaves the empty plaza of Administration Central, Hatcher pauses and looks more closely at the map. It is a map he knows. A thumb-smudged Standard Oil gas station map with a detailed drawing in blue, red, and white. The image once shaped a fantasy in his thirteen-year-old mind: beneath the Standard Oil sign the gas station guy in his Standard Oil ball cap and bow tie holds one end of an unfolded map, with the other end in the grasp of a Tuesday-Weld-cute blond behind the wheel of her convertible. They are both looking at the place on the map where she's going to drive right now and wait for him till he gets off from work. Sometimes it's in the woods along the river. Sometimes his bachelor pad over the paint store downtown. A few years later, Hatcher even spent a summer pumping gas at the Pittsfield Standard station, and at the back of his mind, he was always waiting for that Ford Fairlane convertible to roll in and the blond to honk her horn and ask him directions.

Hatcher begins to unfold the map from the Duesenberg. It unfolds and unfolds. He opens his arms wide to hold it and backs up to give himself plenty of room on the empty concrete. He lays the map out and kneels before it. The Great Metropolis, a vast tapestry of Peachtrees. He lifts the map and turns it over, and on the other side is a tiny-print index of all the streets. He bends forward, bringing his face close to the print, as if he were praying toward Mecca. He can make the names out clearly. He finds the coordinates for Peachtree Way and Lucky Street, lifts and turns the map again, locates the place of the Old Harrowing and Admin Central and plots his course.

His destination turns out to be quite close. The trick is to turn down Peachtree Street Street Avenue off Peachtree Way, and a few hundred yards along, Peachtree Street Street Avenue renames itself Peachtree Avenue Street Street and then makes a sharp left turn and instantly takes on the name Peachtree Way while the parallel stretch of the previous Peachtree Way goes for a couple of blocks under the name Robert. Meanwhile, back on the new Peachtree Way, the intersection of Lucky Street should be coming up soon.

∝

Hatcher walks between dingy brick urban warehouse facades with boarded windows and three-story pilasters mounted by terra cotta demon faces, and the crowd here has lessened only slightly. The street is still full of people pressing ardently onward. But they mostly have long beards and wear rough-cloth cloaks and animal skins. This is an old neighbor-hood, of course. Ahead is the place where it is understood that long ago the Harrowing occurred, when this was the site of merely a foul, sulfu-rous well and an edge-of-town campsite for some of the standoffish Old Ones. And now Hatcher approaches the very place: Peachtree Way and Lucky Street.

On three of the corners, the intersecting streets' grimy buildings end in gaping rubble-filled lots, one concertina-wired, the other two open basement pits. On the fourth corner is a low, curve-edged, metal-fronted deco building. Hatcher pushes through a revolving door beneath a large gilt sign: **AUTOMAT**.

Inside, the two non-street walls are full of small, glass-doored food dispensers. In the center of the floor is a change booth barely as wide as the man within, who is beardless but massively mutton-chopped and dressed in frock coat, high collar, and wide-ribbon bow tie. Hatcher does not recognize Cornelius Vanderbilt. Above Vanderbilt's barred window is an official sign, **nickels**, and propped on the floor against the front of the booth is a cardboard sign with fading handwritten letters promis-ing *MEAT TOMORROW*. From its dinginess, it has obviously been sitting there for a long, long time. All around are tables filled with intently conversing groups of mostly men wearing sackcloth tunics and with the hair at their temples unrounded and the edges of their beards unmarred. A smell of stewed carrots and creamed spinach and sweat and goat hair fills the air. Surveying the room, Hatcher finally turns his gaze to the table in the corner at the window. One man sits there alone, his isolation perhaps due to the fact that he is the only customer dressed in suit and tie. The face is bowed as the man moves his fingertip in a spread of salt on the tabletop before him, the shaker sitting nearby. The top of his head, with its tight right-side part and faint cowlick, is familiar.

"Carl?" Hatcher says.

Carl Crispin looks up. His gaunt face draws even tighter in a flat facsimile of a smile. "Hatcher."

Hatcher moves to the table and sits across from his reporter.

Carl answers what he assumes will be Hatcher's first question. "Once I finally found it, I didn't want to lose it again."

Hatcher looks at the salt. Carl has lettered there: **TAKE <u>ME</u>**.

When Hatcher looks back up, Carl shrugs and backhands the salt from the table in a single stroke.

"A little ritual," Carl says. "We all of us here are searching for the right one."

Hatcher doesn't know what to say.

Carl goes on. "Salt, see. Lot's wife looked back on Sodom and this is what she became. So salt has to be powerful, right? I shouldn't be saying this. I'm going to pay now."

And Carl is pulled up from the chair and he stands straight and his body lifts off the floor and a dozen holes open in the top of his head, two dozen, and his body rotates until he is precisely inverted and he begins to jerk up and down as if an invisible hand is shaking him. From the holes in his head a fine gray powder flows out. His brain, no doubt.

Hatcher wonders what would have happened if he'd reached out his hand at Carl's first rising and held his arm and told him that no one is listening. Would the punishment have stopped?

As it is, though, Carl rotates back to an upright position and descends to the chair. His eyes are empty.

Hatcher waits. And, in time, the gray powder stirs and gathers from the chair, the tabletop, the floor, and rushes back into the top of Carl's head. His eyes come alive.

Hatcher says, "So, Carl. You do believe another Harrowing is imminent."

Carl shrugs and looks out the window. "I'm an awful liar, Hatcher."

"But you can lie about lying then."

"I can lie about anything."

"On air, about this not being a possible story, for instance."

Carl looks back intently to Hatcher. "Or I can lie to myself. I can lie to you about lying because I've lied to myself about lying to you about lying but I could be lying to myself about lying to myself about lying to you about lying which means I lied in the first place."

"The first place being . . ."

"About the new Harrowing. Is there a smudge on my cheek?"

Hatcher looks. "Yes."

"Gray?"

"Gray." Hatcher draws out his handkerchief and lifts his hand. "Should I . . . ?"

"No." Carl is emphatic. "Don't you know what that is?"

Hatcher's hand recoils. Of course.

"I have to stop with the salt," Carl says. "It's cursed. Of course it's cursed. Pretty soon I won't have enough brain left to lie."

"You didn't actually make up the new Harrowing," Hatcher says.

"No. I didn't make it up."

"So was your source . . ."

"He could have lied to me. Or he could have lied to himself. Or he could have . . ."

"I get it," Hatcher waves his hand to stop Carl and sits back in his chair. Of course it could all be a lie. He knows this. He always knows this. And yet Hatcher had some sort of intuition about the neo-Harrowing story. And still does. The news nose knows. The freshman J-Schoolers in a couple of adjoining rooms in Elder Hall at Northwestern would chant that out the windows at the passing coeds. Hatcher's free mind is drifting now, he realizes. It's also free to nurture hope and free to despair in the hope. But he's always felt he has the nose. And it knows.

Carl says, "Hell, the *first* Harrowing might be a lie. You'd be surprised who's still here. Though the biggest guys are mostly out of sight. They're in their own condo somewhere, jammed in bunks with the biggest guys from all the other religions."

Hatcher nods. "I've heard about that too. I figure it's because all the rest of the denizens suffer more if they think somehow they got it wrong. If they suspect nobody got it right, there could be some sort of comfort in that."

"Is that what you suspect?" Carl says. "That everybody is here?"

"I don't know. Sometimes. Suspect, perhaps. But nobody can say if they're *all* here. And if all the big guys are indeed in Hell, it doesn't mean some little guys didn't get spared."

The two fall silent a moment. Hatcher looks around the Automat. "Do you know these people?"

Carl says, "Today it's the writers' workshop. They've all got books. None of them made it into the Big One. Over there, the central table, it's Tobit and Baruch and Ben Sira. They got into the Catholic Bible, but needless to say that's cold comfort for them, like being with a university press when they think they deserve Knopf. These three don't read each other's work anymore. They just kvetch. If you stand up and look to the far corner, you'll see somebody these three should have with them, to be fair, since the Catholics published her too. But not only is she a woman, she has a constant companion."

Hatcher rises and looks across the room. He sees a table with a woman in a gray tunic and headscarf reading from a scroll to a black-haired, bearded, severed head sitting in the center of the table. The eyes of the man are widening and narrowing and widening again in disgust at the woman's reading and he interrupts, saying something that she listens to without reaction, and when he stops, she starts reading again.

"That's Judith," Carl says. "And that's the Babylonian general Holofernes, who she seduced and beheaded. I don't think he keeps his comments constructive."

While he's standing, Hatcher looks more closely at the other tables. Many of them have scrolls being read. "You've got quite a few Gnostics," Carl says. "They churned the books out, I tell you. And there's some guys from Old Testament times who got screwed by the weather or earthquakes or whatever. The Book of Amittai, for instance. The Book of Ishmerai. Lost to the elements. And there are others. They never had a chance. Don't get those guys started or you'll be getting the begats and the goat-slaughter procedures all day and night, and they're all desperate to hear they're as good as the other guys."

Hatcher moves his gaze to a nearby table. Three men and a woman. One of the men is reading from a codex and he's lanky and intense and his long hair falls over his face.

Carl sees where Hatcher is looking. "They didn't make it into the New Testament. The Gospel of Rhoda. Her last scroll was dropped down a well by Paul himself, who never did trust women. The Gospel of Festus got eaten by a camel. The letters of Silas. Don't get him going on the first century post office. And the guy reading. That's Judas Iscariot."

Hatcher looks at Carl.

Carl says, "You were still alive when his lost codex came to light, weren't you?"

"Yes," Hatcher says. "Sadly. It's embarrassing to get scooped by the National Geographic Society. You weren't alive then."

"No."

"You know a lot about all this, Carl."

Carl shrugs and turns his face to the window. "I may be a liar, but I'm a good reporter."

Outside the window, Jezebel's eight hundred and fifty slaughtered priests of Baal are crowding past, all their wounds still open and running. Unseen to Carl and Hatcher, Elijah is being borne along, squeezed tightly in their midst, cloaked in their blood.

"I can see that you are," Hatcher says.

Carl lifts his face and then nods toward Judas. "He's my source on the Harrowing."

"Judas?"

"Yes."

Hatcher takes this in. "Would you mind if I talk to him directly?"

Carl laughs softly and cocks his head at Hatcher. "You're standing on journalistic protocol down here? Asking me?"

Hatcher sees how this would seem odd. He's not sure he would have asked his reporter for permission only a short time ago.

"Of course," Carl says. "Go ahead."

"Thanks," Hatcher says, and he moves off toward the New Testament table.

As he approaches, Judas has stopped reading, and Rhoda is offering a critique. "Everyone assumes it's Gnostics because you did it in the third person. You need to rewrite it in the first person."

"Good suggestion," Festus says, giving Rhoda a little wink. "Make them wonder. We heard he hanged himself right away. But he took time to write this."

"Not to mention the irony," Silas says, also winking at Rhoda.

"What irony?" Festus says with a little more heat than one might reasonably expect. "That's all you ever say. What's irony got to do with it?"

Hatcher is beside the table now and the two men abruptly stop their bickering. All four look up at the newcomer in the suit.

"I'm sorry to interrupt. I'm Hatcher McCord."

"I watch you all the time," Rhoda purrs.

Festus and Silas both scowl. Judas glances over to Carl and then back to Hatcher. He rises. "I'll talk to him," Judas says to the others, and then to Hatcher, "Got nickels?"

Hatcher feels in his pockets. "Yes."

"Come on," Judas says, and he leads them to the back wall. He peers through the window of a food compartment and then another and another, moving along the row. "Not much choice today," he says. "But there never is." He stops and turns to Hatcher.

"Give me thirty nickels and I'll tell you anything you want to know," Judas says.

Hatcher is thrown by this for a moment.

"Just kidding," Judas says. "I need three. For spinach. We can get two forks."

Hatcher gives Judas three nickels, and the ex-apostle feeds them into a slot by one of the dispensing doors. "I'm good about sharing," he says.

They bear their creamed spinach and forks out among the crowded tables, and ahead, a couple of Old Testament guys at a table for two suddenly burst into flames and leap up and run together out the front door. Judas nods to the newly vacated table. "Someone is looking out for us," he says.

They sit.

Judas sticks one of the forks in Hatcher's side of the white china Horn & Hardart bowl and pushes it slightly toward him. The dark green of the spinach can be seen in striations beneath the cream, but the cream itself is faintly wriggling. Judas takes a bite and grimaces. "Jesus Christ, this tastes bad," he says.

He and Hatcher look at each other, stopped by the expletive. Judas laughs loudly. "The Master doesn't mind. He likes a good irony."

"He's coming back here?" Hatcher says.

"For me. It's the deal."

"When did he tell you that?"

"His last night. When he asked me to do this thing for him. Somebody had to do this thing so all the rest of you would come to realize who he was. But see, then he couldn't take me out of Hell the first time round. I just barely got here, and for him to end up being what he had to be, I had to take the heat for a long while. He was crucified for your sins, but I was vilified for your sins. You see what they write about me?" Judas rolls his head. "Oy," he says. Then he motions at the spinach. "Eat up."

"No thanks."

"I don't blame you. It's nothing but vegetables, world without end."

Hatcher nods toward the change booth. "The sign says meat tomorrow."

"That sign's always there and it never happens. Just about everyone in this room thinks they're getting out of here on the next go-round. Most of them are convinced it's about sacrifice. They didn't kill enough goats or bullocks, so they need the animals. They need to do their ritual thing to be worthy. The management keeps promising, but come on. It's not going to happen. Me, however. The Man and I had an arrangement. He needed me to do what I did. I knew His powers. You think I'd send myself to a place like this for thirty pieces of silver? You think anybody's that stupid? He was the Man. I didn't have the preaching skills or the church-building skills, but I had the skill to do what needed to be done, even if it was dirty work."

And what's going on in Hatcher's nose? The smell of animate creamed spinach, certainly. And perhaps that is affecting the workings of his deeply intuitive, Northwestern-J-School-trained, field-tested, Emmy-Award-winning appendage, but hearing Judas Iscariot talk of his expectations, hearing his thoroughly adapted voice, Hatcher isn't sniffing the story so strongly now. Not to mention the irony. Hatcher tries to reason with his nose. Maybe it's the irony that's causing the doubt. Judas Iscariot keeping his faith in Hell. Shouldn't that actually give him credibility? And he's adjusted over the years, as everyone is torturously required to do. Hatcher's own Anne rarely sounds the way she must have sounded in the sixteenth century. They all are compelled to watch television, after all. If Judas had the skills he claims were necessary to do what he had to do in his mortal life, then those same skills would turn him into the Judas Iscariot sitting across from Hatcher right now, keeping his faith, talking wise-ass. And gobbling down the rancid creamed spinach.

"You sure you don't want yours?" Judas asks as he finishes exactly half.

"I'm sure."

Judas compulsively eats on, though every bite is clearly intensely unpleasant to him. Finally he presses his wrist against his mouth and jumps up and runs out the front door. Hatcher sits and waits and lets the possibilities of this story renew themselves. He looks around at all the others here. Also keeping the faith in their own ways, apparently.

Judas returns and sits. He says, "It's not that which goeth into the mouth defileth a man but that which cometh out."

He waits a beat, as if he expects Hatcher to react. Hatcher doesn't.

"Just kidding," Judas says. "Man, if I'm to be judged by what just came out of my mouth, forget about it."

"How do all these others expect to make their sacrifice? Do they think they'll get a shot at the animals before the kitchen deals with them?"

"They're not thinking clearly, most of them," Judas says. "A few think putting their nickels in and pulling out a great piece of roast lamb and then throwing it away would do the trick, under the circumstances."

"And do you think he's coming back only for you?"

Judas shrugs. "Who knows? We can only account for ourselves in the end, right?"

There's one more bite of creamed spinach in the china bowl. Judas has been poking at it with his fork. Now he scoops it up and puts it in his mouth and squeezes his eyes shut at its taste. He swallows hard. "Why'd I do that?" he says.

"You thought someone knew and expected it," Hatcher says.

"Someone always knows," Judas says.

Hatcher does not reply.

Judas leans intently forward. "That's why I'm going to get out. What I did at Gethsemane. He knows why."

"When will he come for you?"

"Soon."

"How do you know?"

"There are signs."

"Like what?"

"I came to learn them secretly," Judas says. "I'm not at liberty to say. But they're happening. Patterns of the pain. Certain arrivals to this place. Cadging nickels, how that goes. Things to come. A screaming in the night sky. You have to understand, man. There's a bunch of holy, picked-out-by-God people still here. Published. And the main players in the books too. All big time. The biggest. Still here. He's coming for *them*, right?"

"I thought he got them before."

"So it was said."

"He didn't?"

Judas shrugs.

Hatcher presses him. "He didn't take them out of Hell?"

"Nobody down here knows for sure. I can tell you there's a bunch of shit-if-I'm-here-and-he's-here-who-isn't going on. But I've got the faith, man. I've got it."

"So you figure there'll be quite a few going out next time?"

"Like you said, you'd think the big boys would be gone by now. But they're not. The direct-from-the-source guys. The holy destroyers of unbelieving nations. The scourge of the infidels and the heretics. And I'm talking the scourgers from *both* sides, from *all* sides. You'd figure somebody got it right. Not a chance. But my guy was full of surprises, don't forget. He could pick any tax clerk or hothead with fishing tackle off the street. Just get your own shit together is my advice."

Judas suddenly stiffens and looks down at his stomach. It swells rapidly and presses tight against his tunic and a wriggling begins there, as if the things in the cream of the spinach have suddenly grown up and are ready to raise a ruckus. "Oh fuck," he says. "I shouldn't have been saying all this."

Judas jumps up and turns and careens around and past the tables and through the front door.

Hatcher sits and tries to be still and think on all this, and he begins to feel a darkness in his head and a faint weakness in his limbs. But these are just his own private feelings going on, he realizes. His body is simply reflecting on these matters as it waits for what he wants it to do next. Hatcher rises and moves to the front of the Automat. Carl is gone. Someone somewhere in the room shouts, "Not convincing? Convince this, shmecklesucker!" Hatcher steps into the street and turns back the way he came.

Behind him, Judas has not burst asunder with his bowels gushing out, which has happened to him before, the most recent time after he spoke to Carl Crispin of many of these very same things. This time, as he rushed headlong into the street, his stomach stopped wriggling and shrank back and he staggered around the corner and sat down on the sidewalk, his back to the metal wall of the diner, and he pulled his knees up under his chin, and now within him, it is the night on Mount Zion, outside the walls of the Old City of Jerusalem: *The others have gone ahead to the upper room of this house and the Master has let them go up first and I wait upon him and he touches my arm and says "Come with me" and I do and we go around to the side of the house in the dark and the air smells of a wood fire and the Master smells of spikenard and I know Mary the Drastically Redeemed has been at him already and I'm thinking he's too easily pampered, he's getting too soft, there's hard work to be done, man's work, and I know he knows what I'm thinking, so I say "I'm sorry, Master" and he says "It's almost over" and it's me now who knows what he's thinking and I say "So we're not going to fight it out" and he says "You know the answer to that" and I do and he says "The stones of this house took long rubbing one against the other before they fit together" and I say "You mean the boys upstairs" and he says "The boys upstairs" and I say "Not enough rubbing" and he says "That would take till I'm gone and come back and gone and come back again" and he laughs and I laugh and I know what's next and he says "I will ask you to do a thing now that will make you wish you'd never been born" and I say "If it's what you need" and he puts his hand on my shoulder and even in the dark I can see the tears in the Master's eyes.*

∝

Up the street, Hatcher is moving quickly. Soon he draws near to Administration Central. The Duesenberg is still sitting at the curb, and though he waited for Hatcher to reappear, since his orders were simply to chauffeur him, Porphyrius is not happy to see the TV minion's approach. He's starting to feel a little hot under the collar already.

Hatcher nods through the window at Porphyrius in his long-practiced, warm, famous-person-encountering-service-person manner and moves to the back door. He pauses and checks the sky. The sun is stalled high up in what Hatcher now sees as a powder-blue sky. He's still not certain about a new Harrowing, but Judas's words are stuck in his head. Get your own shit together. Hatcher climbs into the backseat of the Duesenberg and opens the map, ignoring Porphyrius's glare in the rearview mirror. He finds the location of his nearest wife and gives his driver directions. They creep off into the crowded street.

And though Hatcher feels that this train of thought is wildly dissociated from what he has just experienced at the Automat—overlooking, as he does, the two underlying associative motifs of a striving for Heaven and books—his deep inner voice remembers: *a magic bus, a book with large colored pictures about a bus full of travelers that flies away and I couldn't have been more than three or four years old, and I was sitting in a window seat in my room with bright sun coming in and there was a page where a little boy discovers a golden button on the dashboard of a bus and he says to the driver, Push the button, please, sir, push the button, and the driver does, and the bus lifts off the street to the delight of all the passengers inside and, outside, to the surprise of a little girl and a puppy and a passing bird. And the rest of the book has vanished from within me, except for one two-page spread of artwork, and this has returned in dreams and in the moments drifting toward dreams, perhaps two dozen times over the many years since, and the image is this: the boy is looking out the window of the bus—though his looking out was established on an earlier page, for all these years I've simply known that the boy has pressed himself hard against the window and the other people have vanished for him— and on these two pages is just what he sees, from a great height: a rolling countryside with trees and a farmhouse and barns and a cornfield and, far ahead, a little village with a church steeple and a school and a neighborhood of white houses and the sun high in the sky and, most importantly, there is a truck, a bright blue panel truck with big round fenders and it is on the road through the countryside and it is heading for the little village and on the side of the truck is the word **BREAD** and when I was a child I imagined that it was my father driving that truck, it was my father, the friendly Bread Delivery Man who smiles all the time and whose breath smells of fresh bread, and later, when I dreamed of this scene, the father part had vanished, the driver simply drove anonymously, invisibly, and it was just the bread truck, but it was still in the*

*perfect countryside, and I knew it was heading toward the place where I wanted
to be.*

∝

Mary Ellen McCord—formerly Mary Ellen Gibson but Mary Ellen
McCord even after her divorce from Hatcher as he was being promoted
from anchorman of the evening news in St. Louis, Missouri, to network correspondent in Washington, D.C., and Mary Ellen McCord
even to the day of her not-really-intentional-but-now-that-it-seems-
to-be-happening-oh-what-the-fuck death by drowning off the Cayman
Islands on a Golden Years Singles Cruise with two other unmarried sixty-
something women friends—is being borne along as one of the multitude
thronging Peachtree Street Road Circle. She is trying to get back to her
apartment in the Career Mother neighborhood of the Great Metropolis
in Hell now that she has been reconstituted after enduring the noontime
sulfurous rain that she seems always to get caught in because she seems
almost always to be in the street crowd for reasons she can't even begin
to figure out. But this time she actually recognizes the intersection with
Peachtree Circle Court Loop and she actually fights her way to the edge
of the crowd and actually breaks free to move abruptly into the mouth
of the street where she lives just in time to be knocked off her feet and
run over by a turning 1932 Duesenberg being driven by the greatest
charioteer of the Eastern Roman Empire and bearing her ex-husband.

∝

Hatcher sits on the running board of the Duesenberg, with Mary Ellen's
twisted, broken body a few feet away, and he waits for her to reconstitute. If he had a pack of cigarettes, he'd smoke one now. This is taking
an unusual length of time, with her not showing any signs whatsoever of
snapping back. After the initial recognition of who she is, he hasn't quite
looked at her. Finally it all feels terribly familiar: he hurts her and then

doesn't really look at what's happened; he just waits for things to go back to normal.

He makes himself see her. Not her crumpled, jackknifed body, but her face. He angles his head to the left, sharply, and still more, until his face and hers are aligned across this space between them, eye to eye, nose to nose, mouth to mouth. She looks young. As she was when he was courting her at Northwestern. Suddenly her eyes open. But it's not clear to Hatcher that she is seeing anything. A moment later her eyes close and they begin to move beneath her lids, as if she is dreaming.

And within Hatcher: *She and I stand on the tiny beach at the curve of Sheridan Road near Fisk Hall, the lake the color of car exhaust, the air stinking from the alewives that mysteriously die in large numbers every spring and wash up along the shore, and we're shoulder to shoulder, she and I, but not holding hands, and we're expecting something from each other in light of our imminent graduation, and in light of all the sweet times sneaking her up to the third floor of my rooming house in the still prudish early sixties and clinging to each other very quietly in my narrow bed with the tops of the red maples outside, and I say, "Your folks will be down?" and she says, "You asked that this morning," and I say, "I'm not thinking clearly," and she says, "I'm not either," and I say, "We need to think clearly," and she says, "We need not to think," and I accept this and I say, "Since we're not thinking, let's get married," and she laughs, low, and I let the back of my hand touch the back of hers and her hand is warm and she turns it and I turn mine and we hold hands and the gesture is like a scarlet leaf on the maple outside my window in October and it's the first one to fall and you'd think that would be the most beautiful secret moment of all for the tree—its quaking with red leaves like it's on fire and this first leaf letting go and floating away, free— but it really means that winter is coming in and all the beautiful things will fall away and die and the tree will soon be stark and cold.*

And behind Mary Ellen's closed and dream-restless eyes: *Twilight is coming on and he and I are standing on the little beach near the J-School build- ing and we've never said a word about it but the time is now nearly upon us when we either go on together or we don't, and the lake is dark, nearly the color of his eyes and as deep, and he smells of the drug store aftershave he adores—bay rum, the clove smell of an old man—and I know he will someday get a thing like that right without my having to suggest it, and he says, "Your parents will be down?" and I say, "You keep coming back to that. What's really on your mind?" and I turn my face to him and he turns his face to me and he takes my hand and we both look out to the water and he says, "It's not a matter of my mind," and I say, "We need to think clearly," and he says "No we don't," and this makes me happy and then he says, "I want to marry you," and I lift his hand and I kiss it and it smells of rubber cement from him cutting and pasting his final story for the newspaper, and if I was thinking clearly I'd know this is as good as it's going to get and I should just kiss that hand one more time and let it go and walk on down the beach and out into the lake and just keep walking till I vanish.*

She opens her eyes. She finds her body restored and the promise of more pain perched on the running board of an old automobile. She sits up.

Hatcher rises. Mary Ellen has reconstituted, but her face has turned old, as old as she was when she finally let it all go in the Caribbean Sea. Hatcher makes a vague gesture to help Mary Ellen to her feet, but she waves it off. She stands.

"I'm sorry," he says.

"For what?" she says.

"Running you over."

"Which time?" she says.

Hatcher shrugs. Not from indifference, but she can't see that, of course.

"Right," she says.

"Please," he says. "Any time. All the times. That's why I'm here."

"We're in Hell, my darling," she says. "It's a little late for anything like that."

"Can't we talk a bit?" Hatcher says.

Now Mary Ellen shrugs, wishing to be indifferent. That she isn't, she takes simply to be fresh torture in the afterlife she's living. She turns and walks off along her street. Hatcher follows.

The street narrows abruptly into an alleyway of tenements not unlike his own. The outside corridors stacked at the back of the buildings are crowded with women wandering singly up and down or coming together into small groups and then breaking apart, filling the air with cries of "After all I did for them!" and "I'm a person too!" and "This isn't Hell, I know from Hell already!" But as Hatcher moves along behind Mary Ellen, a murmur starts up, and by the time she begins to ascend one of the circular iron staircases with Hatcher following, all the women above are nudging each other and leaning out over the railings and pointing at him. Now they are crying "He's on TV!" and "What's a man doing here?" and "Who's that motherfucker?"

When Mary Ellen reaches her corridor, she steps out of the staircase but instantly pauses and waits for Hatcher to emerge. She steels herself and offers her arm for him to take. "Stay close," she says. "They'll tear you to pieces. They kept a lot inside in that other life."

Hatcher looks at the gauntlet of faces before him, some once beautiful and some not but all of them leveled now by jowl and wrinkle and blotch and pallor and by the utter ingratitude of men who moved on and children who moved on. Mary Ellen guides Hatcher forward and he takes the pinches and the spit and the hissed words with "Sorry" and "I'm sorry" and "I'm very sorry" until she pulls him in at a doorway and they enter a cramped little room with its walls covered by empty snapshot picture frames. They sit down shoulder to shoulder on a tattered couch that smells, to Hatcher, like dead fish and has always smelled, to Mary Ellen, like bay rum.

"You're chock-full of apologies down here, aren't you," Mary Ellen says.

"Lately," Hatcher says. She's right and this surprises him, but he lets it pass.

"Is that why you've come to me?"

"Sort of."

"Of course. It's a clever torture, isn't it?"

"I don't intend to . . ."

"In all your self-important arrogance, that's one of the weirdest examples, right there. What do your intentions have to do with it? You think I'd assume *you're* the one devising the tortures in Hell?"

"This isn't going well," Hatcher says, reflexively trying one of his little rhetorical tricks from their life together long ago. Play against her anger with understatement.

Mary Ellen knows the trick and simply snorts wearily at it.

They sit silently for a moment. She can't let it alone. But she just feels sad now. "Not well," she says, low. "It's Hell, my darling." She stops. Twice she's called him "darling." With irony, certainly. But also without irony. This makes her even sadder. Which is part of the torture, of course. The "darling" thing was her own similar rhetorical trick from that life together. And it tortured her in much the same way even then.

"I never was religious," she says.

"No."

"This doesn't feel religious, exactly, all this."

"No."

"While I was drowning," she says, "just before the last darkness, I felt peaceful. I wasn't suicidal, really, but I was looking forward to an end to all the crap. I didn't expect to end up *anywhere*."

Hatcher is about to reply, "Especially not sitting on this couch with me," but he catches himself and does not say anything.

"You're thinking it's about you again," she says.

If it's not Satan inside your head, it's your ex-wife. He tries to mitigate his offense with her. "The crap part," he says, and he hears how sorrowful he sounds and he knows Mary Ellen hears it too and she puffs and turns her face away from him.

"Fuck you," she says, very low, and because she has paused briefly before saying it and because he can feel her brace herself ever so slightly, he knows who she's actually talking to.

He reaches out and finds her hand resting on her thigh and he holds it, firmly. He wants to say, "He can't hear you." But he's still not certain everyone has privacy of mind and there's so much yet for him to do. He does say, "Don't let it happen."

He can feel her hand growing quickly warm and he squeezes it tighter. He'll go up in flames with her if need be. "Stop," he says.

She looks at him, her eyes restless again, searching his face, and he looks at her steadily, inviting her to read his mind.

Her hand is intensely hot, her whole body radiates the heat, but there are no flames yet. Her face streams perspiration. But no flames. He holds her hand and her eyes close and still there are no flames. They sit like this for a long while, and at last the heat abates and she opens her eyes.

He lets go of her hand.

"There," he says.

"What do you mean?" she says.

"You didn't let it happen," he says.

"What are you talking about?"

"What you just went through. It wasn't so bad this time."

Mary Ellen's mouth sags open in wonder. "Oh my darling, you are such a man. Such a stupid man. That was one of the worst."

Hatcher doesn't understand.

Mary Ellen says, "Whenever he doesn't like what I think or say, he gives me a hot flash. The mother of all hot flashes."

Hatcher should know by now that intense suffering is a personal thing, even in Hell. Especially in Hell. But his face is still a little uncomprehending.

Mary Ellen says, "The flames are inside."

Still he's lagging behind.

And so she says, "Remember when I was pregnant with Angie . . ."

And she stops.

It has not yet arisen that Hatcher McCord in his mortal life had two daughters, Angela Marie—Angie—and earlier, in his and Mary Ellen's brief but intense Age of Aquarius phase, Summer Meadow. His children have not been in his mind because he has not wanted Satan to get even a faint whiff of them and because—especially with significant time clearly having passed, given the arrivals of Bush and Clinton and others—he could not let himself even begin to wonder if the girls have arrived here themselves. Hell is indifferent to torture based on concern for the welfare of others, so this effectively kept them out of his head altogether when he thought his head belonged to the Old Man. Hatcher's children were living adults when he died. But he has heard rumors that beyond the mountains on the horizon, cut off forever from the denizens of the Great Metropolis, there is even a Great Amusement Park where all the souls that died in the bodies of children clog the roller coasters and theme rides. So what are the chances for Angie and Summer? He can't bear to consider this possibility. They are not children anymore. He has let them go. His old method returns: he doesn't look; he waits for that matter of things in his head to go back to normal. Which it quickly does.

Mary Ellen too has been fighting off thoughts of her daughters, though she hasn't yet quite gotten around to the impression that everyone is in Hell. The pain of the empty picture frames is sufficient unto the day. She cut herself off in invoking her second pregnancy because the man she called "darling" then with no irony whatsoever sits beside her in Hell on a couch that stinks of the aftershave of his youth and because she is looking even more drawn and haggard and wattled and creased for him than she did for herself on that last morning in the bathroom mirror in her cabin on the cruise ship.

The silence of the unfinished sentence about her pregnancy with Angie yammers away in each of them, and to stop it, Mary Ellen says, "You wouldn't understand."

Hatcher does not dispute this, even to say he wants to understand, because he knows she will not understand. And so they sit for a long while saying nothing, not looking at each other. And that was the wrong thing to do as well, it seems to him, for she finally breaks the silence by saying, "You know, I don't even think it's about the public adulation with you. You would be perfectly happy if you were the only person in the world."

Hatcher realizes this is the moment to declare his past feelings for Mary Ellen, and not just because the declaration would surprise the shit out of her and thus undercut her anger, another of his recognized rhetorical tricks. He would actually like to recover that moment by recalling it. He would like to start fixing whatever was so broken in him before. He would like to have a shot at getting out of Hell. So he turns his face to her profile and says, "You may not remember this, you may not believe it now, but I did . . ."

He cannot fill in the appropriate word. But like a fatally wounded animal who lies on the ground still moving its legs, trying to run, he starts again, "Really, Mary Ellen, I did . . ."

She turns to look at him now. Surprisingly, her face has not gone hard at his hesitation. She might be expected easily to fill in the missing word in her own head, the one she would assume Hatcher cannot bring himself to say because he's trying another of his old tricks and is so miserably and arrogantly insincere that he can't even make himself shape the sound in his mouth. But the truth is, she doesn't know what the word is he's looking for. She realizes she should know, but she doesn't. She realizes this is a crucial word, so crucial that she might even find herself inclined to try to give the man she once married a little help, if it's such a crucial fucking word, but she can't think what it is.

Meanwhile, Hatcher says, "Mary Ellen, I . . ." And here he tries just to run directly up on it. Push that sucker out. He can't. In spite of his mind being his own private thing even in Hell, it still is Hell he's in. There are limits. And in Hell the four-letter word he's looking for is not spoken, is not thought. Mary Ellen, I did fuck you. Not a problem. Mary Ellen, I did Roto-Rooter your bodacious cunt. Go for it. But not the thing Hatcher wants to say. It is dangerous even for it to be written here. Let's call it the 'L-word'. And when the L-word is truly called for, not even lesser, permitted words of affection can come to mind.

So Hatcher and Mary Ellen sit shoulder to shoulder, eye to eye, and they each easily recognize the other and they each wonder *Who is this stranger before me?* And then he thinks *What was I trying to say?* and she thinks *What was it I was trying to think of?* And then Hatcher says, "I have to go," and he understands this is so only as he says it. And at that moment their bodies tremble and the couch trembles and the room trembles and the building trembles and the whole of the Great Metropolis trembles and all of Hell trembles as from the horizon comes the grand solar boom of sunset, and the room goes black.

∝

On the slow trip back to Hatcher's apartment, the rear seat of the Duesenberg is dark and the car shudders from the jostling of the night crowd. He struggles to learn something about himself from his visit to Mary Ellen. What. He was arrogant. He was arrogant and self-absorbed. So what was the deal with her marrying him? He must have changed along the way. Arrogant and self-absorbed and stupid. Stupid like a man. But taking these things out of their conversation doesn't do jack shit for him. These are just abstractions. He lived his life with her—made his mistakes—in a body, in the moment, and he doesn't know which moments were the telling ones, and there were so many of them that he can't even recall, and they are all gone, anyway, and there are no more to be had with her. And no one is listening. He would be happy if he was alone in the world, she says. The street is stuffed with bodies, the windows all around him are filled with an ever-changing mosaic of faces. He doesn't see them. He closes his eyes. Half a dozen moon-white geisha faces smear past and are gone, and a Chattanooga Baptist Youth bowling team, and a cornrowed Snoop Dogg trying to mark the Dizzle's rear whizzle but howling from the sizzle of his pizzle. Fo shizzle.

At last Hatcher steps from the car, his camcorder in hand. He hurries into the dark of his alley and along beneath the tenements and he climbs the circular staircase and emerges into his corridor. He certainly does not want to be the only person in the world tonight. He certainly longs to absorb himself in Anne. He will try not to be stupid with her. He even has Henry's address to offer. Can that possibly be self-absorbed? He passes the Hoppers' apartment, and their door is closed. He's happy about that. But that doesn't mean it's all about him or that he wants the doors to be closed on everyone so he can be alone. He puts his hand to his own door and turns the knob.

"Darling, I'm home," he cries even before the door is fully open. And now it is.

Anne sits, in jeans and halter top, at one side of the kitchen table. Lulu, in nothing but her skin and furry wings, sits at the other. Hatcher thinks there might be something quite appealing about this only-person-in-the-world stuff after all.

He's ready to back out of the door, but he understands that's not possible now. He pretty much knows what's on Lulu's mind, so he focuses on Anne to try to read what has transpired and what her attitude is about it.

All he would have to fear from Anne is that she thinks he is anything but forced to go with Lulu. But Anne has never shown a trace of jealousy. It has always been him, and his jealousy has always been of that strange retrospective variety.

He can't read her eyes. But she has her hand upon her throat, thumb to one side, her fingers to the other side, and she's stroking herself there, out and back, out and back, like a man thoughtfully stroking his beard. She probably has never seen a succubus. May not have known they exist.

And in spite of the strange circumstances before him, his free and private mind takes this moment to reflect: *my retrospective jealousy, isn't that somehow a desire to be the only person in the world, with the only exception being the woman by whom my cosmic exclusivity is measured?*

Anne says, "This lady claims she has an appointment with you."

Lulu giggles her deep-throat giggle. "Oh you dear. Calling me a lady. She's so very sweet, Hatcher."

He can only nod.

Lulu says, "And aren't I très discreet? 'Appointment,' my titties."

Anne turns to the faux-Frenchified succubus and says, "I'm not stupid, dear."

Lulu does not giggle at this. She reaches across the table and takes Anne's hand, and Hatcher fears what Lulu might do. The two women look at each other steadily, and Lulu says, "I had an 'appointment' with your King Henry, once upon a time."

"Did he keep it?"

"They all must, you know."

"You're lucky he didn't marry you."

Again Lulu doesn't giggle. To distract the succubus from doing harm to Anne because of her snarkiness and, indeed, to satisfy his own newsman's curiosity, Hatcher puts on the playful voice of their first meeting and asks, "Who else have you done we'd be surprised to know about, you naughty Lulu you?"

"As rotten a fuck as Henry?" she says, still looking at Anne.

"Yes," Hatcher says, calling on all his interview savvy to shift to the subject's preferred tone. "You poor Lulu you."

"Poor Lulu," she says.

"What she has to go through for her work," Hatcher says.

Lulu turns her face to him and she nods again and sighs a loud, booming sigh. She lets go of Anne's hand. She says, "For about a hundred years I was the official harvester of your presidents. We like to use the seed of the big boys all around the world to make our little domestic demons. So you name the guy, from McKinley on through, and I did him, and it all went the way it should go, right through Bush the First. But after that, things started to get freaky."

"Freaky for *you*?" Hatcher says, his incredulity involuntary and dangerous. But he gets away with it.

Lulu nods, pouting. "I have feelings too, mon cheri. With the live ones we're supposed to come in the middle of the night and dope-whisper any companions into a temporary coma and do the boy while he's still snoozing. With your President Bill Clinton, his wife's alone in the master bed, and by the time I can get myself oriented, I'm face to face with a very wide-awake Mr. President."

Lulu pauses for effect.

Hatcher prompts her. "Freaky, Lulu?"

"He took one look at me and dropped his pajama bottoms."

Somehow this doesn't surprise Hatcher, and that must show on his face.

"Only the dead and damned are supposed to go for it, my dear. And then, the next time, I went off to do Al Gore."

"Wait. Al Gore wasn't elected."

"Hello. Poor Lulu had to figure out the fucking electoral college. And after I did, I had to go do a guy whose seed they took one look at and tossed. At that point, I'd had enough."

Lulu digs a knuckle into the corner of a dry eye. A little trick she picked up from her boss. "Boohoo," she says. And then abruptly she flares the hand at her eye and smiles brightly and says, "I am so glad you are dead and damned, Hatcher McCord. You will help make up for the shit work."

And now, without Hatcher even registering her rise and approach, Lulu is in his face, and she gently takes the camcorder from him, and then there is a great flurry of her hands and in a seeming instant Hatcher

McCord is standing naked at his front door, his clothes flung about the room, his camcorder, though, perched safely on the kitchen table, his blue minion tie folded neatly beside it, and beside the tie is Anne, her eyes wide and her mouth gaping.

And in the next instant his naked body is pressed against Lulu's naked body, her two powerful arms clamping him there, and they are out the door and leaping into the air and her great bat wings open wide and beat fiercely and Lulu and Hatcher shoot straight up into the dark and he barely has a chance to turn his head and look behind him as the Great Metropolis spreads open beneath him like the time-lapse blooming of a vast black flower, and Lulu veers, and in the moment that they hurtle over the center of the city, Hatcher at last finds brief voice for all that is happening to him. He screams.

And far below, curled up in the gutter at the side of the Automat on the corner of Peachtree Way and Lucky Street, a sleeping figure snaps awake. Judas Iscariot turns his face upward. He has heard a screaming in the night sky, as it was prophesied, and his faith is renewed.

∝

The city passes away, and below Hatcher there is darkness, and against him there is the massive febrile thumping of a heart—Lulu in excitation, from flight, from him, from Mama waiting—and inside him his own heart beats as feverishly fast as Lulu's, from all that is about to happen, and from Lulu's heart, its ravenousness clear to him.

After a time, he feels them descending, though everything is still black, and then Lulu banks and turns as if deliberately to show him this: red klieg lights scanning the sky from the roof of an eighty-foot Buccaneer Buena Vista double-wide lit bright white from within. He can see in the spill of the light that the place sits in the crotch of two sharp slopes. He is in the mountains again.

Lulu wheels around and then plummets and lands running, and she and Hatcher are abruptly at the front door of the double-wide. She knocks the match-in-the-gas-tank-boom-boom knock. "Tootle ootle, Mama," Lulu cries, and she opens the door.

Inside the trailer, Hatcher is briefly blinded by the light—a thousand naked filaments in a thousand lightbulbs in glass display cases lining the one large room of the double-wide's interior. The light refracts and flares from thousands of snow globes densely packing the cases. And taking up the far twenty feet of the eighty-footer and stretching as wide as the walls is Mama Lilith's bed with Lilith herself sitting with legs spread-eagled, wings unfurled, toes wiggling, and her succubus privates open and steaming like a vaporizer. She is just about to pop into her mouth— with little finger extended—a Toblerone from a box beside her. At the sight of her daughter and the naked Hatcher McCord, Lilith's hand stops and falls, and with slow and meticulous care, she places the chocolate back in the box. Hatcher pulses with foreboding from this gesture.

"Here he is," Lulu says, lifting Hatcher and turning him around and setting him before her for Lilith's frontal inspection.

"There he is," Lilith says even as she levitates from the bed, closing her legs, lifting her wings, and rotating her body forward. She floats toward him, quite slowly really, with the same contemplative air she had putting away the chocolate, and that continues, rightly, to scare the shit out of Hatcher.

Lilith drifts past the display cases. Hatcher has registered the snow globe collection only generically. He has never been a collector of things, and these are snow globes, after all, and he has been understandably riveted by other features of the room. So he has not seen that each snow globe contains an image of a man, the form varying greatly, with Dwight Eisenhower, for instance, being represented in one of these cases by the two-and-a-half inch white plastic figure from the set of Marx Toys Presidents of the United States that Hatcher adored as a boy. The white shakable substance lying at the bottom of each globe, however, is not the powder of fake snow but a dehydrated rendering of something quite personal to the man represented. Lilith, on the other hand, being a collector, is keenly aware of each of these carefully accumulated, classifiable artifacts of her life, and she is twittering with delight at them as she approaches this new man.

Lilith in features and stature is clone-similar to her daughters. But as she draws near to Hatcher, the millennia are obvious upon her. Her all-over bleach job looks more white than blond and her flesh is pasty and liver-spotted. Though she has had a great deal of work done: her face is mostly unlined but forever fixed in a wide-eyed, leering rictus of lust.

"Now, Mama, he's mine," Lulu says, as Lilith arrives before Hatcher and settles onto her feet. Hatcher is filled with the smell of Lilith's perfume: rose and jasmine, both synthetic, and sulfur and semen, both organic.

She looks past him now to her daughter. If her face could physically register an emotion other than lust, it would be doing it now. "My dear," Lilith says, "you must learn to share."

"I am sharing," Lulu says. "I'm here, aren't I? You get to watch."

"Oh, darling daughter, haven't I always been a good mother? How many three-ways have we had, my sweet? Men of my own acquisition, yes?"

"Mama, you got off on that big time,"

"You see what children do?" Lilith says, looking Hatcher in the eyes abruptly. "They twist your maternal generosity and affection into something selfish." Lilith looks back to Lulu. "If what you say is true, then there has never been an unselfish act in the history of creation. Can I take no legitimate pleasure from my generous act? Must I feel displeasure being generous in order for the act to be truly generous? Then are you saying that the only truly generous acts can come from ungenerous spirits?"

"Mama, you just want to fuck this man. But he's mine."

"At least, my darling, a little of his essence for my collection? That's the vigorish, dear. I am the house."

"I could have taken him anywhere."

"You'll give nothing but some quarters for a peep show to your mother who birthed you and raised you and taught you everything?"

Hatcher feels Lulu shudder behind him.

"Oh all right," Lulu says. "Have some diddling. But I get him last. I get to bite."

"Of course, darling. That's for the young anyway."

At some point Hatcher tried to convince himself that in the final analysis, since pain was so extreme in Hell, one pain was pretty much like another. He had to get his addresses from Lulu, but on this point about what he would pay for them, he is realizing he was wrong. He should have known. He has never understood the attitude in people that "It's only sex." That's like saying, "It's only death." There's something uniquely intense about all this, in whatever form.

No more so than in Lilith's double-wide, for she instantly lifts him up and tucks him under an arm and in a flash he is at the other end of the room and he is slammed onto the bed on his back and he closes his eyes and he thinks of England. Literally so. Involuntarily. It's 1968 and the Grosvenor Square protests are just over and the vacationing young journalist has seized the day and taken smart, edited-in-the-camera footage with his Kodak Instamatic and he will soon add a cassette-taped voice-over and win his first broadcast journalism job, and he and Mary Ellen are wandering Piccadilly and she breaks off to go into a bookstore and he is excited by what he knows he will do and he lets her go browse while he wanders on and he passes a cobblestone alley and just off the street a young man is kneeling alone in an army-green field jacket and he is dousing himself with gasoline, and Hatcher pauses, and perhaps all this isn't quite registering on him but now the young man is striking a match and there are no words and no signs, this is a very private act, and perhaps that's why Hatcher still watches and does not think to move, but the privacy does not stop him—nascent newsman that he is—from simply raising his Instamatic, and he films the tiny flare of the flame and the dropping of the match and the man has rested backward a bit on his heels and so the match falls on his lap and the bloom of flame starts from the young man's crotch.

And that's the England Hatcher thinks of as he closes his eyes passively to the sex being visited upon him, because his own quick scorching flame of pain is very much starting in the same place, and the notion flashes through him that perhaps this will be something of an atonement for his newsman's sins, and another pain—damp acid-burn pain—dabs itself again and again all over him—the touch of parts of Lilith's body that he wills himself not to identify—and his own central body part in all this turns abruptly into an unending fount, a great soaring Old Faithful in more ways than one, with the flow geyser-hot, feeling as if the inside channel of him is being ripped up in the process and expelled as well, and now he is aware of a struggle above him, shoving and succubus-hissing and snorting and a sharp "all right you little bitch" from Lilith, and Hatcher knows Lulu has taken over, and a new pain grabs his cheek, a fierce clamping, and he presses his eyes more tightly shut and he could count her teeth if he chose—each is a separate twisting flaming knife blade—and the clamps of pain move down his chest, his abdomen, down and down, heading for Old Faithful as it pours searingly on with the image in Hatcher's head turning from steaming geyser to flamethrower, but Lulu navigates around that spot and down his thighs, the clamp and clamp and clamp of new pain intensifying until it stops for a moment with his right ankle, the last step in a long trail of ongoing pain—the day-after deep throb of puncture wounds—and now he feels his right foot being taken up whole into a wet razor-lined cavern and held for one brief moment and then he hears himself crying out—perhaps he has been crying out all along unawares but now he hears as if from afar his own cry as it fills the room and probably the mountains outside as well—and there is the snapping of bone and the tearing of flesh.

The physical torments of Hell do not allow for the convenient side-door exit of unconsciousness. And so Hatcher McCord, anchorman for the *Evening News from Hell*, newly invested but free-thinkingly subversive minion of Satan, in full consciousness begins to suffer in ways that go rather beyond the poor powers of language to describe, as one foot is devoured and then the other, one leg done in four bites and then the other, the torso done in a dozen large chunks, the throat taken in one bite, and Hatcher McCord's head—including his universally recognizable face—is swallowed whole. And then, last but not least, the famous anchorman's penis remains utterly alone in the center of the bed, spouting on manfully, bravely. After making rather thorough use of this final part for a time, Lulu finally looks at it thoughtfully and then swallows it one gulp. All of Hatcher's parts have now vanished down the wide-gaping throat and into the ever-expanding stomach of the redoubtable Lulu, succubus spawn of Grand Mater Lilith, as the Mater herself flutters nearby watching, having already collected more than enough of his essence for the Hatcher McCord snow globe.

∝

Lulu belches.

"Cover your mouth, dear, when you do that," Lilith says.

Lulu farts.

Lilith rolls her eyes and shakes her head, and with her cupped palm full of Hatcher, she floats off to her arts and crafts corner at the other end of the trailer.

Lulu—her belly vastly distended—lies back on the bed. She pulls a pack of Lucky Strikes from under a pillow and lights a cigarette. She blows a smoke ring and reflects: *I adore having a man inside me. Even if they don't appreciate it and just want to shoot their little load and then roll off you and turn their back and act like you're not even there. And you're so like them, Mama. Deep down, you prefer to watch. The Internet is all you really need. And when you do them, it's just to add to your collection. Oh I did this one. And I did that one. For me, this is the real moment. I cannot hold you close enough, my darling. Come inside me, my darling. We are one, my darling,*

Lulu belches again. This time, with no one to see, she covers her mouth.

Meanwhile, jumbled inside the one large room that is the double-wide of Lulu's inner body, Hatcher also reflects: *In mortal life as well, how often sex went terribly wrong. No. Not always "terribly wrong," sometimes quite subtly wrong and sometimes wrong and right both but mixed so thoroughly that you couldn't tell the difference. But not really "often" wrong either. In fact it* always went wrong, somehow, on some level, even if it was the itch on the heel of your right foot, or what's that distant siren out the window up Riverside Drive or down F Street, or is a two-parter on personal tax deductions during February sweeps a sure thing or a bad risk, all the while you're having sex with a woman who you're never going to see again and you should try to remember or you expect to see for the rest of your life—well, who knows, maybe not that long but certainly indefinitely since you're married to her—and you should try to stay connected to her. And sometimes it was:

Was it good for you?

Yes, was it good for you too?

Yes.

Was it as good for you as it was for me?

How do I know?

Was it the best you ever had?

It was good.

Oh shit.

And sometimes it was:

Are you asleep?

Trying.

Now?

Yes.

Can't we talk?

I'm exhausted.

I want to get pregnant.

Oh shit.

Or instead of "I want to get pregnant" it's "I want it to be like it was" or "I want to get away for a week, alone" or "I want to be famous too"— no, that's too honest—that one wasn't even a question, it was "You never ask me for my opinion" or "What are you really doing for the world" or "I was watching Rather tonight." Or Frank Reynolds. Or, once, Connie Chung. Connie Chung. Oh shit.

And now Lulu shifts on the bed and Hatcher's parts jumble around and his roughly detached head oozes from between chunks of his thighs and his face pops up tightly against Lulu's soft inner flesh. His valiant attempt to remain rational falters: *She is on my arm, my darling Lulu, we enter the conference room and I lay my cheek against her naked shoulder, and the men in the room all rise at our entering and they are pure white from head to toe—faces and hands and suits and ties and hair—as white as the bones of some man that my darling has picked clean in the desert, and I say, "Gentlemen, we've had many fine discussions, the six of us, and Mamie has always been a very gracious hostess, and now I'd like you to meet my darling Lulu—Lulu, this is President Dwight Eisenhower, he's raising both arms to you in electoral triumph, and the man with glasses nodding at you is Harry Truman" and at this Truman lifts both his hands and spreads them as if to measure quite a long penis indeed, and he says, "The fuck stops here" and the Presidents are gone and Lulu and I are crossing the square in Pittsfield, heading for the Rainbow Restaurant for cheeseburgers and cherry Cokes and we pass beneath the awning of the storefront Hotel Parkway and Lulu says, "Let's go in there and fuck" and I say "You bet" but just now my father steps out of the Rainbow and his face is smeared with ketchup and he's popping a final French fry into his mouth and Lulu does a double take and she says "Even better" and she is upon him instantly and his clothes are flying and I really really want to look away before I see my father's cock, especially in the grip of my darling Lulu, and someone taps me on the shoulder and I turn and it's Mamie Eisenhower—the whiteness of her face and hair and pearl necklace and modest fitted woman's suit is dazzling there in the sunlight in Pittsfield—and she lifts her hands and offers me a cup of tea even as my father's voice fills the square shouting "Fuck me, Lulu, yes!" and Lulu cries "At last a real man!" and I drop Mamie's teacup and I run, I run across the square and past the courthouse and on and on till I slam into our front door and I go up the steps three at a time and I find my mother—her late-October-afternoon gray eyes turning on me and brightening—and I sit beside her on the bed where she hugs a terry cloth robe tight around her and I take her hand and I begin to pat it and I pat it and I pat it and she says to me, quite low but quite clearly, "It's all right, my darling. You have everything to give to the world. And everything about you is perfect. Do you hear me? You don't need to worry. You're perfect."*

All the parts of Hatcher's body are beginning to stir now. Lulu puts her hand on the great mound of her distended belly. She smiles, then turns her face, leans off the side of the bed, and throws up for a while. Just as certain physical sufferings in Hell exceed the power of language to describe, so too does succubus vomit, which is just as well. Though Jackson Pollock, in a circumstance similar to Hatcher's, having occasion a little further along in this process to observe the effusion of Lulu's sister Lily, remarked, at its color and form on the floor, "Holy shit. I am profoundly humbled."

This has always been a poignant, though somewhat delusional, time for Lulu. After her ersatz morning sickness passes, she lies back and puts a hand once more on her belly as, within, a reconstitution begins, in this case Hatcher's. She begins to hum "Sympathy for the Devil", though softly, even sweetly, not the Rolling Stones version at all, and Hatcher can hear her from inside, as once did, in this same circumstance, the briefly famous, newly arrived British reality-TV music critic, Simon Cowell, who cried out, desperate to curry Lulu's favor, "Brilliant, you've made it your own." And within Lulu: *My little baby, how boisterous you are, I know you will be a girl this time, I can feel it. A mother knows. I can feel your sweet downy wings trying to unfurl, but that will have to wait just a little longer, my darling, there will be time for that. I will teach you to fly in good time. We will rise together into the hot, sulfurous sky, and we will soar, you close at my side, and we will fly to the great city, and as we approach, I will show you the men below, scattering at the passing of our shadows—how adorable your little shadow is—and we will find a small and lively one for you already here in Hell— a Genghis Khan or a Yasser Arafat or a Sammy Davis Jr.—and you will begin. And you will learn, my daughter. Through them. You will understand who you are. It's what men are for. And so I will also find you a small and thoughtful one—a Voltaire or a Mahatma Gandhi or a Jean Paul Sartre—they are not as lively but they will give you depth—wait until you swallow Jean Paul's sweet brain, my darling, he knows a thing or two about your world—and you will move on from him, of course, you will grow and grow and you will have full-size kings and billionaires and serial killers—but you will always have me to guide you, you won't have some desperate old bitch of a mother who didn't teach you a thing worth knowing and then grasps at everything that's yours. Hell is other succubi, my darling.*

And inside Lulu, as Hatcher begins quickly now to reassemble, he also considers parenthood: *Summer, my little child of dumb-shit flower children wannabes—that was your mother and me—we went a little mad and you suffered for that, and then we went abruptly sane and you suffered for that. And Angie, my little child of a face on TV, my TV face was so much less loving than Mr. Rogers's, so much less charming than Kermit the Frog's. How could I compete with them when I had to bring you the four-car pile-up on I-70 or the fog at Lambert Airport or the latest from the St. Louis County Council meeting? I wonder if I would've been better for you both if you'd been boys. But no. My distraction, my obliviousness would have hurt you even more deeply. As girls you had your mother, who was more important for you, and I was glad for that, I excused myself for that. I did what I did to become what I became and I am so fucking sorry.*

And Hatcher is whole in body again, though naked and curled tightly into a fetal position inside a succubus in a double-wide in Hell. But not inside a succubus for long. Lulu stops humming the Rolling Stones and spreads her legs and props herself up on her elbows and lifts her hips and she begins to daaa-daaa-daaa-da-dummmm the brass fanfare for dawn in Richard Strauss's "Also Sprach Zarathustra." At this very moment, somewhere in the Great Metropolis, Strauss and Friedrich Nietzsche and Stanley Kubrick are locked in a tiny room together listening to the 190 decibel version of the same passage for the ten thousandth straight time. At the other end of the room, Lilith rolls her eyes at Lulu's flair for the dramatic. She jiggles the new snow globe in her hand. Hatcher's own special snow swirls around a small, hand-painted plastic bust of the anchorman. And Hatcher himself suddenly feels a squeezing upon him, and his curled body begins to move.

Lulu stops da-dumming, because even succubi suffer in Hell and this is one of those times, with every cell in Lulu's body feeling as if it is in a vise and being squeezed to pulp, and she screams wordlessly for a while until she manages, "She's crowning!"

"It's just that man who was here," Lilith says.

"Fuck you," Lulu cries.

"Pant pant blow," Lilith says.

"Fuck you," Lulu reiterates, and to distract herself from the impression that her body is being split up the middle by a white-hot gutting knife, she briefly does her best to imitate the horn section of the Berlin Philharmonic, returning to Strauss to introduce what she expects to be her daughter into the world.

Hatcher's whole head emerges between Lulu's legs, and Lulu pauses her pushing and stops the music. Hatcher looks at the ceiling and tries to squinch the muck from his eyes.

Lulu pushes again, and as Hatcher's shoulders pry her open and as the gutting knife renews its work with a special focus on her treasured private parts, she screams "I'll make you pay for this forever, you little bitch!"

And Hatcher moves faster and faster, torso and hips and legs all folded together, and with a splashing all about him and a loud sucking-shut behind him, he slides onto the bed between Lulu's legs.

Lulu falls back flat. Both mother and faux child pant for a while, the latter slowly trying to move his stiffened limbs and the former renewing her pledge to make this daughter of hers forever regret having put her mother through this torture.

Finally, though, Lulu is ready to face the little bitch and she struggles to sit up, just as Hatcher has struggled to sit up between her legs, and they come face to face.

Lulu says, "Oh fuck. Not again," and she fists up her right hand and punches Hatcher square on the nose. He flies across the room, landing about halfway along, and slicked up by Lulu's bodily fluids, he skims the rest of the way to Lilith, who calmly lifts one fat and furry foot—pedicured meticulously, however, in French tips—to bring Hatcher to a halt.

∝

The trip back to the city has certain uncomfortable complications. The sun has risen. It was a short night, this time. And Lulu no longer clasps Hatcher to her body in flight. As they fly off, she holds him painfully by the scruff of the neck, at arm's length, with him dangling full-frontally over the passing landscape. And she's in no rush. And she begins to sing. Defying the fact that she's technically pretty nearly a baritone, in a key intended for a pop-diva soprano, failing painfully but still succeeding in conveying a sobby self-pity, she sings: "All by myself. Don't wanna be all by myself anymore."

She swoops low through a dry riverbed, and in the broken prow of a ship that resembles the *Titanic*, a woman stands shackled and wrapped in furs before the hot sun and she is herself singing—compelled to, as a matter of fact—about how her heart will go on forever, no doubt wishing otherwise, and when she sees Lulu and Hatcher, she stops her song and looks up and is unable to look away. Lulu circles her quite closely and continues to circle until Lulu has sung "All by Myself" six times, from tremulous beginning to excruciatingly botched glory-note climax to simulated studio fade, and from the first bars of the first go-around, Hatcher recognizes the singer on the ship prow, and whatever she is suffering for these thirty-one minutes and eighteen seconds, Hatcher would argue that being dangled naked before Celine Dion is worse.

Then Lulu finally veers away and flies off straight. They swoop up out of the riverbed, still flying quite low. The city is suddenly upon them, spreading from the left horizon to the right. Now, at the city limits, the crowded streets begin abruptly. As the shadow of Lulu and Hatcher passes along the jostling throng, like a coordinated wave in a sport's stadium, the faces of people rise, and Lulu is so low that Hatcher can even see the movements of all the eyes to the dangling part of this dangling man.

It takes him a long few moments of this to get a bright idea. He calls out over his shoulder to Lulu, "Thanks for flying low. I'm afraid of heights."

The brain of a succubus, even at its best, is far from quick-flowing, but post-coital it is downright sludgy. Lulu, still pissed at Hatcher for not being a daughter, beats her wings heavily at this and they shoot straight up until the faces below recede into indistinguishability, as does, Hatcher hopes, his own naked body.

∝

Finally Lulu dumps Hatcher in the mouth of his alley and flies off, dissatisfied as always, with the way these things end. Like all succubi—and many others—she is puzzled how the ravenous sexual desire she so recently felt has turned trivial and empty now that it's sated. She is also puzzled how she forgets this feeling each time and is thus puzzled anew when each man is done with. This is a great deal of self-reflection for Lulu, and as a result, she distractedly flies into a light standard along Grand Peachtree Parkway.

Meanwhile, Hatcher is nakedly beating it down the alleyway and up his circular stairs and along the outer corridor of his apartment building, hoping mightily to sail past a closed Hopper apartment door. He is disappointed on both scores. The door is open, and as he approaches it, his limbs become heavy and his movements turn into an exaggerated slow motion. Peggy and Howard are sitting in their chairs.

"There's the famous TV person," Peggy says. "Try not to be rude."

"Rude my ass," Howard says.

"You never used to use language like that with me," she says.

"What difference does it make anymore?" he says.

"Plenty."

"Plenty?"

"Plenty."

Howard shrugs, "It's not such a terrible word. And you criticize me for saying the word but you don't even notice that the famous TV person's ass is bare?"

"I notice," she says.

"But no matter. *I'm* the one who's wrong."

"He probably has his reasons," Peggy says.

"Reasons? I've got reasons too."

"Good evening," Peggy says to Hatcher.

"Good evening," Hatcher says.

"Forgive my husband," she says.

"Forgive my ass," Hatcher says.

Peggy giggles.

Howard looks sharply at her. He clearly has an opportunity to score big in this argument. But her giggle runs deeper in him now. He can't place the exact moment, but that same giggle once bubbled up sweetly between them, early on. Was it their wedding night? He can't quite bring back the room, the touch, the few words before, after. He thumps his forehead with the butt of his palm. That moment is long gone. That woman is long gone. It's all over long ago.

And Hatcher moves past the Hoppers' door.

He opens his own.

Anne is standing in the center of the floor, facing him, and she is also naked.

"Is someone here?" Hatcher says, his mind following by a few beats the instant suspicion of his body, a few beats in which Anne's face darkens.

"No," she says.

"What is it?" he says.

"My head is on," she says.

"Yes."

"Are you glad?"

"Yes."

"I don't have furry wings," she says.

"That's good."

"It is?" The darkness is gone from her face. Her eyes fill with tears.

"Yes. Very good."

"I am small and dark."

"That's very good too."

"Are you sure?"

"Yes."

"I know what she is."

"I had to go," Hatcher says.

"Yes," Anne says. "I believe that."

"But it still hurt you?"

"Did it?" she asks, seeming not to have thought of this.

"Apparently so." Hatcher is struck by how he seems attuned to her, seems to be saying the right things for once.

"Perhaps worried me," she says.

"Worried this way," he says, gently, nodding at her body.

"Yes," she says. "I'm naked."

"I'm naked too," Hatcher says.

"I noticed," Anne says.

He comes near to her. But they don't touch. It's this next step where things always somehow go wrong.

Anne says, "But she came here so openly. I know she can do that because you're dead. But there seemed to be more to it than she was a fan of yours from TV and happened to be in the neighborhood."

Hatcher hears Anne's voice starting to ice up. He could try to press forward with regards to their mutual nakedness, but the trouble has already begun and he knows it would quickly go very bad. So he says, "She had information I needed, information I couldn't figure out how else to get. I didn't anticipate what the price would be."

Anne cocks her head at him.

"You can believe this too," he says.

"What kind of information?" she says.

He plays his trump card. "Henry's whereabouts."

Anne stiffens, though her voice goes soft. "My Henry?"

Hatcher pauses a moment to absorb the body blow of that possessive pronoun. But he can't simply endorse it. "Henry VIII, former king of England," he says softly.

"You did that for me?" she says.

"Yes."

"Why? I know this drives you crazy."

"If it's what you need."

Anne lifts a hand and lays her palm on his cheek. For a moment he thinks that they will have sex now and it will be good. But the gesture is simply gratitude, he quickly realizes, and the sudden, visible heaving of her chest is about something else.

She drops her hand from his face. "When can I go?"

Hatcher hasn't thought this out. He knows where Henry is and he knows she could never get there on her own.

"I'll have to go with you." This actually sinks in only as he says it.

"Now?" she says.

Hatcher, for several reasons and in several ways, is suddenly feeling thoroughly drained. He has gone weak in the legs and heavy in the chest, and he says, "I've had a bad night."

"Then when?"

"I have to lie down now."

"When can we go?"

"After the evening news," Hatcher says.

This arrangement, uncomfortable for both, floats between them for a long moment. Then Anne says, quite softly, "Thank you."

And Hatcher has never been sadder that the sex between them has never been good.

∝

When Hatcher arrives at Broadcast Central, he heads toward Beelzebub's office. It can't be avoided. He needs a car. He strides along the corridor and he's hoping mightily that Lily is on a sex break. He does not want to face Lulu's sister today. He turns in at the door of the outer office and Lily is there, eating from a box of what one would normally assume are chocolates—small balls, some dark, some milk, some white—but, as has been previously noted, this is Hell and this is a succubus, and so when she smiles slyly at Hatcher and offers one, he declines with something less than gracious reluctance.

"Pathetic," Lily says, and it's clear to Hatcher she's referring to more than his refusal of a treat.

He just keeps on moving, toward Beelzebub's inner office. The number-two demon sees Hatcher coming and he rises from behind his desk. "Hello, my boy. I'm very pleased with the J. Edgar stuff. I do like a good epiphany, you should excuse the expression."

"Thanks," Hatcher says.

"It's Clinton airing today?"

"Bill. Yes."

"And the other Clinton?"

"She's coming up."

"Splendid. Do they blame each other?"

"No."

"Ah. Too bad."

"I've found out where Henry VIII is located," Hatcher says. "I'd like to do him. He's got lots of reasons to understand why he's here, but it'll be interesting to see which ones are on his mind."

"Well well well," Beelzebub says. "Your girlfriend's old flame. That should be painful for you, yes?"

"Yes."

"Good. Good. You intrigue me, McCord."

"I need a car."

"You got it. I like what you're doing with this series. Self-reflection is hell." He chuckles.

Beelzebub doesn't go out of his way to give compliments, and hearing this one gives Hatcher an idea. So he says, "You want me to clear each one with you? There are sometimes targets of opportunity."

Beelzebub gives this only a flicker of a thought. Hatcher feels keenly the power of his secret: this is going to work because Bee-bub can't imagine Hatcher feeling free to have a covert agenda inside his head.

"I'll put Dick Nixon at your disposal for the series. Anytime."

Hatcher restrains his elation, but he does flip Beelzebub a jaunty little salute, in effect dismissing himself.

Beelzebub raises a hand to stop him. "One other thing. You've got a new entertainment reporter. He's been cooking for a while, but I think he's ready for work. He was the mastermind behind an Internet gossip site specializing in Manhattan media gossip. Then he moved up to celebritygenitals.com and was shot dead by a rapper with a tiny dick."

"Who is he?" Hatcher says.

"I'd rather not say. He can still only remember his screen name, and I'm enjoying that."

Having been stopped once, Hatcher waits. Beelzebub says, "Go. Go."

Hatcher does. Lily is staring thoughtfully into her box, and he tries to move by her quickly and quietly. But as he's passing, Lily lifts the box toward him. There are only two left. Milk chocolate balls. She says, "Please."

He hurries past her, saying, "No thanks."

"They're presidential," she says.

And Hatcher, who should be interested in the way the nation went immediately after his demise, hustles down the hall trying to think of anything but.

∝

In the commercial break just before the Clinton "Why Do You Think You're Here," Hatcher ponders how painful it might indeed be, later this afternoon, when he takes Anne to Henry. But he also finds himself wondering if he might get a little spiritual credit for the act, something to begin to qualify him for a one-way ticket at the next Harrowing. That thought immediately seems pathetic to him, but it lingers, working on him, nonetheless. It's why he's seeking out his wives, after all, and he's already planning to use the car to find another one, Deborah, who is nearby.

And now he's back on air and he's introducing the Clinton piece, and his mind is so thoroughly his own again that he can exercise a talent from his mortal professional life: he can roll out the appropriate broadcast-ready words from his mouth while his mind is somewhere else entirely. So as he does his introduction flawlessly, his thoughts slide back to how pathetic he is trying to do a thing or two to qualify himself to be taken out of Hell, and then he thinks no, it's not pathetic at all, it's another example of his self-important arrogance, that he expects to make a couple of selfless gestures and muscle ahead of all the great religious figures waiting in line to get out of Hell.

But Bill Clinton is on thirty-two of the monitors now, and on the central four is Hatcher, beginning to listen to this man, intently, as he always did. Bill is sweating in his cheap hotel room, in his shirtsleeves, his tie askew, and after Hatcher has asked, "Why do you think you're here?" Bill looks sharply away, toward the door, and says, "Is that someone?" And he immediately answers his own question. "No. It's nothing."

Then Bill Clinton composes himself and looks into the camera, and he smiles a small, sneery, Elvis Presley smile, and he says, "The short answer is: Satan is a Republican. But before they stuck me in this room to wait, I personally saw Kenneth Starr around, and Rush Limbaugh, and Newt Gingrich, and quite a few of the others, so I'm afraid that dog won't hunt. Therefore, taking this hotel room into consideration, and what it is I find myself waiting for, and trying to be honest about what the 'is' is, I'd be inclined to say I'm here because I wanted . . . what's the word? Let's see . . . I must be getting old, not to think of that word. Let's say warm affection. That's all I ever wanted with all the women. I need a lot of warm affection. And as for the sex? Well, in the most intense parts of that, I never inhaled. So it wasn't about the sex."

Bill stops talking for a long moment. He tries the Elvis smile, briefly, but it soon fades. Then he says, "What's the point of lying in Hell? Especially to myself. Why I'm here wasn't about me wanting sex. But it wasn't

about . . . that other thing, either, which is maybe why I can't even remember the word. I'm not stupid. If I was after either of those, I would've
said to Paula Jones, for instance, when she came to my hotel room in
Little Rock, 'Darling, I am in a sexless marriage without . . . warm
affection, and I adore that remarkable nose of yours.' That nose being
the thing she has no doubt always hated in her face. She would've been
in my bed in nothing flat, ready to give me both sex and affection, and
she never would've spoken a word about it. But the truth is, with her
and with all of them, it was really about the moment when I knew what
I was going to do and they didn't, and it was about the next moment,
when I dropped my pants or grabbed their tits and they gasped. It was
about the exercise of power. So I suppose that's it. I'm here for the same
reason that when I was sixteen and I shook John Kennedy's hand in the
White House Rose Garden, I knew I would do anything to have what he
had, and I mean the power. And it's for the same reason that if a woman
ever does walk through that door over there, I will rise and I will face
her and I will drop my pants, and being as it's Hell, I know I will pay for
that big-time, but I will still do it."

Then it's back to Hatcher, and he is happy to start the segue into the
final feature, actually helped for the moment by the teleprompter, which
does make sense just often enough to get the news from one segment to
another. Reading instead of improvising makes it even easier for Hatcher's
mind to drift while he speaks, as he retains just enough awareness to
realize if the teleprompter is about to take him way off course. And so
he goes over his plan again to head straight to Deborah after the broadcast, as he reads, "That was the former President of the United States,
Bill Clinton. And I know there are countless millions of you out there
asking the same question, 'Why am I here?' Even if you were quiet, ab-
ject failures, even if you never amounted to enough in your mortal life
to make the slightest public mark on human history, you have to wonder why."

Hatcher's reading slows as he realizes what he's saying. But he doesn't know how to adjust this, and these same countless millions face worse pain in the street every day. Still, he thinks to try to improvise away from Beelzebub's script. But the worst is already out, and he ends up simply continuing to read: "So our new entertainment reporter will expose the private lives of those who have actually accomplished something in the wider world so you can feel superior, no matter for how brief a time or with what pathetic self-delusion. Now here he is, the former Cyberspace Sultan of Self-Righteousness, the Swami of Superiority, the Parasite of Prominence . . ." And the text ends with no name following, not even his screen name, which he is said to remember. But the thirty-two monitors cut to a man in a crowded street with a microphone. His face is hidden by a black and white keffiyeh wrapped sloppily into a terrorist's mask with a square, stubble-chinned white man's jaw exposed at the bottom.

"Yes, Hatcher, hello. I can hear you," the reporter says in a faintly poncy, British whine, "Mineisbigger reporting. But not only can I hear you, I can see you as well, as it turns out. This morning the denizens moving along Peachtree Street Street Avenue Street had a bit of shock when a certain quite famous *Evening News from Hell* presenter appeared, flying overhead, stark naked. Fortunately someone had a camera and we have some splendid footage of the presenter presenting his genitals. I daresay you'll recognize them, Hatcher. They are, of course, yours."

And Mineisbigger goes on for quite a long while with extensive footage and snarky analysis, but Hatcher sees none of it. He lays his hands flat on the desktop before him and lowers his face just enough so he can't see the screens, and he concentrates on making his mind—his true private part in Hell—go blank. He does hear Mineisbigger's coloratura shrieks of agony at the end of the report, as the reporter has likely burst into flames, but Hatcher does not even lift his face to watch.

∝

Dick Nixon and his Cadillac are at the curb in front of Broadcast Central when Hatcher emerges with a camcorder. Hatcher's first thought is *Great, we'll make good time* and he doesn't catch himself until he is in the backseat and Dick is revving his engine and Hatcher realizes he'll get everything he wants done this day only because a wide swath of denizens will be tossed and battered and crushed by the former president's merciless driving. Hatcher tells himself *If he weren't driving me, he'd be driving someone else; if it weren't Dick Nixon torturing them, it would be someone or something else.* And to his credit, Hatcher realizes how, in the freedom of his mind, he is invoking a ghastly classic line of human reasoning. He also hears how that line of reasoning is directed at himself but is also offered as a defense to some higher authority who is presumed to be keeping spiritual accounts for reward and punishment. Will using Dick Nixon to get around in this world keep him from qualifying for the next Harrowing? Indeed, how many of the millions out there in the streets of Hell are here in part because they voted for Dick Nixon? *Am I, in my inner freedom, going mad? Am I, in my freedom, simply renewing my credentials for eternal damnation? Or am I, in my freedom, making progress toward an everlasting release from this suffering?* These seem to be familiar questions from another life. But just moments before he begins, in frustration, to jabber nonsense sounds aloud in the backseat, Hatcher goes *Aw fuckit, I don't know what's right, but I want to see Deborah and let Anne do what she needs to do.* So Hatcher gives Dick Nixon the address of his second wife, and Dick burns rubber and takes off. And having made that decision, Hatcher's mind turns to another, smaller-scale anxiety, which expresses itself in a vague appeal to that vague spiritual accountant: *Oh please don't let her have watched the news today.*

∝

Hatcher's dead and damned second wife lives in a vast, stark, modernist concrete public high-rise housing complex, its dim, jammed corridors a constant, torturously high-decibel cacophony of hip hop and easy listening, klezmer and salsa, grand opera and sea chanteys and blues, cantopop and Nederpop and Hindipop and twee. But Hatcher barely notices all this. He is focused now on his quest. He moves through the crowd on the fourteenth floor fluttering his powder-blue minion tie before him, which readily clears a path until he is standing at the door of Deborah Louise Becker, who remained Deborah Louise Becker even after her marriage to Hatcher McCord, which shortly followed his divorce from Mary Ellen McCord, which was put into motion after several months of a covert affair with Deborah Louise Becker, which began with their having sex on his office couch immediately after she'd interviewed him for *New York* magazine, which was also the first time they'd ever met. Who had initiated the sex on that day and what exactly had been done was a matter of considerable—though, in Hatcher's view, wildly inaccurate—detail in Deborah's post-divorce memoir, *Jerk*. Her subsequent novel, *Fool*, though more advanced in its irony—the "fool" being somewhat ambiguous, applicable in different ways to both the fictional husband-anchorman and wife-journalist—had a strikingly similar depiction of its couple's first sex scene, on his office couch after a magazine interview.

For all the strident criticism of Hatcher in Deborah's books, which he did read out of self-defense, painful though it was, he still needs to knock on this door. He feels in her books she got him wrong, but he suspects that the actual process of writing helped create the distortions. In person, perhaps he can get at something legitimate she knows about him. Because his mother also got him wrong, of course. As much as part of him wants to believe she didn't, she did. He was—is—far from perfect. *You think?* his voice below his thinking suddenly says. *You're in Hell, asshole. I'd fucking say so.* Hatcher knocks at Deborah's door.

There is no answer. Hatcher is afraid she's out somewhere in the street. He knocks again. Nothing.

"Deborah?" he says, loud, over the music all around him.

Nothing.

"Deborah?" he calls, louder.

"She's not in there," a woman's voice says, just behind Hatcher.

Hatcher turns. She's very old and stooped and bony and bewhiskered and her skin is jaundiced the color of a heavy smoker's teeth. She sees Hatcher's tie, and her eyes narrow and she pulls back a bit.

"It's all right," Hatcher says. "I was married to her."

"Which demon of a husband were you?" she says.

"Her second."

"The one on the television set."

"That one." Hatcher did not keep up with Deborah after they split, though he was aware she'd married and divorced once more after him, having also had a too-young marriage before him. He feels a brief pulse of pleasure at her apparent ranting about husbands other than him. He wishes they'd rated books. "Do you know where she is?" he says.

"She threw herself off her balcony about five minutes ago," the old woman says.

"What?" His first thought is that she did it in response to seeing him naked on TV.

"I live next door," the old woman says. "She does this almost every day."

"Thanks," Hatcher says, telling his inner voice to stuff it, as it is about to give him a hard time for thinking his naked body could inspire a suicide for any possible reason. He focuses on Deborah lying broken outside and he moves off quickly.

The old woman watches him go: *Leap, yes leap, my friend, I have leapt too, we all of us in the balcony rooms leap and leap and O if I could but seal off that end of my room, the terrible open end, the wide sky beyond, I dream of my cell in the convent, the narrow walls, the high, small, knifeprick of sky, the bed, the bowl, the cup, only these. And I remember—though it has been a long long time now—the days of my one husband, my own demon, the baron of . . . where? Sussex. Yes, some baron of Sussex. It is torture, this fading of my memory. O if I could but picture his face more clearly so I could hate him all the more. My husband who put me aside with lies so I was left with only death or the cloister before me. And the ringing takes up, the ringing in my head: the Sanctus bell, the Host rising, the only man's body for my last many years, His holy body. He was my last husband, who looked the other way, I always thought, whenever I laid my mortal body down with the body of my Abbess in the warming house in winter where we covered ourselves in ash, and in the granary in summer where the wheat clung to us in our sweat. But even my last husband put me aside in the end, in spite of my prayers in the final moments to be forgiven. And though it's true that even as I prayed, if I'd had the strength and the chance I would have sought her sweet kisses once more, He should still have forgiven this body of mine with its terrible weakness, for His Father created my body this way and if His Father could not resist creating it thus, how could I resist thus living in it?*

∝

The hundred apartment buildings in the housing project float on a sea of concrete. Hatcher rounds the corner of Deborah's building and enters the fifty-yard-wide margin reachable by jumpers from the balconies, a place called The Landing Strip by the denizens. It is splashed with dark stains. The crowds between the buildings mill about in clusters that shape up and fist fight or knife fight or simply scream and foam and rage and then break apart and form new clusters, always stumbling about in the shadow of the buildings, but never ever moving into The Landing Strip. So from the moment Hatcher turns the corner, he sees Deborah up ahead. He rushes toward her.

She lies broken in a widening pool of blood, her cheek pressed hard against the concrete, her eyes open, seemingly sightless but blinking, her arms at elbow-flared angles, her legs cracked and splayed but bent under her at the knees so that her back and butt are lifted slightly. Her left hand is twitching. Hatcher arrives beside her and kneels in her blood so he can extend a hand and gently palm the side of her head just above her ear. Her hair was always soft and thick, and it still is, though it is gray. She did not kill herself at the end of her mortal life. That she's doing this now, over and over, makes his hand tremble against her.

"Debbie," he says.

Her eyes move slightly toward him, and they close.

He does not know how to take this. But he keeps his hand on her, even as her blood continues to gather around his knees.

"I'm sorry," he says.

Her eyes move beneath her closed lids as if she were dreaming.

Hatcher and Deborah stay like this for a long while, until finally her blood stirs around him, even drawing itself out of his pants legs, and her body begins to jerk and shiver and the blood flows back into her and her body straightens and mends, and Hatcher takes his hand from her head as she moves and slowly flexes her limbs and finally gathers herself into a sitting position. He shifts from his knees and sits beside her.

She says, though softly, "Leave it to you to show up when I'm at my worst."

"It was unintentional," he says.

"It was instinctive," she says.

She still isn't sounding as angry as Hatcher would expect. But he has no answer for this.

"Sorry for what?" she says.

"Whatever I did to us."

Deborah humphs at this. "I hear that in the hallways around here once in a while, and it always surprises me."

"Hear what?"

"'I'm sorry.'"

Hatcher looks away, beyond the Landing Strip. There are skirmishes all over. Immediately before him, several gangs of young men, black and white, have been forced to swap some of their past styles and are murderously fighting over it: the whites are in the zoot suits and the hoodies and the sagging pants and the bucket hats and the neck bling and the do-rags and the dreadlocks, and the blacks are in the leisure suits and the chinos and the boaters and the Hush Puppies and the ascots and the crew cuts. Beyond them are old people jostling and wailing and cursing. And Hatcher recognizes an instance of what he has come to understand as his own arrogant self-absorption, for it never occurred to him that others in Hell are apologizing. Surely Hell is never having to say you're sorry. But Deborah apparently has heard it—no doubt because here in the projects, the crowds are always upon her—and so, once in a while, someone says I'm sorry, even as they think Satan is listening in, even as they expect to be punished for it. Hatcher's chest fills with a complicated warmth about these people before him now, though they are fighting and cursing each other. They are struggling on, even in Hell, and sometimes they regret what they do or what they have done, and they say so. Hatcher is breathless now over all of them, and he turns to Deborah and he lifts his hand to touch her head again. She bats his hand away, though lightly.

"What are you doing here?" she says.

"That's what I'm trying to figure out," he says.

"Oh please. You think I'd ever wonder about *that*? I mean here." She flips her chin at the apartment building.

"Trying to figure out what I'm doing in Hell."

"Read my book."

"I did. I didn't believe it."

"Then I can't help you."

This isn't what Hatcher expected. He expected her to defend the truth of what she wrote. He expected a heated renewal of all that. "You don't believe it either," he says.

"Of course I did," she says.

"Did. But not now."

"You were a shit."

"I believe that."

"*Are* a shit."

"Just not that particular shit," he says.

"What difference does it make anymore?" she says.

"I don't know."

He lifts his hand again toward her.

"Stop," she says.

He stops.

"Go away now," she says.

Hatcher turns his face from her. He sees a young black man in an Arrow button-down shirt and Birkenstocks and a Brylcreemed pompadour who is faced off with a young white man in Ben Davis gorilla cuts and a Michael Jordan jersey and dreads. They are pushing each other in the chest.

"Please," Deborah says.

Hatcher does not intend to ignore her. He just feels utterly inert inside. He can't bring himself to ask the questions he wants to ask. But he can't bring himself simply to walk away now either. All he finds he can do is focus on the two young men. Just as he expects the thing between them to escalate, the young black simply grabs one of the white youth's dreads and tugs it, but not hard, and he shakes his head in outsized disgust.

"Hatcher," Deborah says, knowing he won't answer. She closes her eyes and her shoulders droop. He has come to her in Hell simply as a reminder that her insignificance is eternal. Who better.

The young white reaches out and musses up the black's pompadour and jerks his hand away, exaggeratedly wiping at the grease. The two of them look at each other and start to laugh.

Deborah hears the laughter. Her irritation at Hatcher fades and she turns to the rare sound. They will pay, she knows. The two young men stop and give each other an oh-shit look, and they take a deep breath, and the hair on each of their heads bursts into flames.

Hatcher turns from the two men flailing in pain. Does it have to go that way?

He and Deborah face each other once more.

"Look," she says, "I don't know what you want from me. Absolution?"

"No."

"It wasn't your fault I was so unhappy. Okay? You helped. But it wasn't all about you. At first, you were so important—in the world—it made me important too. I was trying to be somebody, and you already were somebody. Then I wasn't becoming what I hoped to be. You had your work and I admired you so much for it. Until I hated you for it. You know I still try to write? Even here. What's that about? I have to do it in spray paint on my walls. Maybe you wouldn't have been able to help me through all that, back when we were alive. But you never thought to try. You were oblivious. You were so . . . *you*."

They sit in silence for a long moment in the middle of the Landing Strip, unaware of the din nearby, aware only of the beating of their own immortal hearts, thumping heavily in their immortal chests, aware of the slip of rancid air into their immortal lungs.

Hatcher thinks: *We only hurt each other.* "Why are we here?" he says, softly.

"We were always here," she says.

"Yes," he says.

"I wish I were dead," she says.

And just then there is a whoosh of air upon them and a cracking thump and they are spattered with thick wetness. They look. The medieval nun who lives next to Deborah has jumped, and her broken body is beside them and her blood is upon them.

∝

And this puts an end to Hatcher's time with his second wife. She crawls to the nun, to touch her, speak low to her. He stands up.

"Please," Deborah says. "No more."

She says it softly and without looking at him, so he thinks she's speaking to the old woman. And maybe she is. But then he realizes she's talking to him as well.

"I'll just wait a moment for her," he says. His clothes and face are maculate with her blood, and he does not know how near he has to be for it to find its way back to her. So he stands close by while Deborah strokes the old woman's head, and Hatcher has the urge to touch his wife again. But he doesn't. He can't. She is done with him. All that is done.

But inside her: *The Mayor's office at City Hall and Ed Koch presiding, mugging his way through, and Hatcher says "I do" and I'm fluttering inside and I'm ready, but before Koch turns to me he twinkles at Hatcher like he famously does and he says "How am I doing?" and my friends and Hatcher's friends all laugh and Hatcher says "Great. How am I doing?" and Koch says "Great!" and everybody laughs again and Koch turns to me and as much as I am happy that I rate the Mayor of New York City as I marry the hot young anchor who beat Rather and Mudd-Brokaw and Reynolds-Robinson-Jennings six weeks running in the Nielsens this spring, I understand with a terrible sudden grinding in my head that nobody has the slightest clue who I am, who I really am, not the Mayor of New York, not these friends laughing, not the media waiting in the street, not the vast public out there reading and listening and watching, not the famous man who is about to become my husband. Nobody. And no matter how much I try, they never will.* Deborah squeezes her eyes shut hard, and her mind with it, even as she continues to stroke the head beneath her hand.

Meanwhile, Hatcher has looked away, briefly, to the crowd, grappling on. And then he looks back to the apartment building. Sometimes you can see something but not see it, and then once you do, it is overwhelmingly clear. He looks to the next building down and to the one beyond the crowd. And it is all the same. He turns his face once more to Deborah's building: The walls are jammed with words, outside on all the surfaces reachable from the ground or from the windows or balconies, and inside too, he recalls now, in the corridors, on every inch of the inner walls and the ceilings and the floors. Everywhere, the housing project is teeming with handwritten words. And like the crowds of Hell themselves, the words are a wild profusion of shapes and forms, bubble letters and rustic capitals, cuneiform and cyrillic, Spencerian and wildstyle. They are spray-painted and brush-painted and knife-bladed and charcoaled everywhere. And what they are *not* is political or religious, they are not angry or profane. They are names. Just personal names. Just simple assertions of self on the walls of Hell. BLADE and BJÖRK, KILROY and AJIT, TAKI 183 and CELADUS CRESCENS, MAMA DIVINE and DAZE, JULIO 204 and NOVELLIA PRIMIGENIA OF NUCERIA, S. MAGEE and W. M. McCOY, SERGEI and MAHMOUD and CHAN.

Hatcher cannot find the tears he wants to shed. He cries out. Wordless. Just an animal sound, trying to name a thing that has no name. The sound of a Neanderthal, who is filled with a terror and a longing and a grace he cannot understand about his mate or his child. And the blood of the nun is stirring on Hatcher's face and hands and clothes. And it flies away from him. And he turns and he goes and he rounds the corner of the building and he hurries along and he passes BUFFY and DAFYDD and BUBBA and MENACHEM and LADY PINK and FLY. Hatcher stops, trembling. He looks at the wall. A space. A small space in the crotch of the V in EVA 62. He pounds around on his chest feeling for a pen. He's wearing his anchorman suit and has one somewhere. There. Fallen into the bottom of an inner coat pocket. He digs out his Bic ballpoint and moves to the wall and he leans into Eva and is deeply grateful for the space inside her. He scratches and inks and scratches until the pen tip is no good for ink but it can still scratch and he puts his name on the wall: HATCHER.

∝

Hatcher readily passes the Hoppers' closed door, but his legs go heavy and his movements turn lugubriously slow as he approaches his own apartment. Not long ago, he would have heard the old, aggrandizing voice-over narrator in his head. But not anymore. He simply thinks: *I am taking Anne away now to lose her.* And there is a sad silence inside him, and he stands before his door, and his hand is pausing on the knob. And he thinks: *But if that's so, then not to take her away would make keeping her meaningless.* He opens the door. It does not even occur to him to call out their ritual darling-I'm-home. She is not in sight. He does call "Are you ready?"

She appears from the bedroom and sucks the air from his lungs and up flutteringly into his throat and head. She is wearing a gossamer white Edwardian tea dress, all cobweb linen and openwork lace with a scarlet ribbon tied at her waist, and her hair is done up beneath a wide-brimmed straw French sailor hat with a silk band in matching scarlet. He wants to say he was wrong. The address he has is wrong. He has no idea where Henry is. But her eyes are bright with expectation. It is not for him. There's no going back.

"I haven't seen that," he says, nodding at her dress, though he realizes its appropriateness for where they are headed.

She looks down at herself and raises her face with a faintly puzzled expression, as if she hasn't seen it either. She opens her mouth to speak but doesn't know what to say.

"You look beautiful," he says, and even he hears the sadness in his own voice.

She clearly doesn't, for she brightens at once. "Thank you," she says.

∝

The Raffles Hotel in Hell sits in the desert outside of the Great Metropolis, facing the mountains, blindingly bone-white in the sun. Like its progenitor in Singapore, it is done in French Renaissance-cum-tropics style but on a vast scale, with six stories of arched and ornamented windows growing narrower and narrower as they ascend toward the hipped and balustraded roof until, in Hell's version, on the top layer, they become federal prison slits, though with scrolled finials. At most of the thousands of those windows along the hotel's half-mile front façade, the guests press their faces against the glass. Many of them were colonial empire builders, and they are sealed, cooking, in their suites and are serenaded endlessly by Satan's cockroaches singing "Rule Britannia" to the Dutch and "Deutschland Über Alles" to the Brits and "Het Wilhelmus" to the Germans and so forth.

There are some who are condemned to roam the hotel, though that group slowly changes over time. These denizens often linger on the wide veranda beside the front entrance. They sit on sulfur-soggy rattan furniture and drink caustic gin slings, many of the men in claret-stained linen suits and many of the women in lingerie dresses not unlike Anne's, but dingy and smelling of semen from encounters they cannot remember. Old, imperialist-white-man punkah wallahs stand nearby fanning the hot air over everyone with thin, burningly weary arms. There is no shade. The sun drills into every corner of the place, on all four sides at once. And there is a bar-lounge featuring all the stand-up comics of Hell— which is, it should be clear by now, tantamount to all the stand-up comics who have ever lived and died—and presently headlining Jerry Seinfeld. The audiences are plucked temporarily from the sealed rooms and inevitably find themselves even less amused by the comics than they have been by the singing cockroaches.

It is in front of this hotel that Dick Nixon roars up in the Fleetwood, trailing a vortex of desert dust, and fishtails to a stop. All along the veranda, the arrival draws attention. For instance, Jefferson Davis, wearing a long black dress with a fan-front bodice and pagoda sleeves and with a black shawl over his head in hopes of eluding capture, ceases swatting Abraham Lincoln's hand from his knee, and he and Abe, whose linen suit is stained with blood, look toward the car. And the tiny, waist-cinched Gibson Girl in the far corner—Agnes Gonxha Bojaxhiu, known in her mortal life as Mother Teresa—and the florid-faced, high-collared professional snark, Christopher Hitchens, separate their lips, having felt compelled for quite some time to neck, and they wipe hard and yuckingly at their mouths. She squints to see who might emerge from the car, while Hitchens, with her attention diverted, quietly swoops up what's left of Teresa's gin, downs it, and replaces the glass in front of her.

Anne and Hatcher step from the backseat of the Cadillac. They go up the steps, aware of all the attentive faces, both of them nodding slightly in the same reflex, got-no-time-thanks-for-noticing way that earthly queen and news anchor learned to affect with the public. They push through the wide front doors and into a brutally bright lobby lit by the sun pouring down a six-story atrium.

They pause, shield their eyes, and move to the registration desk, where Sally Sue Plunkett, former front-desk girl at the Motel 6 in Des Moines, Iowa, known behind her back as Surly Sally, is hating this job as much as she did that one. At the approach of these two, she lowers her face and fiddles with a dozen brass keys, representing recent departures for other quarters of Hell.

Hatcher and Anne arrive and stand shoulder to shoulder before this early fortyish woman with curly hair the color of an Iowa corn-fed beef-steak. They wait a beat or two, but the woman is not looking up.

"Miss," Hatcher says.

Sally is arranging the keys in a circle.

"Can you help us?" Hatcher says.

Sally opens the circle at the bottom and makes the outline of a straight, long hairdo of the sort she always wanted.

Anne slams her hand on the counter.

Sally jumps and raises her face snarling. "What the fuck do you want?" she says.

Hatcher lifts his powder-blue tie at her.

She clearly recognizes it but simply glowers, saying nothing more.

Hatcher says, "We're here to see Henry...I'm not sure how he'd be known here. Henry Tudor. Or Henry VIII."

Anne quickly adds, "By the Grace of God, King of England and France, Defender of the Faith, Lord of Ireland."

Sally shoots Anne another what-the-fuck look. "He's not in his room," she says.

"You know this from your head?" Anne says.

"What of it?" Sally says.

"Do you know where he is?" Hatcher says.

"Yes," Sally says, but no more.

Hatcher puffs. Basic interrogatives. Elemental interviewing. He didn't think he'd have to jump through that hoop with a clerk at the front desk. He attributes this to Hell, though in truth, he would have had to do this with her in Des Moines as well. "*Where* is he?" he says.

"He went in to catch the Seinfeld," Sally says, nodding across the lobby.

Hatcher turns and follows the nod to the door of the **Ass in a Sling Lounge**.

"Henry is mine," Sally says. "I plan to marry him." And her head instantly falls off, disappearing behind the desk with a thud on the floor.

Hatcher and Anne pull away from the front desk and move across the floor toward the lounge. He can feel her seething. He cares about Anne and wants to say something reassuring, but this is all too strange and complicated for that. It is enough that he's brought her here.

They step in at the back of the lounge. The room is dark and filled with cigarette smoke and the dim shapes of denizens from the hotel. At the far end of the room is a klieg-lit Jerry Seinfeld on a tiny stage, the familiar, wryly conspiratorial smile in that long, narrow face held there by willpower, getting a little trembly around the edges. Because the place is utterly silent except for a scattering of deep smoker's coughs. It is a silence that Hatcher can instantly sense has not been broken at all. They are not between guffaws here. Seinfeld hasn't elicited so much as a snicker. He is dying up there.

But he goes on. "Have you noticed? Everyone seems to be here in Hell. What's up with that? I ran into my sweet little Aunt Rachel the other day. She always had a good word for everyone, even for my Aunt Sophie, who had hairs growing out of her chin and encouraged her Pekinese to chase the neighborhood kid in the wheelchair as he rolled by, the way the big dogs in the street would chase cars. Aunt Sophie is in Hell, of course. Too bad her dog isn't. I saw her out on the Parkway last week. She was on all fours running alongside Stephen Hawking and barking at his wheels. But Aunt Rachel—who also had hairs growing out of her chin, come to think of it—so chin hairs are either irrelevant in Hell or really really crucial—but chin hairs notwithstanding, Aunt Rachel was sweet as can be. I'd go to her house for lunch and I'd try to leave the end crust of my hot dog bun, which was hard as a brick. She always bought out-of-date buns at the day-old store. How do you get into the stale bread and donut business anyway? What makes you think of that? Maybe it's that certain kind of underachiever kid we all know. See, he's content to eat hard bun ends. So he has a childhood epiphany at the dinner table. He picks this thing up to gnaw on and he looks at it and he goes—someday I can do this. But Aunt Rachel would see me scooting the end of my bun away and she'd say, 'Don't you know there are starving children in the world who'd be happy to have that? Clean up your plate.' So I'd say, 'Then by all means, let's get an envelope and mail this thing to some kid who'd appreciate it.' And Aunt Rachel would just roll her eyes. She was that sweet. But there she was the other day, over at the Lake of Fire with her shoes off and her feet turning the color of a boiling lobster from the hot sand. So I say to her, 'Aunt Rachel. What are you doing here?' And she says, 'It was all your fault. I let you waste food.' It's bad enough I'm in Hell. I've got to feel guilty on top of it? And what good is guilt down here anyway? What's going to happen? I'm going to go to Hell? Well, I hate to say it, but look around. And about Aunt Sophie's Pekinese . Yitzchak. You'd think *he'd* be here, wouldn't you? You know some dogs are just made for Hell. But have you seen any dogs? There's not one. I think it's because they always cleaned up their plates. You ever see a dog leave a shred of food behind? And cat poop is their favorite. Right at the top of the doggie nutritional pyramid. Just ahead of snotty tissue. The Recommended Daily Allowance of cat poop for a dog is 225 grams. That's the size of a Burger King Double Whopper. And it's especially desirable if the poop's been buried in the yard for a while. Day-old is fine with them. Month-old? Not a problem. It's like vintages to them. Oh, here's an impressive little calico poop from May. And this April tabby has a splendid bouquet. And they eat it all up. Every morsel. That's why they're in Heaven. If I had my life to live all over again, I'd eat cat poop at every opportunity. And I wouldn't leave a bit on my plate."

All through this, at every beat when a laugh was possible, Seinfeld paused ever so slightly, the stand-up's subtle elbow in the ribs of his audience. But the room has remained absolutely silent, save for the coughing and an occasional hawking of a phlegmy throat. This time, though, Seinfeld draws out the pause. He looks around, blinking in the light, and he waits and waits. Anne, meanwhile, has been peering into the darkness, looking for Henry. Hatcher thinks the act is over, and he has to decide whether to stay or to go when these two reunite, which will be torture either way.

But Seinfeld resumes, in the same monologist's bright tone, "See, what I'm thinking is, we always misunderstood religion. All the religions of the world were, in fact, just these great big objects of performance art. Like going to Lincoln Center or the Met. So whatever religions knew about the universe, it was all metaphor. But how we all ended up here is that we've got this irresistible urge to turn metaphor into dogma. Like we read *Huckleberry Finn* and we become Twainists and we go, Every year you've got to lash some logs together and float down a river or you'll end up in Hell. And if you *don't* do the river thing, if, for instance, you've read *Moby Dick* and you're a Melvillean and you think to save your soul you've got to go fishing every Sunday instead of floating on a raft, then I'm going to hate your infidel ass. And you're going to hate mine. And if I don't have a religion? Well, I've got the antidogma dogma going and I'll hate your ass anyway. That's why we're all in Hell. And speaking of asses, I'm working mine off here with second-rate material while you just work the loogies out of your fucking throats."

Instantly, someone from the darkness shouts, in a thick British upper-class accent, "You can't say 'fuck'." And a heavy glass ashtray flies into the spotlight and catches Seinfeld on the left temple. He staggers back and another ashtray hits him bloodily in the nose. A dozen more ashtrays fly at him and he covers his head with his arms and he turns and staggers off the stage and disappears into the darkness.

The lights come up. The crowd stirs and rises—all men in morning dress—and they flow around Hatcher and Anne muttering "Rhubarb, rhubarb, rhubarb." Anne studies the faces going by, and Hatcher is watching her watching them when the crowd thins and she shifts her gaze and her eyes widen and she stiffens. Hatcher looks. Two men are dawdling up from the front table, talking to each other. They are both dressed in iron-gray, single-breasted cutaways with pearl-gray vests and silk top hats, which they are patting into place. They are moving this way. One of the men is slender and narrow-faced and is wearing a black patch on his right eye. The other man, hobbling painfully, is vast and thick-necked and red-faced, and in spite of the fact that his specially tailored vest and coat could hold at least three of the eye-patched man, the fat man still threatens to burst from them. And though he is clean-shaven except for a small mustache with waxed twists at the end, and though the reddish-gold hair that has just disappeared under his hat is parted in the middle and lacquered with Wildroot, it is clearly Henry.

This is not the slender, strapping young Henry of Anne's girlhood. Or even the notably expanding Henry of their marriage. This is the bloated and syphilitic end-of-his-life Henry that Anne, wide-eyed, is seeing now. Satan is not exactly known for never closing a door without opening a window, but Hatcher understands the primary torture here will be for Anne and Henry, and this will be a benefit for him. *Let them both suffer* a voice somewhere in him says. Hisses, really. And Hatcher feels light. He feels he can just bound out the door and go sit on the veranda and cross his legs and sip a gin sling and stare contentedly into the desert. And the drink will taste very good, while these two rancorously finish with each other, for all eternity.

Henry and the other man are upon them. As soon as the king sees Anne, his face bloats in a smile that is instantly lost in the folds of chin and cheek. He cries, "My once mistress, once friend, my once wife, once betrayer—or was it I who betrayed you?—my once joy, once torment, have you found me in Hell to torment me truly now so as to have your righteous revenge? For yes, I betrayed you, and to understand that betrayal is hell heaped upon Hell, my once wife. How's that pretty throat? I'm sorry to allude thus now to your final wound, a wound I ordered, it is true, a wound I later conjured before my mind's eye many a time as if it was our first fuck, and I am sorry to allude to that as well, but I find in this place that I cannot choose my own words and I cannot leave from speaking, except when I am listening to comedy that is not comedy at all and that leads me to yearn anew for my axman so that I might silence these solitary jesters who come before me, but I cannot find an ax when I need it, I can only find, as I listen to them, rotten pustulous things in the back of my throat, which surely rise from these poxed and cankered legs of mine, the legs that ruined me. O my legs, my once queen, my later queens had to deal with them, but at least you were spared the burden of my pus." And all these words rush from Henry as if in a single breath, and he still does not pause but turns his face to his companion and moves seamlessly from pus to command. "Sir Francis, my dear Vicar of Hell, take this man to the veranda and provide him with drink, I must have a word now with this once inadequate womb before me, this slut, this girl-yielding cunt, though the girl she yielded had quite a reign, as I've heard, a greater reign than mine, they say." And Henry begins to quake even as he talks on and the man called Francis has Hatcher by the elbow and Hatcher is happy to go, for the rancor soars now on strongly beating wings.

And so Hatcher crosses the lobby of the Raffles Hotel with Sir Francis Bryan, Henry VIII's longtime drinking buddy and master of the henchmen, poet and roving diplomat, sent to the Pope when Henry first sought a Catholic divorce for the sake of Anne, and a master of jousting as well, which is how he lost his eye. The eye is unrestored in the afterlife, though Bryan has come to see that as an ironic benefit—one less body part to hurt when it is time for everything to hurt. "Sir Francis Bryan, at your service," he says.

"Hatcher McCord, presently at your disposal."

Bryan chuckles. "He will do that."

"You're his vicar?"

"Lay vicar, I must stress."

They step out onto the veranda. A table at the front is being vacated by an elderly couple in hunting jodhpurs who stagger off the veranda and out into the desert, clutching at their stomachs.

"Some people shouldn't drink," Bryan says.

The two men move toward the vacated table, and on the way, Hatcher is surprised to find Bill and Hillary Clinton sitting together.

She's staring vacantly out to the mountains. Bill's mouth is drawn down sadly and he's stirring his gin with the tip of a forefinger. Hatcher stops beside them. Hillary ignores him, but Bill looks up from the slow swirling of his drink. "Hello, Hatcher," he says.

"Mr. President. You escaped the hotel room."

Bill Clinton tilts his head very slightly in the direction of his wife. "She showed up."

"I see."

"It seems it was her I was waiting for all the time."

Hatcher doesn't ask the question that instantly springs to mind. Hillary is still quietly averting her eyes from both men. Bill licks the tip of his finger and returns to stirring his drink with it.

Hatcher looks toward Sir Francis Bryan, who is claiming the vacated table. Hatcher is about to move off, but he is still a journalist, after all, and he must ask the question.

"Mr. President," Hatcher says.

Bill looks up.

"Did you drop your pants when she arrived?"

Bill smiles. "It surprised the hell out of her."

And with this, though she continues to look out across the desert as if she were alone, Hillary extends her hand and lays it on Bill's arm. Bill looks at his wife's hand, and Hatcher cannot see—but rightly assumes—the faint lingering of the smile.

Hatcher heads off to the table, and he knows that the tender gesture he just saw pass between the presidential couple will, in this place, only lead to larger pain and mutual torture. But in the freedom of his mind, Hatcher holds the gesture apart from all that will surely follow, and he too smiles a small smile.

He sits down with Sir Francis Bryan, and they are both facing the mountains. A monocled and mutton-chopped white man, a former Governor-General of India, wearing a dhoti overhung with a starvation-distended belly, instantly arrives with a tray and two gin slings, which he puts on the table. He bows deeply and backs away.

Hatcher nudges the drink away with his knuckle, shuddering at what the Raffles Hell might be substituting for the cherry brandy. He looks at Bryan, who has taken off his top hat and placed it on the table in preparation for his drink. Bryan is a bald man with the fringe of his hair close-cropped and with a faintly aquiline nose. He swirls the dingy ice in his gin sling, takes out the swizzle stick, and compulsively downs about a third of it in one gulp. He turns away to gag and cough and spit. When he has recovered somewhat and is sitting upright again, his hand still clutching at his burning throat, he glances at Hatcher's drink, untouched, migrated toward the center of the table, and he looks at Hatcher and narrows his good eye while raising the eyebrow over his bad one.

"Some people shouldn't drink, vicar," Hatcher says.

"I thought we all must, in this place," Bryan says.

Hatcher understands. His freedom of mind is showing, but he does not take up the gin. "It's torture for me not to touch the stuff," Hatcher says.

This satisfies Bryan. "Of course," he says. "You know how I came to that nickname with His Majesty?"

"Not because you were of holy demeanor."

Bryan laughs. "Indeed not. His Majesty and I and Thomas Wyatt and Nicholas Carew and George Boleyn and some others were great companions and full of jests, and His Majesty once asked me as we sat at dinner, 'What sort of sin is it to ruin the mother and then the daughter?' And I replied, 'Sire, it is a sin like that of eating a hen first and its chick afterwards.' The King laughed loud and heartily at this and said when he was done, 'Well, you certainly are my vicar of Hell.' And we all laughed louder and more heartily still, and the name was imprinted upon me thereafter."

Hatcher has been forcing his mind away from what might be happening inside the hotel. But what he has heard in this anecdote is the power of sexual privilege possessed by the truly prominent and wealthy, experienced to some extent by Hatcher in his earthly demi-celebrity, but not nearly as strongly as by kings and billionaires. He turns his mind to the likelihood that he will leave this place alone today.

And inside Sir Francis Bryan: *Sire, Geoffrey Plantagenet married Matilda, granddaughter of William the Conqueror, and they begat Henry II, King of England, who begat Eleanor Plantagenet, who married Alphonso IX, King of Castile, who begat Eleanor of Castile, who married Edward I, King of England, who begat Edward II, King of England, who begat Edward III, King of England, who begat Thomas of Woodstock, Duke of Gloucester, who begat Lady Anne Plantagenet, who married Sir William Bourchier, who begat Sir John Bourchier, who begat Sir Humphrey Bourchier, who begat Lady Margaret Bourchier, who married Sir Thomas Bryan, who begat me. My blood is the blood of four kings of England and our Norman conqueror, and through them my blood is the blood of Charlemagne the Great and Clovis the Great and Boadicea, our great Briton queen who rose up against the Romans before there was an England. And yet it is the way of mortal life that I was destined to end up merely playing the role of Your Majesty's jester and go-between instead of you playing mine. But Hell is oddly comforting in that regard, sire, for it appears that we are all of us here, all the seed of all the righteous, world-bestriding, wealth-wielding, nation-making, genocidal men since the beginning of time. And they themselves are all here too. And as for the drastic differences of privilege and power that make human beings so inescapably and arbitrarily unequal for that brief mortal span? Those differences are mere surface ornamentations now to our eternal suffering. Thus sayeth your vicar, sire.*

Unbeknownst to Sir Francis Bryan—and unnoticed by Hatcher—Bryan's own seed, twelve begats along, sits a few tables over, a man with an aquiline nose writing in a Moleskine sketchbook with a Waterman 494 sterling silver Bay Leaf fountain pen. With Noodler's Antietam red ink, flexing the Waterman's nib, thickening the downstrokes, the man writes: "It has been long enough." And he pauses. He turns and says to his table companion, a bent and liver-spotted Graham Greene, whose mind has wandered in the few seconds of silence that has fallen between them, "What were we saying?" Greene is thinking about the Nobel Prize never won and about the lost bougainvillea and white-washed villa walls in Anacapri. He turns his face to the man with the Waterman, which is still poised in the air. "I don't remember," says Greene. "Neither do I," says the other man.

And a few tables down, Hatcher thinks: *It has been long enough.* And Hatcher pardons himself and rises and turns and heads for the door into the hotel. As he passes the Clintons, Bill catches him by the arm, stops him. "She's wrong about how I won," Bill says.

"I'm not wrong," Hillary says, still scowling out at the desert.

"You're wrong," Bill says.

Hillary looks at Hatcher. "It's not about smart. It's not about articulate. You look at your working masses, the ones who really decide, and those qualities are actually disadvantages. He won because of the cheeseburger. Cheeseburger, cheeseburger, cheeseburger. He famously ate cheeseburgers. He ate fucking cheeseburgers for them all. He ate cheeseburgers and they believed in him."

Bill says, "It's not that which goeth into the mouth empowereth a man but that which cometh out. It was me. My words. Me."

"All those cows died for you," Hillary says.

Hatcher gently pulls Bill's hand off his arm and he moves away. At the door, he hesitates. But he pushes through into the lobby, and up ahead he sees the hurried veering of people around low-to-the-floor activity lit brightly in the center of the atrium, activity he does not recognize at first glance from this distance. There is no rubbernecking in Hell. Suffering splashes over, spills out, spreads immediate contagion, and everyone knows just to look the other way and move quickly on. But Hatcher hurries quickly toward the pain, for he begins to see what it is.

It is Henry lying massively on his back, his pants off, his legs bare. Anne is crouched beside him, on the far side. She is stripped down to a handkerchief-linen teddy. But in spite of Hatcher's impulse to expect the worst in this realm, it is instantly clear to him that what's happening here is not about sex. He draws near and can see that Henry's massive legs are haphazardly swathed in strips torn from Anne's tea dress. She is quickly, quakingly wrapping the last bit of it around Henry's right calf. The pieces of the dress are going dark from a profuse flow of fluid.

Hatcher stops before the two of them. He can see between the bandages that Henry's legs are a patchwork of ulcerous sores pumping out a thick, striated mixture of blood and pus. Anne is panting and moaning and wrapping, and her hands are smeared with Henry's fluids and she can't keep up, this last bit of her dress is in place and his suppuration goes on and on and she cries out and she lifts upright on her knees and she strips off the teddy and she is naked, utterly naked, and she begins tearing at the linen, pulling it into strips and bending down to Henry again and wrapping his legs.

And Henry's head is to the side, and his eyes are closed, and he is singing, softly but clearly, the song he wrote as a young man, the one Anne thought she heard a few nights ago outside the window. "Pastime with good company, I . . ." and he hums across the word no one can think of in Hell and he sings on ". . . and shall until I die. Company is good and ill, but every man has his free will."

And Anne is moaning, fumbling with the cloth, unable to go on. Hatcher hesitates. But now he circles Henry's legs to the other side and goes down on his knees next to Anne. He bends to her ear. "You'll never keep up," he says, gently. "It's Hell, my darling. You've done what you can."

She looks at Hatcher, her eyes wide, restless, uncomprehending. Her hands are trembling furiously, full of the strips of her teddy. Hatcher takes the end of one of the strips and pulls at it. Her hand is clenched tight, and he tugs the cloth firmly and she lets it go. He turns to Henry and finds a patch of his ulcerous flesh, oozing profusely, on the side of his calf. Hatcher lifts the leg and the pus flows over his hands and he lays the strip of cloth on Henry's leg and he wraps it around and half around once more and that's as far as it goes, and he eases the leg back down, and Henry sings "Pastime with good company I . . . sway . . . I swoon . . . I swisser my swatter . . ." and Hatcher turns to Anne, who is staring at him, steadily. When his eyes meet hers, she glances at Henry's legs and back to him. He takes the end of another strip of cloth and pulls gently at it. Anne holds on tight. "I caused this," she says.

"No you didn't," Hatcher says.

"Not in life. Now, I mean," she says and her voice is steady.

"It's what we all do," he says.

"He cut off my head," she says.

"Yes," he says.

"Let's go," she says.

Hatcher's chest pumps up instantly full at this and lifts him and he cups her elbow and they stand up together. He strips off his suit coat and puts it around her shoulders, pulling the coat to, buttoning the buttons so it will cover her loins, and she bends into him and they move around Henry, and before they are halfway across the lobby floor, all of Henry's bodily fluids have lifted away from them and flown back to the former king.

∝

At the Cadillac, Hatcher opens the back door and sees the camcorder lying in the shadows. The pretext that got him here was to do an interview with Henry, and he utterly forgot. With a mind free to think and plan for itself, he realizes this absorption with his own agenda is a grave danger. He reaches in and takes the camera, and he turns to Anne. "I still have this to do," he says. "I'll have Dick take you home."

She nods.

He guides her into the backseat and tucks his suit coat around her. "Can you do this alone?" he says.

"Yes," she says. "Thank you."

He moves to the driver window. Inside, Dick Nixon has fallen asleep, his head sharply angled to the side, as if his neck is broken. Hatcher raps at the window. Nixon snaps upright, and he rolls down the window. "I am not a crook," he says.

"Mr. President. Are you awake?"

"I am not asleep," he says.

But Hatcher isn't sure. He waits a few moments while Nixon blinks and looks around and then back to Hatcher.

"Are you ready to go?" Nixon says, clearly focusing now.

Hatcher says, "Take Anne back to the apartment and return here for me."

Nixon nods and rolls up his window and the motor instantly revs to life and the tires dig wildly and the Cadillac shoots off, leaving Hatcher standing in a cloud of desert dust.

He's glad Nixon will hurry. He doesn't look forward to lingering here.

Hatcher turns and goes up onto the veranda and through the doors. Ahead in the foyer, Henry is still on the floor. Hatcher approaches. Sir Francis is holding Henry's pants and waiting for the king to stand up. But Henry sits, fully reconstituted but unable or unmotivated to rise. This interview doesn't have to be good. Hatcher just has to have something for the record. He crouches before Henry and looks at the former king through the viewfinder. Henry seems not quite aware of where he is. But Hatcher thinks his state might actually be a good thing for this feature. He starts the camera.

"Sire, I'm here at the request of Beelzebub himself and for the sake of Our Supreme Ruler's own TV station. I have one question to ask you, and you can talk for as long as you wish. Why do you think you're here?"

In spite of what he has just gone through and his post-reconstitution daze, Henry begins speaking at once. That and the seeming indirection of Henry's words make Hatcher think that he really hasn't heard the question, "O meats, my abundant meats, I miss your pleasures deeply in this afterlife, where once, in life, I had faith to believe I would have you yet again, my lamb and ox, my rabbit and deer, my partridge and pea-cock and pig, my hedgehog and heron and swan, my bustard and black-bird and hart, all of you and more. Those of you who ran free, I hoped to hunt you down, to set a pack of hounds of Heaven or Hell, whichever was my fate, upon a great rangale of red deer, or by my own hand with longbow or crossbow to pierce the heart of a wild boar, and then to sit at table and tear your sweet flesh with my hands and eat. I am ravenous yet for my meats, but I know now that every arrow shot, every dog unleashed, every hawk set forth, every side pierced and throat cut and belly sliced open, I should have done them all in the name of God, I should have made each a sacrifice to the God who was hungrier even than I, and if I had done so, perhaps I would be eating meat now in Heaven instead of starving in this meatless Hell."

Henry looks straight into the camera and wipes the back of his hand heavily across his mouth. He heard the question. And Hatcher thinks of cheeseburgers, of Bill Clinton winning his presidency by eating cheese-burgers, and how sad a figure he is in Hell without them.

∝

Hatcher finds a far corner of the veranda and puts his back to every-one, wanting to be alone now, making his mind go blank, feeling he knows very little about himself, really, and not expecting to learn much from the one wife left to see. But he will try. He will try. He does not have long to wait before he hears the rush of the Fleetwood and the grinding of its brakes. He goes to the car and gives Dick Nixon Naomi's address.

Naomi Jean Delancey—later Naomi Jean Rutherford, the not-yet-forty trophy widow of a didn't-quite-get-to-seventy shipping magnate, and then, three years later, the third and final wife of network anchorman Hatcher McCord—lives in a warren of alleyways next to the Central Power Station, the narrow passages twisting and always dark from the shadow of the buildings and from the vast, lolloping, pitch-black plumes of power station smoke, the natural color of Naomi's hair in her prime. Hatcher moves along a shabby-carpeted inner corridor redolent of piss, its darkness broken only by three widely spaced bare lightbulbs hanging from the ceiling on fraying cords. As he passes, doors open and women peek out, haggard faces with hair disarranged, but disarranged, Hatcher realizes, from former haute coiffure. He knows this neighborhood. This is the Central Park West of Hell. High society. Naomi adored her Chanel and Dolce&Gabbana and also her Lagerfeld and Westwood and Mugler. She adored the Dakota. She adored Hatcher, mostly, though he came to feel that was largely for the opportunity he gave her to radiate at parties, in her couture, in the presence of Hatcher's most important news subjects, presidents and ambassadors and movies stars and kings.

He is at her door now. He hesitates. Can she shed any light on his sins? She was no trophy at all to him—he knew she was smart—and she knew he knew it and she clearly appreciated that, but she finally did leave him a couple of years before he died and it wasn't for another man, but for the death of him he can't remember why, exactly. They ran down, she didn't like his cigars, she was too smart, finally, to stay interested in primarily glittering in her clothes. Something. They both had affairs—that may have been it, but it was quietly mutual, and surely that was a symptom, not a cause. She was dating a U.S. Senator when Hatcher's heart stopped, and he wonders if she came to the funeral—he wonders if any of his wives came to his funeral.

He knocks on the door. There is no answer, but he thinks he hears sounds inside, a vague scuffling. He knocks again. He can hear nothing now. Nevertheless—perhaps this comes with a free mind in Hell—he senses her just on the other side of the door. He could be wrong. He knocks again.

"Naomi?" he says.

Naomi is, indeed, on the other side of the door, terrified, always, about being in Hell, particularly because she is wearing a polka-dot pink summer dress with an elastic waist that would have cost twenty-five bucks out of the Sears catalog in the year she married the anchorman, and she has not been able to take this dress off for many risings and settings of the sun and the pink has turned mostly gray now from the grit which settles through the ceiling and walls from the power station. At the sound of Hatcher's voice, which she recognizes at once, she lays her forehead quietly against the door: *Not like this. I am not who I am, wearing this. I am not who I am in the company of the person who has just now slipped into the bedroom. But in this dress, in this society, I am this other. And I was another I, once. I chose myself and dressed me in myself and I was I. Though I had to make do at times. My sweet young self, debuting in the Continental Ballroom in the Peabody Hotel in Memphis in a white satin gown that Mama and her Memphis-Main-Street tailor and I figured out, and it had a strapless bodice and a ruched midriff and lace appliques, and I put the me of that dress on and I melted perfectly into the floor in a full court bow before the society of my mama's boozy peroxide-bleached friends and the U of M's boozy sun-bleached Sigma Chis and the Citadel boys in their uniforms and buzz cuts, and it wasn't until later that I realized how not-me I was, though in a way that was me at nineteen, I suppose, but I was more me later, much more, I was me in a power-black Thierry Mugler with wide shoulders and collar points and flame cutouts and a waist corseted down to breathlessness, to breathless dominating otherness, and I was in the society of the people who ran the world. The world. The world that came and went. And now I am I in another world. I am forever a cheap cotton dress the color of Pepto-Bismol.*

Hatcher knocks again. "Naomi? It's Hatcher," he says.

"I'm not here," she says.

"Then let me in and I'll wait for you," he says.

"I don't expect to show up ever again," she says.

"Is there someone else I can talk to?"

"You don't want to."

"I do."

"Believe me, you don't."

"It's your worst about me I'm looking to hear," he says.

"It's worse than that," she says.

"I don't care," he says. There is a long pause. "It's Hell," he says, trying to put the shrug that just went through his upper body into his voice.

He feels exhausted. He leans his head against the door. Though he sensed her here even before she spoke, he does not sense that his right temple is lying against the exact spot on the door where, inside, the center of Naomi's forehead, just below the hairline, is touching.

They both stand there like that in silence for a time. Finally, he says once more, softly, "Naomi?"

And she opens the door.

He sees her dingy polka dots and knows how she is suffering.

She sees his powder-blue tie, and her hands claw at the bodice of her Sears dress, bunching the cloth, pulling it toward her throat. "So," she says. "You're still traveling in the right circles."

This time she can see his shrug.

They don't move. She is blocking the doorway with her body.

"May I?" he says.

She looks around her, a little uncomprehending. She turns her body to the side.

He steps in. She closes the door.

There are a few pieces of tattered Goodwill-bargain-back-room furniture and there are a thousand roaches crowding along the baseboards like the people in the streets. As soon as Hatcher sees them, they all stop, rise up on their back feet, and look in his direction. He knows how they must torture Naomi. He lifts his tie at them. The whole throng of roaches sings out in unison, "Cheese it! The cops!" and they instantly flow into the join of the baseboard at the floor and vanish.

Naomi has watched this and turns her face to him. Her eyes—still darkly beautiful in spite of the age lines—are wide with surprise.

"The right circles," Hatcher says.

"Thank you," Naomi says.

She closes the door, and the two stand awkwardly where they are.

"Can we talk for a few minutes?" Hatcher says, looking toward the little setting of spring-sprung and stained metallic tweed sectionals. He misses Naomi's eyes sliding away to the bedroom door and then back again.

"Okay, Hatcher," she says, and he doesn't catch how she says his name just loudly enough to be heard in the other room. "You can stay for a few minutes."

They sit at right angles on a two-piece sectional sofa, with a matching chair at the other angle. Naomi has her arms crossed over her chest, covering as much of her dress as possible, her hands laid on her throat as if she were about to choke herself.

Hatcher is trying to shape the question in his head and wondering if he should begin with an apology. The apology set Mary Ellen off from the beginning, though he learned some things along the way.

But before he can speak, Naomi says, "You freaked me out today."

Hatcher's mind starts to sputter. He feared this with Mary Ellen and at least that bit turned out okay. But Deborah saw the news broadcast.

"How . . . ?" she says, and then she hesitates, searching for a way to finish the question. Her hands descend from her throat and squeeze at the polka dot dress. And some other part of her finishes the question in a way her conscious mind, which she has been consulting, cannot. "How can you be you in just your skin?" she says.

Neither of them knows what to say next.

And then Hatcher's mother bursts in from the bedroom. "You freaked me out too!" she cries, based on no consultation at all with her conscious mind. "What a pathetic dick. Dangling there like that. Your father's was so much more interesting. How could I ever have thought you perfect?"

His mother is standing straddle-legged before him now in her terry cloth robe, her arms akimbo, her storm-cloud gray eyes looming before him, and Hatcher has lifted his feet onto the seat cushion and is crawling his butt up the back of the sectional couch and wishing the sulfur rain was pouring down outside so he could escape into it.

His mother cries, "I haven't seen that part of you since your were a little boy in the bathtub. But what a wretched disappointment. Of course, I should have known. You're in Hell. I'm here too, and it's all your fault. You were supposed to be perfect. I thought you were. Because I knew I was. You were a reflection of me. But you weren't perfect after all, and so you turned this into my destiny as well. And it was probably because of your miserable dick. You could never be worthy of *this*."

Hatcher has reached the top of the sectional and as his mother grabs each side of her robe and begins to rip it open, he falls backward off the couch. He quickly rights himself and stays low, scrambling along the floor on hands and knees, making straight for the door. Down here he sees he's being observed from along the baseboard by a row of cockroaches shaking their heads in disgust.

"Come here," his mother is calling. "Face facts."

And he's up on his feet and wrenching the door open and careening down the dim hallway. And not for a moment does he think this was planned by Satan. Even the Prince of Darkness isn't wickedly smart enough to have invented this torture for him. He could only have done this to himself.

∝

When Hatcher bursts from the downstairs door of Naomi's tenement, the alley is black with night. He pulls up sharply. When did this happen? There was no sudden silence, no trembling city, no solar boom of sundown. For night to have come when he was windowless and deeply distracted and he missed its coming, that should be closer to the expectations he brought with him from life, should provide a little bit of wistful relief, but in fact this sneaky night he has rushed into scares the shit out of him. He gropes along, bumping into passing bodies, seeing very little, just a dull red glow at a distant turning of the alley, and a heavy shoulder thumps against him and Hatcher says "Sorry," and he does not remember ever saying that before in the jostling crowds in Hell. He's been saying it a great deal lately, he realizes, but to the women from his life. Except to his mother. Not to his mother. He shivers now and he rushes faster away from the tenement, and a bump and sorry and another bump and sorry again, and he turns at the red glow and there's another red glow at another turning ahead, and for all the sorrying he has sorried since he knew he had a free mind, he has done nothing, he's afraid, to earn his way out of Hell, if such a thing is even possible, and Mary Ellen's voice trails through him *you'd be perfectly happy if you were the only person in the world* and maybe his sin was as simple and as basic as that, maybe taking that one step back to report on the people of the world was the same as not being among them, he was in a separate universe, one that was superior in its separateness, and he was happy being alone there, and you were supposed to take women to you and so he slept with them and he married them, and you were supposed to make children and he did, but maybe all that was simply to avoid facing the truth about himself, maybe he went through the motions of connection—fucking and marrying and fathering—so he could live with his precious aloneness and not feel damned. But he was damned. He was damned indeed. And maybe it's why we're all of us damned, he thinks. Maybe a mother can join herself to an image of a son until she can't, and a man can join with a woman till he can't, and the *can't* part of it means it's not doing the mother or the husband any good anymore, for herself, for himself, for his arrogantly self-absorbed self, you just want to get away from the other and you'll stop at nothing till you do. And with all this thinking, he finally thinks none of it sounds right, none of it, and he thinks maybe the thinking itself is the problem, your mind is free but it's free all to itself, you're never more alone than in your mind. Only in our bodies are we together. Maybe it's all about the *thereness*, there's nothing more *there* than every moment lived in these tortured bodies in Hell, and there was nothing more *there* than the life we led in these bodies on earth. And the problem was, we tried to think it out when we should have just held on to each other, and if we held on, all the pain and all the pleasure was the same, it was all one complex thing that was okay, that was really okay, but it was okay only if you took all of life in through your senses and stayed in the moment, holding on. But even as he thinks this now, even as he thinks of the alternatives to thinking because he thinks the problem is thinking, it feels untrue in just the same way again. And he thinks: *Fuck me.* And he thinks: *Fuck you. Fuck us all.* And he is at the corner and the glow isn't there anymore and he turns and far ahead is another turning and the glow is there, the red glow from the power station in the center of the Great Metropolis in Hell, and he thumps into a dark figure, a man's chest as hard as the boulders in the mountains, and Hatcher says "Sorry" and he puts his hands out and grabs the figure at the arms, as if he's afraid he'll knock him down, when in fact it's Hatcher who reels, whose air thumps out of him, and he gasps another sorry and he means it, and he veers away, veers away and moves on.

And behind Hatcher, the hard-chested man stands where he has stopped. He realizes it was Hatcher McCord, anchorman for the *Evening News from Hell*, he has just bumped into. But that is of no consequence to him. He pauses for his own leisurely purpose. He reaches into the inside pocket of his tweed sport coat with suede elbow patches, and he pulls out a pack of Luckies. He pops one up, puts it into his mouth, and snaps his fingers. A flame licks up from the tip of his thumb, and he lights his cigarette, his face briefly illuminated, still the faintly jowly face of an overreaching politician who could only manage three percent in the Iowa caucus. Satan waves the flame away from his thumb and blows a careful series of smoke rings, invisible in the dark. And he looks around him, seeing everything: *I move unseen among you, my children, and I can smell you as you stumble along in the dark. You stink of your humanity, and it is very good, for so very many of you are perfect: you despise yourselves, and yet at the same time you are full of self-righteousness. And you do not recognize your own shape-shifting sanctimony. You do not understand it is the life force of your anger and your hatred and your violence and your aloofness and your indifference and your pride and your intolerance. And the ones among you who seem not to be perfectly mine, who are wise enough to know that self-righteousness is my life's breath inside you all, you roil with anger at my perfect ones, you hate them, and you take comfort in your superiority to them, and so, in your wisdom, you become perfect as well. You all have my sweet stink about you. In your own unique ways you are all perfect, my darlings.*

Satan takes a last drag on his Lucky Strike. He blows the smoke out his nose and his ears, and he flips the butt, its glowing red end tumbling through the dark.

∝

After Hatcher finds his way to the Fleetwood and then to his apartment, the night is thick upon the Great Metropolis, and in the back alleys of Hatcher's neighborhood, the weepings and thrashings are muted behind closed doors. Even the Hoppers' door is shut and the snarking is soft, and he opens his own door to a dark apartment. He steps in but does not speak. He feels his heart begin to pound in his throat. He should have come straight home with Anne after she broke away from Henry. Fuck the interview. Fuck his cover story for Beelzefuckingbub. At least he should have rushed here after filming Henry, instead of tracking down still another wife. His wives are dead to him. Anne is the woman he wishes to be part of. And he staggers at the thought. What's the angle in that for his alleged self-absorption? Though it's impossible to be alone while in Hell, he is free to acknowledge the desire to be. And yet.

He gropes in the air for the pull cord to the hanging bulb. He finds it. Pulls. The room dimly presents itself, and he turns his eyes toward the kitchen table. He recoils. Her body sits there in her green velvet Tudor dress and her neck is ragged along the axman's line and her head is gone. He looks at the tabletop. It's not there. He looks around the room. Nothing. Her body is motionless, her hands crossed in her lap.

"Anne?" he calls.

There is no answer.

"Darling, I'm home," he cries.

No answer.

He draws near to her body. He leans forward and picks up one of her hands. It's warm. He bends to it and kisses the knuckle on her middle finger. The hand does not respond. He puts it gently back on top of the other one.

Anne's head is not on the floor near the chair or under the table. It is not on the kitchen counters or in any of the cabinets. He sweeps around their little living room and it is not on or beside or behind their couch, their chairs. He is doing this systematically, going outward from the body that had to find its sightless way to the kitchen table.

He goes into the bedroom, which is dark. The TV is off. He shuffles his feet gently to the end table and turns on the lamp. Her head is no-where to be seen, not on the floor, not on the bed, nowhere. Hatcher moves to the closet and opens the door.

And he is looking directly into Anne's face. Her head sits on the shelf. Her great, dark eyes are full of tears. Her cheeks are wet.

"Anne," he says.

She closes her eyes and squeezes out a rush of tears.

"I wanted to do more," she says.

"I know," Hatcher says.

"I wanted to be more," she says.

Hatcher lifts his hand, reaches out, draws the back of his fingers across her wet cheek.

"Motherfucker," she says, softly, sadly. She closes her eyes. And after a moment, she says, "Mea culpa. Mea maxima culpa."

And Hatcher makes a loose fist and thumps his right forearm on his chest. And again. And a third time. On her behalf. And his own.

After this, Anne lets Hatcher put her back together and she takes off her gown and he takes off his suit and they lie beside each other naked in the bed in the dark, and on this night they do not even try to have sex. They lie listening to each other breathe until they both, surprisingly, fall asleep.

∝

And the next day, from Broadcast Central in the Great Metropolis where all rivers converge, all storms make a beeline, all the levees look a little fragile, and the anchorman, Hatcher McCord, is looking particularly fragile tonight, the *Evening News from Hell* is well under way. Cerberus has rabies again and is raging his way through Everland, the densely occupied molester estate on the edge of the city. Michael Jackson and Gary Glitter inadvertently swap severed penises in the aftermath. Bobby Fischer, though always playing white, is mated for the thousandth straight time by a chess-playing computer named Hadassah. The Chicago Cubs lose.

And with the news finished and the preview aired of the Barbara Walters-Oprah Winfrey boiling-tar-pit naked wrestling match and with the eventual end of a classic This-Is-What-You-Want-But-You-Can't-Have-It-In-Hell commercial—a long, relooping version of the McDonald's commercial where everything the Hamburglar touches turns into a McDonald's Cheeseburger, including his own head—Hatcher goes to a live remote with the new entertainment reporter, who thinks he has finally remembered his own name, although only the first one. Hatcher improvises the lead-in: "Now, at the site of the free Power to the Denizens Concert, our only partially brain-dead entertainment editor is reporting live. Take it away, Nick."

The entertainment reporter formerly known as Mineisbigger and now known as Nick, still unable to remove his terrorist mask, is standing in a bright light with his microphone. Behind him is a welter of bodies lunging and fighting and slashing—there are obviously sharp weapons involved because there are pulsing plumes of blood everywhere and flying body parts—and beyond, distantly, is the stage, also crowded with a brawling mob. Nick says, "Yes, Hatcher, the vast crowd here at the free concert finally couldn't contain its anger. They've listened for several hours to the All Star Polka Choir made up of Presley and Hendrix, Joplin and Marley and Jagger, Cobain and Shakur and Lennon and Madonna, Houston and Selena and Coolio and Morrison—both Morrisons—all dressed in lederhosen and Alpine hats and playing accordions and fighting among themselves about who will sing lead vocals on such classics as 'The Polish Sausage Polka' and 'In Heaven There Is No Beer.' As you can see, the crowd couldn't take it anymore, the flash point being Madonna's version of 'Who Stole the Kishka.' But Hatcher, I've got an exclusive interview here and some hot news about the *Evening News from Hell*."

And with this, Nick looks off camera and makes a motion, and Robert Redford, dressed in white shirt, dark suit, and bright red tie and beaming a fixed smile that makes the deep creases of his face seem somehow boyish, steps into frame beside Nick.

Nick says, "Bob. I understand you're in negotiations to become the new face of the *Evening News from Hell*."

Redford nods gravely. "That's right, Nick. I've always wanted to play a network anchorman."

And now the crowd behind them swells, and a tsunami of blood and body parts washes over Nick and Bob and the camera.

Hatcher, with absolute, suave anchorman cool, says, "Thanks, Nick. That was Nick Mineisbigger reporting live, though presently decomposed, from the Power to the Denizens Concert."

And Hatcher goes on with the news and he finishes the news and not once does he give his bosses even a tiny, corner-of-the-mouth twitch of a clue that he is concerned about his job. Nor does he show even a brief eye-sparkle of a clue that he is pleased to be thus torturing Satan and Beelzebub over their inability to read their subjects' minds. And he is surprised at himself over his inner calm. He does not want to give up this chair. But he knows whatever is afoot may end up with him keeping his job and thereby torturing Nick and Bob primarily and him only if he lets it. But any way it plays out, he is ready to accept that and go on.

∞

So when he steps out of Broadcast Center, he finds Judas Iscariot crouching near the door. The ex-apostle leaps up at the sight of him and rushes forward. He talks very fast, his hands fluttering before him. "You're here. That's good. At last. I had a hard journey to get to you and it'll be a hard journey back and there's not much time, there's no time, man, time is slipping into the future. I figured I owe you this. But just for you, you know, off the record, deep background. You understand? Deep throat stuff. So here's the deal. I heard the screaming in the night. A bunch of the other signs had already occurred and that was a big one. I heard a screaming in the night sky and there was just one more thing and that one thing came to pass today. You know what finally shows up at the Automat? Lamb chops. Lamb chops. Behind every little door. Every last one of them is lamb chops. Only three nickels away. And nobody's buying. We're all crying, 'Sacrifice! Sacrifice!' And we all just sit there fasting when there's finally meat, and we're all righteous at last. Then one dumb shit—Thomas, of course—he puts his three nickels in and we're all going, Don't do it, man, but he's doing it, and we're white-knuckled and gritting our teeth, but it's okay, the righteous thing is only about us, see, about each one of us individually. Thomas can fuck himself over if he wants to, but that's just him and it's not about us. So Thomas sits down and he starts eating, and after a moment he jumps up and he cries out, 'It's tofu! It's just tofu!' Like he would know tofu, right? Like they can make a whole lamb chop out of tofu, right? I don't think so. I don't think so. And so the old boys tear him apart. Limb from limb. And they throw his parts into the street. And that's according to the prophecy as well. Trust me. So it's going to happen. Soon. Real soon. He's coming back for us. Come to the Automat and look at those chops and turn away quick. Maybe you can hitch a ride out of here.'

Judas starts backing away. He says, "I'm sure of it this time. We're all of us sure."

And he vanishes into the crowd.

∝

Hatcher gets the car just in case he can figure out the wild seething inside himself. He sits in the backseat and does not yet tell Dick Nixon where to go. He's unsure why he's hesitating. Judas's druggie persona, perhaps. His own unworthiness. But I'm still a newsman, he tells himself. I need to step back and observe and report. I at least should go watch the others being taken away from here, even if I am not worthy. Or watch as they watch and nothing happens. Even for that. Judas seems to believe deeply that a Harrowing is imminent. As, apparently, do the others from the Book. And all the prophets were wild-talking eccentrics. Judas is from that tradition. Trying to think it out, Hatcher finds himself panting and restless in the backseat of the Fleetwood. *I have to stop thinking*, he thinks. *I have to stay in the moment and in this body and I have to act.*

He leans forward and is about to knock on the partition and head for the corner of Peachtree Way and Lucky Street. But if it's true. If this turns out to be true. He can't go without Anne. He knocks on the partition. It slides back. And Hatcher directs Dick Nixon to swing briefly by the apartment. The car leaps forward. Hatcher still seethes inside, but now from an intense awareness that he is heading in the opposite direction from a way out of Hell. He turns his eyes to the window. He watches the flying, broken bodies as he cuts a great thumping swath through all the damned in order to get Anne and escape.

∝

Hatcher dashes up the circular stairs and along the corridor and he's embarrassed to wonder this, but he wonders if he's running along this corridor for the last time, for the last time ever, and he sees the Hoppers' door is open, up ahead, and he does not want to slow down for anything and he pushes his legs, and this time they stay strong and quick even as they pass the Hopper apartment. But in his peripheral vision he sees the couple sitting there in their overstuffed chairs. And he stops himself. And he steps back, and he stands in their doorway.

Peggy is saying to Howard, "It's true. It's always been true. From the first time on. You never tell me you . . ." And she catches on the word.

Howard says, "There you are. How can I be expected to tell you something that you can't even remember yourself what it is."

"Pardon me," Hatcher says.

The two Hopper faces turn to him.

"You should come with me . . ." Hatcher begins.

"Oh we couldn't do that," Peggy says instantly.

"No," says Howard. "Thanks, but never."

"We can't get up," she says.

"Not at all, ever," he says.

"This is where we are," she says.

"Right here," he says.

"I understand," Hatcher says and he moves to his own door and he's surprised at himself over the impulse he just followed and he tells himself there's nothing he can do for anyone else. He can do only for Anne now, if this is real, the best he can do is for Anne and for himself.

He touches the knob to his door. And the Hoppers suddenly terrify him: Will Anne go?

He steps in.

Anne is near the bedroom door, her back to him. Her head is on. That's good. She is wearing still another Edwardian tea dress. That's not good.

"Anne," he says.

She turns to him and she consciously puts on a little smile. She has something to say and he is very glad he has something to say first, and because it is the only way to keep her, he leaps fully into faith. It's real, he tells himself. It's going to happen.

"Wouldn't it be better," he says, "to leave Hell altogether, with me?"

She looks at him wide-eyed, as if the axman has just been called off. "Can you do this?" she says.

"Yes," he says. "But we have to go now."

She does not say another word but is beside him and they are rushing along the corridor, perhaps for the last time.

∝

And once again Hatcher finds himself grateful for Richard M. Nixon's merciless driving. But as they plow into the writers' neighborhood, the impulse that put Hatcher in the Hoppers' doorway comes upon him again, with an even stronger moral imperative. He does not think it out but leans forward and knocks on the partition and directs Nixon to an address nearby, and they soon pull up in front of a grimy brick tenement. He tells Nixon to keep the engine running.

"Where are you going?" Anne says, the first audible words she's spoken since the apartment.

"I owe somebody something," he says.

When they first got in the car, Hatcher told Anne where they were heading and with only a nod of recognition to him she began to quietly pray for absolution, softly pounding her chest in mea culpas. Now, as he opens the door, she says, "Do we have time?"

"Yes," he says, though, in fact, he's not so sure. But he does owe Beatrice.

He dashes for the entrance, realizing this is the street-side front of the tenement that Virgil led him to a few nights ago. He pushes through the door and he staggers to a stop and he has to consciously adjust his center of gravity to keep from falling down. The whole place is tilted to the left, and mounting before him is a wide staircase paneled in William and Mary oak and with an iron banister with grillwork of ormolu garlands, and a steam horn sounds in the distance and a ship's bell is ringing and a multitude of voices are crying out, wordlessly, far off, and a smell of salt water fills his head and he feels a chill on his feet—a rare sensation in Hell—and he looks down and water is spreading out from the deep shadows on either side of him, lapping at his shoes, and Hatcher knows this is the Grand Staircase in the first class section of the *Titanic*. No, he cries to himself. This is, in fact, a typical, cheap illusion, a movie setting in Hell of the Grand Staircase in the first class section of the *Titanic*.

Nevertheless, Hatcher's first reflex is to run. To turn around and bolt from this place and get back in the car instantly and take off. But he tells himself not to play the game. He doesn't have to play the game. He has a mind that is free. But movie illusion or not, this is the only staircase he has to work with, so he dashes up, past the bronze cherub holding a lamp, onto the landing and up another flight, a vast cut-glass dome above, and he is not looking closely but he can see that all of it—banister and paneling, cherub and stairs and dome—are covered in a thin coat of green slime and he's smelling mold now and rot and he goes up to the fourth floor and cuts down the corridor.

The carpet is thicker under his feet and the walls are paneled oak but it's the same layout as the film noir tenement, and the corridor—the whole tenement—lurches a bit and his own free and independent brain isn't doing a fucking thing to make this all go away and he sprints for the door at the far end and he arrives, breathless not from the sprint but from a rising fear as cold as the North Atlantic. If he gets sucked into this little Hell game, he may miss the Harrowing. The door says 4D. There are vague rustling sounds inside. He knocks. The sounds stop but no one is coming to the door and no one is talking and he calls out, "Beatrice." And there is silence.

He does not have time for this and so he tries the knob on the door and it turns and he pushes in. Not to a first class state room on the *Titanic* but to the same seedy tenement apartment 4D as before, with the same sagging couch in the center of the floor. But the room is tilting. It is full of the smell of the ocean. And on the couch is Beatrice, naked, on her back, her legs hooked over the shoulders of the dingy-white naked marble body of Publius Vergilius Maro, also known as Virgil, who continues quietly to pound away Roman style at Dante's girlfriend.

They do not stop their fucking but they do both turn their faces to Hatcher. The faces show no trace of pleasure, of course.

Hatcher finds himself compelled to shoot his cuffs. He pats his pockets, but he can find no smokes, so he simply squares his shoulders and says, "I thought we had an understanding, doll. But what do you expect in this crazy world? I don't blame you. You figured you had a chance for happiness and you took it. Me, I can only offer you a long shot. The longest of long shots. A way out of Hell. So here I am. But you have to make up your mind now. Because chances have a way of disappearing on you. Especially when the odds are long."

Hatcher hears himself. He's not saying this quite the way he expected.

But Beatrice seems to get it. And she doesn't. "I can't go with you," she says, her voice quaking from the boffing being administered by Virgil. "I can't. The ship's going down and all the lifeboats have sailed."

From behind the closed closet door, where last time a Renaissance Pope imitated a police car siren, Celine Dion begins to sing, "My heart will go on."

And Hatcher backs out of the room, closes the door, turns, and takes one stride and another down the hallway, passing the door behind which, if he stopped to listen, he could hear the beating of his own heart.

∝

When the Fleetwood takes the sharp left turn as Peachtree Avenue Street Street turns into Peachtree Way on the run up to the corner of Lucky Street, Hatcher opens the driver compartment partition and sees the back of a crowd up ahead. Before they pound through the candidates for Heaven, he tells Dick Nixon to pull over to the curb and stop.

Hatcher grabs Anne's hand and throws the door open and they slide out of the car and move quickly up the street. The back of the crowd is all cloaks and animal skins and sackcloth tunics, and as Anne and Hatcher approach, they can hear a clamorous bleating as if from a vast drove of goats, and Hatcher thinks of animal sacrifice—this has been an ongoing theme of the past few days—and he wonders if there are actual goats now being slaughtered to buy the Old Ones a way out of Hell.

But that's not it at all. He and Anne reach the back of the crowd and start pushing their way through the rough cloth and the skins and the fetid stink of ancient bodies, and it's instantly clear that the sounds are coming from the Old Ones themselves. They are huddling hard together and lifting their faces and crying like goats, and it's tough pushing through, the bodies are thick and unyielding, and Hatcher vaguely remembers a Bible verse about the Son of God coming in glory and separating the sheep from the goats, and Hatcher feels in his chest and in his arms and in his throat and behind his eyes a powerful swelling of belief. He believes. Yes. He believes that a way out of Hell is just ahead, and he presses in front of Anne and holds her hand even more tightly and he puts his shoulder heavily ahead of him and he pushes hard and they are moving, the bodies are sliding aside, parting like the sea, and he and Anne break at last from the drove and into an empty stretch of street, empty but for half a dozen bearded men in tunics cracking whips and driving back this crowd found unworthy of Heaven.

One of these goatherders cocks his head in surprise at seeing these two Moderns fly out of the crowd, but he does not try to stop them. And Hatcher and Anne rush on toward another crowd of the Old Ones in front the Automat. Hands are shooting up and waving and falling and shooting up again and the cries of this crowd are "Me!" and "Me!" and "Save me Lord!" and "I am worthy!" and "I am worthier!" and "I am worthiest!" and a body—a very old man in a bear skin—comes hurtling out of the crowd and he is carried along toward the drove of the damned faster than his feet are moving, and he is already bleating, and another body flies out, a woman in a long dark robe and with a scarf covering her face and her goat voice is thin and full of vibrato.

Hatcher and Anne reach this other crowd and stop. Hatcher looks around for Judas. He is about to call for him, but Anne pulls at Hatcher's hand. "Over there," she says, and she draws him to a thickening of this crowd, and the two of them stretch up and they look and they can barely see the very top of a liver-brown head of hair in the empty center of this crowd—distance is being kept from this man—and the man cries in a loud voice, "Ye fed me!" and another man's voice yelps in joy, and the loud voice cries, "Go ye forth to the Chariot of Fire," and Hatcher can see the tops of the heads of the far part of the inner circle of the crowd open for the chosen one making his way toward Lucky Street. And then

the loud-voiced man cries, "Ye gave me no meat!" and another voice wails
in anguish but the wail quickly morphs into a goat cry and a body flies
from the crowd and back down Peachtree Way. Hatcher and Anne look
at each other with the same thought. Are we hearing the voice of the
Son of God? Even as they think this, Hatcher also thinks the voice sounds
faintly familiar and he tries to remember some moment, somewhere in
his earthly life—did he have a miraculous encounter?—did he actually
hear the voice of Jesus in his life?

"We have to get closer," Anne says.

Hatcher takes her hand and steps before her and reaches forward to
try to part the bodies in front of him. But he feels Anne's hand wrench
out of his. He looks back to her.

"You need both hands," she says. "I'll be right behind you."

He nods and begins to turn.

"Wait," she says, wrenching him around. "This," she says and she
lays her hand on his tie.

He looks down. The powder-blue shocks him like blood from an
unexpected wound.

He grabs at the knot at his throat and tears it open, untangles the
tie, and stuffs it in his jacket pocket. "I never did . . . ," he says. "I never
even . . . I never."

"That's for Him to decide," Anne says.

They look at each other and then in unison they strike their chests
three times in the mea culpa.

And Hatcher is ripping and shoving and punching and pounding his
way through the crowd, one layer, and another, and once, he glances
quickly back and Anne is there, shoving away, and another goat is iden-
tified up ahead, and another sheep—Hatcher is no longer listening to
the words of the Son of God, not till he can stand before Him, not till
then, but he knows the work of winnowing is going on and Hatcher plays

over a little litany of I-nevers as he struggles with the crowd, which still has many layers before him.

Now a voice nearby says, "He's on the move," and another takes it up, louder, "He's moving!" and another shouts, "He's done! He's leaving!" and then a wild chorus of "No, Lord!" and "Take me too, Lord!" and even "I'm more faithful than that camel turd you just chose!" and even "You'll understand if you just read my book!"

And the crowd surges and carries Hatcher along and he senses his crowd skills are still good, though they let him slide out of the flow, not with it, but that might be okay, to get to the margin of the crowd and head for the Chariot on his own, but as he feels he needs to make a move to the side and get out, he reaches back for Anne and grabs a hairy man's arm—Esau's, in fact—which pulls away, and Hatcher looks over his shoulder and Anne is nowhere in sight and the crowd is surging forward and she is nowhere and he calls out "Anne!" but the sound is lost in the din of the men all around him.

She's gone. She's lost to him for now. So he presses toward the edge of the crowd, angling through the seams, and as he moves readily, he thinks that maybe it's for the best, surely it's for the best, surely she will have a better chance if she's not in the company of Satan's anchorman, but surely he has a chance too, surely the Son of God has seen into his heart in Hell and knows he's been trying to separate himself from the spirit of the place, and didn't he do something pretty good against the odds down here? Hatcher thinks so, but he can't remember now, he can't quite remember what it was, exactly, but surely God knows, surely God can see into his heart, can hear his mind.

And as Hatcher pops out of the crowd and tumbles to the pavement and skids along, it comes to him in a terrible rush: if Satan can't hear our thoughts, can't read our deep inner selves, maybe God can't either. Maybe it takes meat.

He scrambles to his feet. The crowd is surging past him and around the corner. He is standing before the door to the Automat. But it's a little late, he knows, to go in and effectively not buy a lamb chop. He takes a step toward the corner and his hands are at his sides and suddenly his left palm feels a complicated metal something. He lifts the hand and finds two car keys on a looped key ring with a heavy bronze fob engraved DICK. Nixon is disappearing around the corner up ahead.

Hatcher follows and he turns the corner and the crowd thickens and he keeps his head down and works hard to push through, and then, as with the first crowd, he breaks into a sudden sizable empty space. Another line of whip wielders is trying to keep order, and again they ignore a Modern coming through, and ahead are the chosen, queuing up. Dick Nixon is hustling toward the line, and now Hatcher feels something, a large physical presence, and he stops and turns his face and looks up, and across the street, sitting in the rubble-filled lot at the corner, looming high over everyone, is a vast, primitive rocket ship, an amped-up Wernher-von-Braun-model V-2 with an extra pair of wings mid-body and portholes all along the side and a door at its base, a narrow door— though wider than the eye of a needle—with a metal staircase ascending to it.

At the bottom of the stairs leading to the door of the rocket, his back to Hatcher, is a man in a flowing crimson robe, the man with the liver-brown hair, which hangs down to his shoulders, the man of the loud voice, the Son of God, guiding the line of the chosen, placing a gentle hand in the small of each passing back. Including Dick Nixon, who enters even as Hatcher watches. Nixon made it. Hatcher tries in his mind to put Jesus with this machine, and again he looks up the long, gray body of the rocket. It is streaked in black, as if with reentry scorch marks. And up near the nose of the rocket is a word in Old German typeface, running at right angles to the ground. Hatcher angles his head to the side to read it: 𝕳𝖊𝖗𝖆𝖚𝖘𝖋𝖔𝖗𝖉𝖊𝖗𝖊𝖗. He can't figure the word out by cognates. But he thinks perhaps this is the hand of Wernher von Braun showing itself. And if von Braun is in Heaven making chariots of fire and if Dick Nixon has made it as well, then maybe Hatcher and Anne have a chance.

Anne. Hatcher snaps his head back toward the crowd, but he can see only bearded male faces. He takes a step in that direction. He is about to call out her name. Then suddenly she's beside him.

"We can approach our savior together," she says.

"Anne." He tries to take her in his arms, but she presses away with her hands stiffly on his chest.

"There'll be time for that later," she says.

He pulls back his hands.

"You have to get me out first," she says.

"You may do better going to Him alone," he says.

Her brow furrows as she contemplates that.

"I'll follow," he says.

They turn toward the Chariot of Fire. Jesus is bouncing along the line now, coming in this direction, his exhortations not quite audible from this distance. He has one hand on his beard as he rushes along. His hair does not flow with his steps. Something seems off.

"It's all about our minds, man," a voice says behind Hatcher. "It's all about the human mind."

Hatcher turns. It's Judas.

"What we remember," Judas says in a rush. "What we forget. We choose those things for ourselves and it all has to do with what we want. And what we fear. You know? What drives us. What we gotta have. What we're scared shitless to have. And they can always fuck with us, the powers that be. The powers can fuck with us because of our minds."

"Isn't He going to take you?" Hatcher says.

Judas ignores the question and he talks ever faster. "See, our minds aren't really us. They've got their own agendas. If you can keep your head when all about you are losing theirs and blaming it on you, yours is the Earth and everything that's in it, small is the number of people who see with their eyes and think with their minds, if only we could pluck out our brains and see only with our eyes."

And now behind Hatcher he can hear the voice of Jesus, that familiar voice. "Hurry, my lambs. Hurry. It's time."

And Judas says with sudden, calm slowness, "I've been through this before, man. I remember now."

Jesus's voice is very close and Hatcher begins to turn.

"A hundred times," Judas says.

And Hatcher is facing Jesus, who is very near. And the liver-brown hair is a bad wig. And the beard is fake. Plastic, hooked loosely over the ears. And inside the overlarge robe is a small, dark-skinned man with a smarmy voice that Hatcher remembers from a special exposé they ran on the alleged fakery and fraud of his miracle services. Jesus is a creepy little self-denominated evangelist named Benny Hinn. Hinn looks Hatcher in the eyes and he says, "Come along, my lamb. Come along." He looks at Anne. "You too, my dear." And Hinn turns and he starts pushing the people at the back of the line, and the chosen ones stampede forward for the rocket ship.

"It's a different dude each time," Judas says softly. He's standing at Hatcher's side now. "They always seem to actually believe they're the Man Himself while it's going on."

Hatcher looks toward Anne, who is standing in absolute stillness at his other side, her mouth tight and drawn down.

And so the three remain for a while. Hatcher McCord, Anne Boleyn, and Judas Iscariot watch as the last of Benny Hinn's chosen lambs enter the door of the rocket, and then Hinn himself steps in, turning at last in the doorway to make the sign of the cross before disappearing into the darkness and closing the door behind him. Faces appear at the portholes. One of them is Dick Nixon. One of them is Carl Crispin, whose fingers appear beside his chin and wiggle farewell to Hatcher. Then the rocket begins to make a deep, thunderous sound, and it begins to tremble, and great plumes of black smoke roll from its exhaust port, and the rocket begins slowly to lift from the ground, and it rises and rises and the three observers tilt their heads far back watching and Judas says, "We need to go inside now. Quickly."

And Judas leads them along Lucky Street toward the Automat, even as all the other petitioners for Heaven are surging past them toward the place where the rocket took off. But at the corner, Hatcher stops and turns and looks up at the distant Chariot of Fire with flaming exhaust, soaring high into the powder-blue sky of Hell, glinting in the faux sunlight. And suddenly the rocket vanishes in a vast, booming bloom of white smoke.

"Hurry," Judas says, pulling at Hatcher's arm, and the two of them and Anne push through the Automat's doors just in time to avoid the dense, flaming rain of metal shards and body parts falling all over the neighborhood.

∝

Through it all, through the clanking and thwacking and squinching in the street and through the cries of the Old Ones left behind as they stagger in from the carnage outside, Hatcher and Anne and Judas sit at a back table and say nothing. Eventually, after all the pieces of the *Herausforderer* and its passengers have finished falling from the sky, and after the ones who were not chosen and who escaped maiming and burying under body and rocket parts out there are sobbing and wailing inside the Automat, Anne turns to Hatcher and says, "I have to go now."

Hatcher does not look at her. He knows where she must go.

He feels the Cadillac's keys in his pocket. He knows Dick Nixon is scattered around the neighborhood.

"I'll take you," he says softly.

And they rise.

Judas reaches up and touches Hatcher on the arm. "I'm sorry, man," he says.

Hatcher wants to say something encouraging to Judas, and he begins, "The next time . . ." but he realizes he doesn't know how to finish the sentence. Perhaps with ". . . it will really be him and he'll know you."

But before Hatcher can find those words, Judas finishes the sentence himself. ". . . I will have forgotten all about this."

Hatcher nods. "Good luck," he says.

"I hope you'll remember not to believe me," Judas says.

"If I do, I'll remind you," Hatcher says.

"Deal," Judas says, and he makes a fist and extends it. Hatcher does too, and they bump knuckles. When he pulls away, Anne is already waiting at the door.

Hatcher crosses the floor, and Anne is looking outside. He stops beside her and she touches the door handle.

"Wait," Hatcher says. She pulls her hand back. He reaches into his pocket and pulls out his powder-blue tie. He lifts his collar, puts the tie around his neck, lowers the collar, and ties a perfect Windsor knot, growing sadder with each wrap and tuck.

∝

Driving the Cadillac Fleetwood, his head is full of the red and black flying bugs named after the word that is never spoken in Hell, known in some places as honeymoon flies. Hatcher can't even remember when it was or why he was there, but he was driving a rental car along a highway in northern Florida, and it was the season for these bugs, and when they reach maturity, each finds a spouse and the two of them begin to fuck and they never stop. They attach their bodies, male and female, at the tip and then spend the rest of their lives together fucking. Awake or asleep, sitting on fence posts or flying around, they never stop fucking. And even when the male dies, which, in the natural course of events, always occurs first, the two of them continue to stay sexually connected, the female dragging the dead male's body around until she lays her eggs. And in their season, they fill the skies, flying around in coupled pairs. You drive your car to a constant ping and ping and ping, the sound of death as you hit and crush the mated couples. And there is no way to avoid this. For you to live, for you to move from one place to another, means you are the bringer of death, the creator of thousands of tragic romances.

It's the sound Hatcher thinks of now as he drives the Fleetwood. He is driving fast to a constant thump and thump and thump of bodies in the crowded streets of the Great Metropolis. He has to drive fast. He's sorry to be visiting pain on these denizens, but if it wasn't him it would be something else. And he knows now that this is it forever. Nothing makes any difference about anything and you always get put back together to be hurt some more, so he might as well get this over with quickly. He must, in fact. Because inside the car there is only silence. Anne is sitting next to him, and they have nothing to say to each other, and this simple silence now between them as he drives her to the Raffles Hotel to be with Henry for eternity, this silence is the worst torture he has experienced in Hell. If only he could die and have her drag him around forever. Or if they could die together in a rush of wind and a car horn and they could just stay dead, coupled and dead.

And the constant thumping stops. They are free of the city streets and rushing through the desert and the Raffles is not far. And the closer they get to Henry, the more deeply this ongoing mystery settles into Hatcher: why, in life and in afterlife, we seek—we even create—the things that hurt us.

"It won't be long," he says.

She does not answer.

He glances at her. She is looking out the side window at the passing wasteland.

"This is the last of us," he says, softly.

In his periphery he can tell that she turns her face toward him. But he does not look at her. He cannot bear to do that right now.

"Yes," she says.

"He cut off your head," Hatcher says, even more softly.

"Yes."

Then why are you his forever? That's what Hatcher wants to know. But he cannot summon the energy to ask.

She waits a long while before she speaks. "Will says that April is the cruelest month."

"That was a later guy who said that. He's here too, somewhere."

Anne shrugs this off. If she can shrug off Henry taking her head, she can shrug off Shakespeare stealing a good line.

Anne is silent for a moment, and then she says, "Well, January is the kindest month. The world outside you fits what's inside. It's a grim place, the world, but it's the world. At least you're not a freak, at least you're part of it."

And that's all Anne and Hatcher say to each other.

Hatcher turns in at the road to the Raffles and he drives them fast in a great whirlwind of dust, but as the vast white sprawl of the hotel looms ahead, he throttles back drastically, he squeezes the steering wheel hard, and he slows the car down. He regrets this now. He wishes he could have just walked out of the Automat and left her there to do what she had to do but not be a fucking part of it, not carry her here himself. But as soon as he wishes this, he knows there was a deeper imperative. He had to seek out the thing that hurts him most.

And they are stopped in front of the Raffles Hotel and the engine is off and the car is ticking and the blood on the grill and on the windshield is flying away and Anne is opening her door and she is getting out of the car and he is sitting behind the wheel and he is not moving and though there is no death in Hell, he knows that he and Anne are dead to each other.

∝

Hatcher drives back to the city and parks the Fleetwood on Peachtree Way in the same spot where Dick Nixon parked for the Harrowing. Hatcher gets out and walks toward Lucky Street. The rubble of body parts and rocket parts is all gone. The street is full of the bearded men in tunics and animal skins pressing on to nowhere. Hatcher barely looks before him as he walks but instead scans the passing crowd. He reaches the Automat and takes a few steps beyond so he can see up and down both streets. He does not notice Judas Iscariot, who is curled up and sleeping fitfully in the bright sun in the center of the rubble-strewn lot from whence the Fiery Chariot departed, remembering the event of this afternoon now as his Master's first return and a promise made to come back for him someday. But Hatcher isn't looking for Judas.

He goes back and pushes through the revolving door into the Automat. The writers' groups have resumed. The group in the Catholic Bible but not the mainstream one, the prolific Gnostics, the Old Ones whose books were lost, Judith taking criticism from a severed head, and all the rest. The New Testament writers who got dumped or lost. But that's not Judas with his back to the door. It's the man Hatcher is looking for. Hatcher approaches the table, and Dick Nixon is explaining to Festus and Silas and Rhoda how his mother was a saint, a Quaker saint, and so was his wife, and how if he'd been at the foot of the cross, he wouldn't have run away, and Hatcher puts his hand on Nixon's shoulder.

The ex-president looks up. Hatcher reaches down and puts the Cadillac keys in Nixon's hand. Nixon looks at them.

"You are not a crook," Hatcher says.

"I know," Nixon says.

∝

Hatcher climbs the circular iron staircase toward his apartment, slowly, the heaviness of his legs already upon him, the outer curving of the stairs blinding him over and over as he circles toward and away and toward the full, overhead sunlight in the alleyway. The day seems to be rewinding itself. It seemed later, earlier. And he emerges into the corridor. He stops. Ahead is the Hoppers' closed door. And then his own empty apartment. Anne is gone. He stuffs his hands into his coat pockets, even before he realizes he's searching for something. One last thing left undone before he's ready to face the rest of eternity. In an inner pocket he finds the list of addresses.

He has seen his wives. And his mother. He shivers again at that. He has seen Beatrice and Virgil, whose delusional preoccupation when he came for them was of no consequence. They had no worse a fate than he, going down with a faux *Titanic* while having what surely turned out to be unsatisfying sex. He has not seen Dante, who, however, is a professional liar. Hatcher has no interest in finding him now. But there is one more address, from the impulse to help Sylvia Beach. The address of the former companion she longs for, Adrienne Monnier. She should have this.

Hatcher turns away from his apartment now and descends the stairs and rushes along the alleyway and into Grand Peachtree Parkway. He turns toward the neighborhood of the writers. He makes good time along the margin of the crowd, as always, until the run of store fronts and apartment stoops begins. He slows down and studies the windows going by and soon he finds himself before a hand-lettered sign: SHAKESPEARE AND COMPANY. He stops. But a single glance inside makes him lay his forehead sadly against the glass. The store is empty. The shelves are bare. Sylvia, like all the other bookstore owners in Hell, has almost instantly gone out of business. He curses himself softly. He secured Adrienne's address but not Sylvia's. He thought he knew how to find her. And in the cursing of himself, Hatcher backs away from the shop and a shoulder bumps him, from the edge of the crowd, and he thinks to go to Adrienne, at least, and tell her that Sylvia is somewhere in the writers' neighborhood, and this leads to more unfocused steps and then another shoulder and another step and he is drawn into the great, onflowing current of the street crowd.

And quickly Hatcher McCord is sucked toward the center, though he finds that he doesn't care. He doesn't have the energy to do it right now, but he knows he can always slide back out when he wants. But at this moment he is wedged front and back and right and left by these four denizens: Isabella Andreini, former actress and member of the Gelosi Commedia dell'Arte troupe of late sixteenth-century Italy; William W. Ross, former Fuller Brush door-to-door salesman of Altadena, California, and the 1948 Western Region Salesman of the Year; Spec 4 Jason Stanley of South Bristol, Maine, and former clerk-typist at the Long Binh base camp about thirty clicks up Highway 1 from Saigon; and Jezebel, former wife of King Ahab of Israel. And this moment happens also to be the very moment that a mid-day sulfurous rain begins.

A flaming spot flashes onto Hatcher's face and he knows what's happening and he has never before been caught in the rain, never, and he tries to move but the crowd implodes and it is too late and another flame on the forehead and a spray of pain, serrated blades, a thousand of them, ripping through his face and his shoulders and his chest and then the drenching of pain, and things slow down, things slow way down, as every cell in his body shreds and dissolves, and he feels each one separately, he could count each cell though they are as great a multitude as the stars and each one is raging as hot as the bright flaring center of a nova. And the four denizens pressed into Hatcher are also dissolving and they flow together, these five, and in the rain you never lose your consciousness and all the bodies dissolving around you are part of your body and your body is part of theirs, and inside Hatcher, even as he is dissolving, a voice speaks: *I am between wives and my ratings are high and I am with a tiny-boned*

woman with dark skin and a black bindi between her eyebrows and we are naked
and she says she did not know who I am she says she never watches the evening
news and outside the window a flare is falling from a guard tower on the perim-
eter somebody is nervous about Charlie and I look at Hoa which means flower and
she has just stepped out of the black silk pantaloons that all the hooch girls wear
and she is no whore she says and I say I know and I rip open my gown and I tear
it from me as I go mad from the scorning of my passion and the eyes of my noble
audience the Grand Duke of Tuscany and his bride grow wide and I am wrapped
tight in a body stocking but their eyes are on me as if I am really naked and she
is naked right there in my Fuller Brush Illustrated Catalog on page six and she
has her hair pulled up and tied in a red ribbon and the very end of the hand-
somely designed unbreakable plastic handle of a number 401 Shower Brush is all
that covers her nipple and just barely and he lays me down beneath an almond
tree and we are naked and we share a quince before we touch I bite and he bites
where I bit and I lick that place where he bit and bite in a new place and we make
our mouths sweet make the very air we breathe from our bodies sweet before we kiss
for the first time and this is before Ahab comes to me and brings his god whose
breath stinks of old blood and if I never leave the almond grove without becoming
the wife of this other man if I marry my own if I marry the body that first holds me
and breathes sweetly and deeply into me then perhaps Baal can save me from the
knock on the door and she has the look I've always wanted to see in a woman's
eyes she has that look even from the first moment and I sit with her on her couch
and our shoulders are touching and she stops on page six and she smiles faintly
and she touches her hair at the back and she orders a number 401 Shower Brush
and she orders a number 386 Flesh Brush and she says its name slowly drawing
the word out Flesh she says I want a Flesh Brush and I say number 386 and I write
down her order and I shake her hand and I leave because I am the fucking Western
Region Salesman of the Year and if I do what I think of doing when my gown is
ripped and is falling at my feet if I take my hands and clutch the body stocking
and dig my fingers deep and I pull it apart and rip it from my body so I can stand
truly naked before the Duke and his bride perhaps I can be fully true at last to

*who I am for I went upon the stage so that I could be naked and I could be seen
and she is naked and we touch and that is the last time and afterwards I don't
know where Hoa has gone and the other hooch girls shrug when I ask about her
and I can only lie on my bunk and watch the flares in the night sky and dream of
me coming home from the lobster boats and she is waiting for me my flower of a
wife and she takes me to the bath and strips me naked and she scrubs the smell of
fish off me with a brush and she takes the tip of her finger and she touches me in
the same spot on my forehead as her bindi and she says that's where all the expe-
riences of your life have gone where you will find everything that you are and we
touch and we touch and though we never say a word about it we both know we
will never do this again but before she leaves she cooks for me she tears the chicken
apart with her hands and she cooks with asafetida and it smells like tar it smells
like Pittsfield when I was young and when everything was new it smells like the
tar from the streets but it tastes wonderful and she is gone*

And in this moment, all the souls in the streets of Hell are indistin-
guishable, they are shimmering primordial puddles that stink of sulfur
and are full of regret, they are full of eternal regret.

∝

A short time later Hatcher finds himself standing in the middle of Grand
Peachtree Parkway, exhausted, achy, dazed, and near him are Isabella
Andreini and William W. Ross and Jason Stanley and Jezebel and they
are likewise exhausted and achy and dazed and these five are conscious
of each other, they look into each other's eyes and then quickly away
again, vaguely aware that there was something between them but they
don't know what, exactly, though Hatcher works at remembering, and
he does, briefly—like remembering a dream upon awaking and then
forgetting it utterly a few moments later—Hatcher briefly remembers
the shared longings, the shared selves, and he thinks he understands, he
thinks it is only in pain that we are all truly connected, and when the
pain ends, we are alone. Utterly alone in our heads. And as soon as he

thinks this, he forgets it. But only in his mind. His hands flex and they remember. The crowd begins slowly to flow forward. His legs move and they remember. The others push among Hatcher and Isabella and William and Jason and Jezebel and the five disperse in the crowd, their bodies separating, their minds and hearts separating. And in their minds it is as if this never happened.

And Hatcher slides across the crowd as it flows onward and he emerges onto the sidewalk in front of empty bookstores. One of them has a sandwich board outside: Hell's Belles Lettres. He is at the alley mouth where Virgil led him to Beatrice. Is this a bookstore that's surviving? He steps to it, but the door is locked and the blind is down. No. Nothing lasts in Hell but the promise of pain. And he lifts his eyes, and there, on the corner on other side of the alley, its red neon sign spewing bright sparks, bright even in the mid-day sunlight, is the establishment called **BURGERS**.

Hatcher snaps straight upright. **BURGERS**.

BURGERS is open for business.

BURGERS.

He crosses the alley mouth and stops and turns and faces the door that leads into the only hamburger joint in Hell. He lifts his hands before him and he looks at them and he flexes them and he looks at the door. He steps to it and puts his hand to the knob and he turns it and he pushes and the door swings open and his legs move. Inside, there is a sizzle in the air, things frying, pungently meaty things, out of sight, and yet the place is empty. He closes the door behind him and he steps farther in. He stands in the center of a linoleum floor full of Formica-top tables, all of it white, achingly white from bright fluorescence overhead. He waits and he realizes there is no way in Hell he is going to figure out what this is about. He just has to move across the floor and through the door before him.

But he waits. He waits and he listens to the faint buzz of the ballasts above him and he realizes that he can no longer hear the perpetual street roar. Grand Peachtree Parkway is just behind him and he can hear nothing but the buzz of the light fixtures and a distant sizzle. And a doorknob rattling. Also behind him. But the knob is not yielding. Hatcher slowly twists around toward the sound, but by the time he can see the front door, whoever was trying to get in is gone.

He turns back to where he now feels strongly he must go. He squares his shoulders. He shoots his cuffs. And laughs just a little at himself for this. And he moves forward. He puts his hand on the knob and he opens the door, and he finds himself in a short, white-walled corridor, with another buzzing fluorescent bulb and another door straight ahead, only a dozen paces away. He does not hesitate. He moves on. Passing on the left is a door marked **WOMEN** and two paces farther, on his right, a door marked **MEN**. There is nothing else. The entrance ahead, he assumes, is into the kitchen.

And he is before it. And still another knob yields to him, though this door feels very heavy as he starts to push, and it is faintly luminous, he sees, and he pushes hard to get it to move and it does, barely, he puts his shoulder against it and it is cool to the touch, it is emanating a coolness onto his face, a sweet coolness, and once the door starts to move, it feels not as heavy and now less heavy still and now actually easy and now the door is so light it feels as if it is opening itself and it swings suddenly wide, carrying him shoulder-forward for a step and then he takes another, just to keep himself from falling, and he rights himself and he stops, and the door thumps heavily closed behind him, and he is standing in a kitchen. A classic, compact, stainless-gleaming, fast-food kitchen with deep fryers and grills and bun toasters and sinks.

And it is air-conditioned. The hamburger grills are sizzling loudly and Hatcher can see the rows of burgers there, and it's real meat—the air is full of the smell of all-beef patties—but there is no heat, there is only a soft undulant coolness all around. And there are no people.

Hatcher steps farther in. "Hello?" he calls.

But there is no answer.

He looks at the burger grill, beside him now. All the patty tops are pink. They have only recently been put there. But even as he watches, all the burgers rise in unison from the grill and rotate themselves in the air and they descend, and they hiss and pop and fry noisily on.

Hatcher lifts his face and breathes deeply into his body the cool conditioned air. Not since he died has he felt this. Not since he died. And he does not let himself think. He calls out once more, "Hello?"

Nothing.

He walks forward and emerges from the kitchen to find himself behind the order counter. Before him are rows of free-standing molded plastic booths in red and yellow. The window posters push Happy Meals and Quarter Pounders with Cheese. The windows themselves are storefront, looking out on the sidewalk of a city street with a glass office building façade directly across the way. Halfway to the front door, a to-go bag with the Golden Arches sits in the middle of a booth table. What Hatcher does not see is another person. Not in the restaurant. Not passing by outside. He steps around the order counter and suddenly senses someone to his right and he looks and he jumps back at a wild head of red hair and a red nose and a broad red mouth and he has been away from his life on earth long enough that it has taken him this brief moment to recognize Ronald McDonald, in yellow jumpsuit and red-and-white-striped shirt, and another brief moment to understand that the clown, though life-sized, is not real. He is molded plastic. He stands watching over the dining area with his right arm extended and his hand cupped, perpetually ready to administer a comradely hug. And suddenly a rich, deep, mellifluous male voice speaks from the general direction of the clown, "Welcome."

Hatcher comes near to Ronald. This is clearly no sentient being. But someone might be watching through the clown from some remote place. Hatcher says, "Hello?'

But Ronald says no more.

"Hello? Anyone there?"

Nothing. No one.

Hatcher looks out into the street. The air in the dining area is cool, the smell of the hamburgers is very good, and the silence feels like his head is lying on a down pillow. What part of Hell is this? And he knows the answer. He knows the answer to that, but he does not let even his deep inner voice speak it.

He moves toward the front doors. When he passes the to-go bag, he can feel it radiating heat. Not like any heat he's felt in these past many risings and settings of the faux sun of Hell, but the heat of putting your feet up on your desk and unloosening your tie and somebody steps in and sits and you talk about the Yankees or the Jets with that heat kissing your fingertips through a bun and sweetly stirring your tongue, and this to-go bag is giving off not only heat but the smell of two all beef patties, special sauce, lettuce, cheese, pickles, onions on a sesame seed bun. And Hatcher stops. And he knows this is for him. He picks up the bag.

He steps into the street. In the air is a hint of ripe peaches. And of coffee brewing. He looks up and down. No people. No cars. No birds, either. The sun is high but it feels mellow on his head. He walks toward the corner, and across the way is an urban park lush with live oaks whose broad limbs wear a dense cloak of Spanish moss.

And he is standing in front of Starbucks. And he steps in. And there is no one. But sitting on the center of the first table to the left of the door is a Venti that he knows—instinctively now—is a Toffee Nut Latte with extra foam. He knows it's for him. He picks it up and it is sweetly warm in his hand, and he steps back outside, and he crosses the street and begins to follow a fieldstone path, and it is rising gently toward the center of the park, and he stops suddenly. He sets his McDonald's to-go bag and his coffee down on a stone, and he steps off the path. There is no grass in Hell. Even at Satan's hunting lodge it was fake. This appears to be real.

The broad, flat, dark green blades of Saint Augustine grass. He kneels down and puts his palms on the ground and it is soft and it yields and the smell of the soil and the real grass well up into him, and he stretches out forward and presses his chest and the side of his face into this living ground. He lies there for a long moment and then slowly rises, and he does not brush himself off but picks up his bag and his cup, and he continues along the curving path up the rise. And at the top is a chair. A familiar chair.

A low-slung Toshiyuki Kita recliner, the "Wink," exactly the same as his reading chair after becoming the anchor of the *Evening News from Hell,* the first thing he bought strictly for himself in his Dakota apartment. He shared that apartment with someone. Someone who wasn't crazy about this chair, but he was, and he bought it. It makes no difference who didn't like it. He approaches the chair slowly, and he touches the twin yellow headrests, which always felt to him like his own two hands clasped comfortably behind his head, and he crouches down and eases onto the chair, settling into the broad sitting groove of its purple body. And he looks out at a wide azure pond in the center of the park, and beyond is a dense stand of water oak, and beyond the trees is a stacking of high-rise buildings, a cityscape of glass, with the sunlight reflecting there, but softly, and one skyscraper rises high above it all, its lean dusky brown facade a stacking of vertical piers going up to a gilded pyramid of open latticed girders that seem stuffed with the baby blue sky.

Hatcher eats his Big Mac. Pittsfield Kobe. He drinks his Starbucks latte. The caffeine rushes in him and he lets the foam evaporate on his lips. And when he finishes eating and drinking, he rubs the heels of his hands on the arms of the chair. And his thumb thinks to look for something, a little rub spot on the right arm. And he finds it. This is his chair. His. And he knows he is in Heaven.

And he has still seen no one else. He lifts his head a little. He looks off to the trees on the right. He looks off to the trees on the left. He looks at the pond, and he scans the far tree line. There is no one. And there is silence. Which is all right. He feels his body letting go. He lays his head back into the two soft hands of the chair. And he sleeps.

∝

He wakes to stars. The night has come, and it is cool, and the air is full of the smell of Confederate jasmine. The tall buildings beyond the trees are dark, but the pyramid atop the skyscraper is lit brightly in gold. It floats in the sky before him like a fiery crown. Hatcher rises from his chair, and he walks back down the path, and there are bright lights all along this thoroughfare. He has always felt most comfortable in big cities. He steps in at Starbucks, and his evening latte is waiting on the table.

He goes back outside, and he stands in the center of the street, and he feels luxuriously slow inside. He sips his coffee. He takes his time. His coffee stays hot to the last drop, but not so hot that he can't sip it as deeply as he wants, which he does, even at the very last, filling his mouth full and holding it warmly there and then letting it slide down. And all the while, he watches the bright golden crown floating above this Great Metropolis of Heaven.

And when he is finished with his coffee, he knows simply to open his hand, and he does, and the empty cup drifts off. And with a bit of a shock he realizes, as he stands there, that nothing hurts. There is not a single part of his body that isn't feeling sweetly fine. And still he can't take his eyes off the Great Skyscraper of Heaven. And suddenly the building below the pyramid, merely implied till now in the darkness, begins to come alive with light. The windows. The thousands of windows before him begin to flare into golden brightness. Quickly, in no discernible pattern, high and low and middle, left to right and right to left, the windows burst into light like the explosion of a Fourth of July rocket. It's all for him, he feels. He begins to walk toward the building. And part of him is thinking: *That's where everyone is.*

∝

Hatcher passes through a street of restaurants and he sees all his favorite cuisines. Indian and Italian, Afghan and Vietnamese, even Eritrean. All the restaurants are brightly lit, all of them are empty of people, and each of them, he suspects, has his favorite dishes waiting in the center of a table. He passes through a street of clothing retailers. All lit. All empty. And then he enters a residential street of ornate, rusticated limestone urban mansions in Renaissance and Classical revivals, and he laughs at himself for thinking of these as architectural revivals. Everything's a revival in Heaven. It's a bland and esoteric little wisecrack he has made to himself but he laughs out loud. He can laugh now, even at bland and esoteric wisecracks. And his voice echoes in the street. He stops, struck once again by the silence. The houses are all dark. But they are suddenly less dark. Not from within but from without. They are beginning to lighten before his eyes. From the darkness, balustrades and friezes and Corinthian columns and Ionic columns and parapets and French doors are emerging. Softly, quickly, quietly, night is turning into day.

And he walks on, and soon, in the full light of morning, he is standing at a broad, maple-lined setback before the Great Skyscraper. Red maples. The building is vast above him, pulling his chest upward as he lifts his face to look. And then he walks beneath the maples. These are the trees of his time in Evanston, the trees that watched him holding . . . someone . . . in his arms. He can't think who. He is under the maples. He is feeling peaceful. He approaches a high granite archway, and he pushes through the doors and crosses a marble lobby, his footsteps echoing all around him. And again, there are no people. He had the thought they might be here. Perhaps they still are, up above.

Hatcher enters an elevator. He has fifty-five floors to choose from. He starts with a middle one. He pushes **27** and the elevator fills with sound—the music of Brian Eno—the muted trickle of electronic sighs and cries and drippings. Music that once enchanted Hatcher. Music he played often. Music that drove someone crazy, he thinks, though he can't think who. He can't even think of some choices of who. He doesn't feel the elevator moving, but the lights for the floors are flashing quickly upward. And then **27**. The doors open. He steps onto plush carpeting. A broad window to the left looks out on the city. That interests him, but he's more interested in this nagging thought that there are other souls quietly waiting somewhere. Or is it a hope? Thought, he thinks. Just a thought. He heads the other way and moves around a large desk in front of a wide reception wall that has no company name. Nothing.

He heads down a corridor of offices, the doors all standing open, the windows inside showing the tops of other buildings, the offices flashing by looking identical. Mid-corridor he stops at one. He stands in the doorway. It has a desk and a high-backed leather chair and a computer, with its screen dark. It has in-and-out trays with nothing going in or out and an empty pen holder on the desktop and a potted ficus standing in a corner. But there is not one personal item. And it's the same in all the other offices, he's certain. There is no sign of any other soul. He wants to look out at the Great Metropolis of Heaven, and he thinks to step to this window now, but he doesn't. The absence of any apparent human touch pushes him away.

He turns and strides back along the corridor and past the reception desk and out the door and along to the elevator. He pushes the UP button and the elevator he arrived in opens up instantly. He steps in. He pushes **55**.

And floor **55** turns out to be entirely unpartitioned and unfurnished, one vast carpeted space with wide, tall windows, and Heaven to its horizon is out there waiting for him. He crosses the floor, heading for the center of the far wall where he can see the bright concentration of morning light. East, he presumes.

Hatcher arrives at the window and draws close, his breath showing up faintly there, and he looks out: the sun is still low, where it's rising, and he can see a horizon, at least a place where sight ends, and it seems lushly green at that far point. Hatcher stares directly at the sun—a liquid golden orb that appears more luminous than thermonuclear—and its light touches his eyes like a soft breeze. Hatcher looks sharply downward, and nearby is a clustering of lower high-rises, their roofs pristine and their glass facades crystalline, and farther out is a broad park, dense with trees—a park different from the one with his recliner, this being the opposite side of the city—and beyond the park is another neighborhood of freestanding mansions, from this height mostly dormers and pitched roofs and parapets and stacked chimney caps and turrets. And lifting his eyes beyond the mansions, Hatcher finds an abrupt end of the city. A rolling green landscape that he does not take in at once.

Instead, he looks back down on his new Great Metropolis. Something clearly noticeable is there but it waits, still, to claim his attention. Slicing through all that he is seeing of the city is a web of broad, immaculate thoroughfares, laid out straight and true, and he has been taking them in, these streets, as he notices the neighborhoods, but now he sags forward against the window with a realization. He presses his face there and lays his palms against the glass as he understands that the streets are utterly empty. He has seen this in one way or another over and over since he's arrived, but only now has it finally accumulated into a deep and overwhelming and unmitigated conviction. This building is empty. All the buildings are empty. All the shops. All the houses. All the streets. Heaven is you, alone. *I am alone.*

Can this be? he asks inside his head. It is not a rhetorical question for himself. He is speaking to God, a thing he has not done in a long time. There is no answer. Not even in Heaven. It was not long ago that he skidded to this conclusion. No one is listening. No one. Alone, indeed. But there's coffee and cheeseburgers and good weather and a good chair.

Heaven. Somebody would assume he's a happy man now. Somebody. He tries to remember who said something like that. Said he's happier alone. Something. Someone. He doesn't know who. He even feels himself losing hold of the notion that anyone at all said anything like that. He tracks the empty boulevards with his eyes now. He looks up and down and up and down. He searches every one of them. Someone else should be here. But he can't remember any faces to imagine down there. He's even losing an image of crowded streets of any kind. He gasps. He knocks his head against the glass. Hard. And again, harder. It doesn't hurt at all.

And now he lifts his eyes beyond the city. That rolling countryside. There's something about it. But it's distant and he can't see. And as soon as he thinks this, he realizes that there is an object standing next to him. He turns. A telescope. He steps behind and puts his eye to the viewer, and the instrument is already focused exactly where he wishes to look. And he sees a rolling countryside with trees and a farmhouse and barns and a cornfield, and far ahead, a little village with a church steeple and a school and a neighborhood of white houses and the sun high in the sky and, most importantly, there is a truck, a bright blue panel truck with big round fenders and it is on the road through the countryside and it is heading for the little village and on the side of the truck is the word **BREAD**. It is exactly the scene from his book, from his favorite book when he was little Hatchy, little little Hatchy, somebody's perfect little nookykins. Somebody.

Hatcher rears back from the telescope and deep in his throat he makes a guttural grinding whatthefuckisgoingon sound, probably not heard before in Heaven. But no one is listening anyway. He puts his eye to the viewer once more. The truck. When he was a little boy reading this book over and over in the window seat in his room with the sun falling on the pages and when he was taking delight in that truck, he thought someone was driving it. Who? He can't recall. It was part of the delight, once upon a time. For someone in particular to be driving. He looks at the truck.

The truck is moving but it doesn't seem to be any farther along on the road. It is moving when he looks at it, but when he compares it to the landscape, it is opposite the near edge of the cornfield. Which is where it was a moment ago. Okay. Okay.

Hatcher backs away from the window. He turns and he jogs across the wide floor and out into the hallway and he punches the elevator call button and the doors open and he gets in and he heads for the lobby, thinking somehow this place will grant his present wish.

∝

And it does. In the form of a 2006 fire-engine red Maserati Spyder, Hatcher's last car, sitting at the curb outside the skyscraper. Hatcher gets in, puts the top down, and starts the engine, revving the Hell out of it and thrilling to the red-line roar going up his accelerator leg and into his crotch. And he rips into gear and takes off, peeling down the street along the setback and fishtailing a right turn and screaming past the high-rises and through the park, and then the Italian Renaissance mansions and the Chateauesque mansions and the Beaux Arts mansions all vanish in a blur as he Maseratis through the empty streets of this city without stoplights, and he is into the countryside and he's leaping the sweet little green hills and racing past the farmhouse and the barns, and the cornfield is up ahead and so is the blue truck, and Hatcher downshifts and he comes up fast on the back of the truck and he shifts down again and he brakes, and they are doing twenty, he in his Maserati and the bread truck.

The road is narrow. Too narrow to pass. And so they drive like this for a while and the cornfield does at last go by but then another cornfield begins and when that one is gone, there is another, and he can go on like this for as long as he wants, he realizes, following the blue bread truck through the perfect countryside. Hatcher can smell the bread for a moment. He has a warm lolling in his limbs. Now the air smells of fresh cut grass. He feels as if he's sitting in his recliner on the top of the rise. Even the Maserati has stopped complaining about second gear.

Hatcher wonders: why am I doing this? Why did I race out here to catch the blue truck? It's okay. It's pleasant, following the truck. It's very pleasant. And what's that new smell? Teaberry gum. It smells like Teaberry gum out here. Whatever happened to Teaberry gum? And he knows if he opens the glove box, he will find packs of Teaberry gum. His head is so sweetly mellow he can hardly think. But some little unadjusted something in him cries out, in a wee tremulous voice: *what the fuck?*

He pounds his head against the steering wheel. No pain but he jars a little something loose: the driver of the bread truck. It's about the driver. And Hatcher lays on the horn. He honks it loud and hard and he stops his car and he wants the truck to stop, and it's Heaven, so he gets what he wants. The truck stops.

Hatcher gets out of his car and closes the door with a tight little thunk, and this sound thrills him as it always did. But he fights off the invitation to mellow out about that. He is standing in the middle of his childhood landscape. The car is ticking as loudly as his Krazy Kat clock with its big black eyes restlessly darting back and forth. And he knows what's happening. He's forgetting the ones in Hell. In Heaven, there's no place for the memories of the damned. They have been judged. They have been placed where they belong in their own torment. The sharp shards of them that still stick in you are things that need to be plucked out. They would only fester. They are the sins of the world. They are the pain and the suffering and the imperfections and they are fading away, happily so, happily happily happily. Hatcher is forgetting everyone.

But not yet. He moves forward, heading for the cab of the truck. He passes before the **BREAD** and the smell of it fills him up so achingly full that he has to stop, he cannot move his legs, he is chewing the air, it is so thick with the smell of the bread, and he knows he can stand here for as long as he wants, he has eternity, he can linger for centuries chewing the smell of bread in the air and it will be as the blinking of an eye and it will only be Hatcher and the bread and the gentle sunlight. And that little voice again: *fuck this, who's driving?* And Hatcher's legs are moving again and he approaches the cab and he is panting, he is this far into Heaven and he is summoning up anxiety and he knows he needs it, he knows that when he fully lets go of the fear and the trembling and the pain, he will lose everyone forever, and his little Heaven voice pipes up *that's good, that's good, you're perfected at last and you are pleasing to the one who created you and that's all you need* but he stops by the panel truck door and his heart is pounding and that's also good, that's better for now.

The windows are tinted. He cannot see in. He clasps the door handle. And he knows the truck will be empty. There is no one else in Heaven. No one else. Surely the truck is driving itself. Neither was there a driver in the bread truck in the book in the window seat with the sunlight while Hatcher's . . . someone was downstairs, and with his . . . other someone off somewhere . . . Hatcher pounds at his head with the heel of his hand, trying to remember. And he does. With his *mother* downstairs. With his *father* off somewhere. And when the father comes home, he will be worthy of Hell. And Hatcher twists the handle. He opens the bread truck door.

And his father is sitting there. The old man's hands are clenching the steering wheel hard and he is dressed in a brown uniform with a hat on his head like a police patrolman's hat and his face turns to Hatcher and the hat has **BREAD** written across it and Hatcher's father says, "You crazy motherfucker what the fuck do you think you're doing chasing me down and honking your fucking horn you motherfucker I have half a mind to jump out of this truck and kick your fucking ass."

And Hatcher says, "It's me, Dad. It's just me."

And the old man's eyes narrow. He can't quite focus his eyes. "Hatcher?" he says.

"Yes."

"Where have you been?" his father says. "You're all grown up." But there are flames licking up from his father's shirt collar now, and the face is dissolving, it's vanishing in the flames, and it is gone, his father has gone back to Hell, and the bread man's uniform crumples into the seat.

And Hatcher is filled with the smell of bread. And above him is a beautiful blue sky. And up the road is a perfect little village. And he wonders if perhaps there are even people there to give bread to. Hatcher reaches out and picks up the hat. He puts it on his head. He can drive away now in the bread truck. Drive away into eternity.

∝

And on the outskirts of the Great and Placid Metropolis of Heaven, there is the sound of an engine. Not a bread truck. A Maserati. Wailing to the red line and racing like a sonofabitch into town, past the mansions, through the park, past the high-rises and the Great Skyscraper and past all the great shopping and great eating, and Hatcher McCord, along with the great automotive passion of his life, screams to a stop in front of Starbucks. And Hatcher jumps out of the car and he does not get his coffee, which is waiting for him, but instead he dashes up the block and he pushes through the doors of McDonald's and he whisks past his Big Mac sitting in the center of the center table and past Ronald McDonald who says "Welcome" and Hatcher is around the order counter and one stride into the kitchen before he tosses a "Fuck you" over his shoulder to Ronald. And Hatcher races by the grills and the fryers and he is at the back door and wrenching its handle and it is heavy, this door, fucking heavy, but Hatcher finds the strength and he pulls and pulls and it's getting easier and the door is open and he is beneath the glare and the buzz of the fluorescent light and dashing along the little back corridor as the door to Heaven thumps heavily and forever shut behind him, and he is opening one more door and he flings himself in, and he stops, panting, in the center of the floor of the only hamburger joint in Hell, and all along its baseboards, ten thousand cockroaches are cheering. Hatcher nods at them and they nod back.

He catches his breath. He is sweating, and his legs are cramping up. But it's okay. Hatcher moves to the front door, and he opens it, and he steps out. Grand Peachtree Boulevard is jammed with the damned, and they are howling and they are cursing and they are flowing always onward toward something they want but can never name and can never have.

And Hatcher McCord, anchorman for the *Evening News from Hell*, opens his arms wide, and he cries out above the din, "I love you all."